OUT
of the
SMOKE

Matthew Wainwright

THE WAKEMAN TRUST, LONDON

OUT OF THE SMOKE
Text © Matthew Wainwright, 2020
Illustrations © Jaime Dill, 2020

THE WAKEMAN TRUST
(Wakeman Trust is a UK Registered Charity)

UK Registered Office
38 Walcot Square
London SE11 4TZ

USA Office
300 Artino Drive
Oberlin, OH 44074-1263

Website: www.wakemantrust.org

ISBN 978 1 913133 10 8

Cover design by Matthew Wainwright

Printed by CPI Group (UK) Ltd, Croydon CRO 4YY

Contents

Victorian London is a lawless city. Street gangs engage in running battles in broad daylight, while pickpockets, burglars and sneak-thieves plague even the wealthiest boroughs. The Metropolitan Police force, still in its infancy, struggles to hold back the rising tide of violence and petty crime.

Children are the worst affected. Homeless, orphaned, uneducated, and frequently starving, they must choose between back-breaking work—twelve-hour shifts on the factory floor, or else squeezing up narrow chimneys—or a fight for survival on the streets. Either way, life is short and brutal, and few see adulthood.

Most people in positions of power would prefer not to acknowledge their existence, much less reach out to help them. But one man is determined to do all he can to lift up the downcast and shed light into the darkest slums: a man known as "the Poor Man's Earl"...

"They wandered in the wilderness in a solitary way;
they found no city to dwell in.
Hungry and thirsty, their soul fainted in them.
Then they cried unto the Lord in their trouble,
and he delivered them out of their distresses."

Psalm 107.4-6

Loosed from my God and far removed,
Long have I wandered to and fro,
O'er earth in endless circles roved,
Nor found whereon to rest below.
To Thee, my God, at last I fly,
O bless me, Saviour, now draw nigh.
                                    Charles Wesley

To my ever-patient wife

PART I
THE SILVER SPOON

"Thou shalt not steal."
Exodus 20.15

1
Up, Up, Up

"GET IN THERE!"

Gerard tightened the rope around Billy's ankle with a sharp tug and shoved him towards the sheet-draped fireplace. Billy stumbled and almost fell, but he bit back the retort that came all too easily to his lips. It wasn't worth arguing with Gerard: he would only get fresh bruises for his trouble. Gerard was the master sweep, and Billy was just an apprentice; apprentices kept their mouths shut and did as they were told, or they regretted it.

He ducked behind the sheet. It was dirty, and it stank, but at least it shielded him from Gerard. He crouched, bending almost double as he stepped over the grate and into the remains of the last fire. Mercifully the ashes were old, warm on his bare feet rather than burning hot—but he would have barely felt them anyway. Years of burns and scrapes had turned his soles into a mass of calloused skin, along with his palms, his knees, and his elbows.

From his crouched position he peered up into the chimney, a black hole in the dim light. There were only two ways he could go now: up into that cramped hole, or out to face another beating.

Unless he got stuck. Then it would be neither, and he would stay where he was until they got him out, dead or alive.

Billy had seen it happen before. The lad had been just eight years old, and a sweep for only a couple of weeks— sold to Gerard by his father for a few guineas. Billy had never even asked his name. The boy had cried when Gerard made him go up his first chimney, and had carried on crying when he wedged himself fast. It was only when the crying stopped that Billy knew he would not be coming down again.

He had watched as the mason took apart an upstairs wall brick by brick, until finally the body tumbled on to the floor in a cloud of soot and ash. Billy had watched them wrap it in a sheet and carry it down the backstairs and into the street. After that? A quick burial in one of the common graves, most likely. That was what happened to sweeps. They were cheap, replaceable, and soon forgotten.

Not to Billy, though. Hardly a day went by when he didn't think about that lad—not out of pity or remorse, but as a warning, a reminder of what happened if you were not careful up there.

He reached up with both hands, feeling for the smoke shelf, a cramped ledge above the hearth that drew the air through the fireplace and up the narrow flue that formed the spine of the house.

Above the smoke shelf, the brickwork sloped up sharply towards a square black hole, barely ten inches wide, which was the opening of the flue. Once inside he would have to worm his way through unknown dirt and grime, twisting and turning around any number of tight corners to reach the top.

Billy grasped his stubby sweep's brush in one hand, and with the other jammed his cap down over his face. There would be no need to see, up there in the flue. It was black as pitch anyway, and no way to go but up.

He took a deep breath, raised his arms, and slowly wriggled himself into the hole.

Gerard was the closest thing to a father Billy had ever known—if a father was a drunk with squinting eyes, yellow teeth, and a wiry black beard as thick as the brushes that were his livelihood. Billy had been sold to Gerard when he was five years old; 'indentured' they called it, all legal, with papers signed before a magistrate. He supposed his parents had been either too poor or too overwhelmed with children to keep him, but either way the result was the same: from that moment he had belonged to Gerard, and he was a climbing boy whether he wanted it or not.

He did not remember anything much of his life before then, nor of his first few months with Gerard. He had a fleeting memory of a tiny room up a narrow flight of stairs, and of being constantly cold; but after that the next thing he could remember was the first time he got stuck, and the pure unmingled terror of realising he had brought his knees up too far, jamming himself in the shaft. It had not been a bad jam—he had freed himself in a minute or so—but he had never forgotten the blind overwhelming panic, the feeling that the flue was squeezing him like a vice. It had taught him that life in his new world was fragile, and that a chimney would swallow him alive if he gave it half a chance.

Six years he had been with Gerard now, and hundreds, if not thousands, of chimneys climbed and swept. The fear no longer gripped him—he saw each flue as a challenge, an adversary to be wrestled and beaten—but he never forgot the spectre of death hovering nearby, ready to pounce.

Sometimes he dreamed that he was climbing a flue, and that just above him was Death himself, a grinning skeleton holding a scythe and an hourglass. Death would not say anything, would not touch him or hurt him, and Billy was never afraid. All the old skeleton would do was check the hourglass now and again, patiently watching the grains of sand trickle away.

As it turned out, he was a rare prize for Gerard: one of those boys who reaches a certain height then grows no further. He was no taller than boys three years younger than him, and his sparse diet kept him lean. His wiry frame and short stature meant he was able to squirm through the narrowest of flues and around the tightest of bends, and his age and experience had made him tough and unafraid: he was the perfect climbing boy.

As one of the older boys he got to eat on most days—a crust of bread here, a slop of stew there, beer to drink and, if he was really lucky, the odd swig of gin—but even so the pangs of hunger were constant and unyielding.

He knew what it was like to be one of the little 'uns—lads of five or six, red-eyed, gaunt, noses streaming, trembling like leaves, watching him greedily as he gnawed on his scraps. He felt sometimes that they would eat him if they could. He knew that was what they were thinking, because the same thought had come to him when he was their age, when other boys had been the ones crouching in the corner with an end of mouldy bread. If a scrap happened to slip through his fingers they were on it like rats, fists flying, elbows gouging, teeth biting in a desperate frenzy.

He didn't blame them. If they didn't fight, they wouldn't eat. All they were doing was surviving.

Billy climbed, jamming his back against one wall with his forearms and knees against the other, inching slowly, caterpillar-like, dislodging the filth that had accumulated from months or even years of fires burning in the hearth below.

Up, up, up: scrubbing, scraping, hacking at the soot and smut, shaking off the dirt and grime that showered down all around him. Up, up, up: inch by inch, scraping his back on the burned brick, ignoring the pain.

He stopped, panting, and rested with his feet against one side of the shaft and his knees against the other. It was a risky position—boys got jammed doing it—but it gave him a chance to catch his breath, and to ease the burning pain in his arms and shoulders. He could not stay for long, but even a few seconds was respite enough.

There were few moments in the day that he really had to himself. Back at the House (their name for the bare loft Gerard called home) all the boys slept and ate together, piled one across another on the soot-stained sheets they tied across the fireplaces and draped over clients' furniture. Out on the streets they went in pairs, older and younger, calling out, "Sweep! Sweep!" in the cold dark before dawn, with Gerard not far behind to make sure none of them bolted.

But up in the flue Billy was truly alone, hidden from prying eyes, just him and the darkness. Here he could have a few seconds to himself, and those few seconds were worth more than gold.

A yank on the rope around his ankle nearly dislodged him, and he pressed himself hard against the brickwork as his heart hammered. That was Gerard. Even a few seconds' pause was too long. If he waited much longer there was the risk that Gerard would set a fire in the hearth to drive him up, like he did with some of the little 'uns.

"All right! I'm going!" Billy yelled back down the shaft, then braced his shoulders, raised the brush, and started up the flue again.

Up, up, up: clearing, scrubbing, chipping, coughing. Up, up, up: burrowing, squirming, panting and sweating until, at long last, he felt a coldness on his up-stretched hands and a few seconds later they emerged from the top of the flue into the fresh air.

Billy wriggled himself the rest of the way and pulled himself up and out of the chimney pot so that he hung by his armpits. There he rested for a moment, looking out over the darkened city.

The black night sky above him was slowly turning to muddy blue-grey as a new day dawned. A sea of rooftops spread out all around him, rising and falling, the scattered chimney pots like bobbing buoys; already thin streams of grey smoke had begun to rise skywards from them, as the morning fires were lit in kitchens and bedrooms across the city. His eyes followed the crowded mass of buildings down towards the river, where the great dome of St. Paul's Cathedral rose serenely over the sleeping metropolis, and for a few seconds he felt oddly at peace.

He closed his eyes and breathed in the freezing air,

catching the familiar smells: the acrid bitterness of chimney smoke, the sharp undercurrent of sewage, the barest hint of a briny breeze from the nearby Thames. At times like this he could almost forget the hell that awaited him below.

A shout echoed over the rooftops. Billy turned to see another blackened face poking out of a chimney pot a few houses along the street. It was Tosher, one of the other boys in Gerard's gang, and the only person Billy would have called a friend.

"Hey! Billy!" Tosher shouted, grinning and waving. He was a year older than Billy, and a few inches taller, but far skinnier. Above his soot-stained features, a shock of bright red hair stuck out at all angles. Tosher's hair was a running joke in the gang: so thick, the little 'uns said, that Tosher didn't need a brush to clean a flue, as long as he took off his cap before he started up it. Tosher didn't mind being the butt of the joke—he just laughed along with them and shook his hair so that a cloud of soot and ash rose all around him.

Tosher had been with Gerard the longest out of all of them, so now Gerard trusted him enough to lead his own gang of sweeps. All the boys wanted to go with Tosher: he actually enjoyed the climbing, and would not let them go up unless the flue was too small for him to fit. He also hardly ever beat them, unless he really had to.

"How was yours?" Tosher called.

Billy shrugged. "Fine," he said. "Yours?"

"Tight." Tosher grinned, as if this was a good thing. "Nearly got meself jammed. Had to squirm like a beast to get out!"

He cackled, but though Billy smiled he could not laugh

with him. There was something about Tosher that was not quite right—he savoured the risk that came with being a climbing boy, loved the suffocating darkness, the tight spaces, the constant struggle against danger and death. Billy did not savour these things: every time he went up the flue he reminded himself that he was never more than a moment or two away from a grisly fate.

"Here!" Tosher called, putting a hand down the chimney pot and rummaging around. "Look what I got!"

He drew something out and held it aloft. It was too far away to see, but it glinted in the dawn. Billy squinted, trying to get a better view.

"What is it?" he shouted.

But Tosher had already slipped whatever it was back inside the chimney pot. He gave an exaggerated wink, tapping on the side of his too-large nose. "All in good time, Bill! All in good time!"

Billy sighed. Typical Tosher. He was never happier than when he knew something Billy didn't. "I'd better get back," he called, pointing downwards. "Gerard's been on my back today. Says I've been slow."

As if in response, the rope around his ankle jerked, almost dislodging him from his perch. He grabbed hold of the chimney pot and peered down the flue.

"I'm coming!" he yelled, as loudly as he could, then gave Tosher one last wave. "See you at the bottom!"

He paused to take one last longing look at the spreading light of dawn as it spilled over London, then lowered himself back into the darkness for the long descent.

2
The Silver Spoon

THE JOURNEY DOWN WAS, if anything, more dangerous than
the journey up. Flues did not exist in isolation: they ran up
the backbone of a house like a river with many tributaries,
the flues from three or four different fireplaces all merging
together as they rose towards the roof. The possibilities were
ripe for losing your way as you descended and encountered
places where the flue divided; it was easy to slip down the
wrong flue to find yourself behind a bricked-up fireplace, or
else encounter a blockage of the soot and ash you had dislodged yourself on the way up.

Billy was always careful to make a mental map as he
climbed, noting any openings and remembering whether
they were to the left or to the right. He was also careful to go
down facing the same direction as when he came up, so as
not to get left and right mixed up—simple precautions, but
they stood between him and a choking death.

Not that it was easy to keep a clear head when Gerard
was tugging on his ankle the entire way down, threatening
to dislodge him and bring him tumbling to a bone-breaking

end.

"I'm coming, I'm coming!" he yelled, bracing himself against the pull of the rope as the tugs grew stronger and stronger. The calluses on his knees and elbows tore against rough brick as he slid and skidded the last ten feet and landed with a jarring impact on the smoke shelf.

"Are you trying to kill me?" he shouted, flexing his bleeding arms. Immediately he regretted the outburst. There would be a fist waiting for him when he got out now, for sure. He slithered off the smoke shelf and dropped into the hearth, soot billowing up around him in a soft black cloud. Better to get it over with. At least he was ready for it this time.

He ducked under the sheet, bracing himself for the blow, but it didn't come. Gerard was too busy berating the two little 'uns who were desperately shovelling soot into grimy black sacks, to be taken away and sold to farmers for fertilizer. One of the lads was constantly spilling his, and despite the room being swathed in grimy sheets he had still managed to spatter the walls and furniture with dirty flecks. As Billy straightened up, stretching his aching back, Gerard snapped and smashed his fist into the boy's ribs, doubling him over with a whoosh of expelled air.

"What d'yer think yer doing, you weasel?" Gerard snarled. "That's coin, that is!"

The lad struggled to get up, gasping for breath and clutching his bruised side, but Gerard swung again and this time he crumpled to the floor.

"Gerrup!" Gerard bellowed, aiming a boot at the boy's curled form and catching him on the leg. "Gerrup, you maggot!"

Again the boy tried to get to his feet, and again Gerard's boot sent him sprawling. Billy had seen enough. If Gerard kept kicking the boy he would kick him to death. He darted forward and barged into Gerard, knocking him aside and sending his next kick wide of the mark. The boy scrambled away to the other side of the room, scattering black soot as he went, as Gerard rounded on Billy instead, his face bright red and his beard bristling with fury.

"Gerard, look," Billy began, holding up his hands. "I'm sorry for that, but they ain't any good if they're dead or crippled, right? I'm just saying—"

He got no further. Gerard's meaty fist lashed out, meeting the side of his face and knocking him back into the sheet that covered the fireplace. Billy put out his arms to break his fall, his ears ringing and his sight blurred, and caught the edge of the sheet, dragging it from the mantelpiece to fall in heavy folds all around him. As he hit the floor he curled instinctively into a ball, ready to take the kicks that were sure to follow—but instead heavy hands parted the sheet, and he looked up to see Gerard standing over him, leering through a mouthful of rotten teeth.

"See?" Gerard growled. "You bounce right back, don'cha? Gerrup, you lazy idiot. And get this cleaned up."

Billy struggled to his feet. His ears were still ringing, and his head was still swimming from the punch he had received, but at least he was spared a further pummelling—for now. He gingerly touched the side of his face, and felt the skin swelling around his left eye. There would be a beautiful bruise soon, but it could have been worse: the little finger on his left hand was permanently curled inwards from the time Gerard had kicked him and broken it, a few days after his parents had sold him. It had been over something minor—Billy couldn't remember now; probably something to do with not working fast enough, or crying too much when Gerard bullied him into going up the flue—but it had taught him the first and most important lesson of being a climbing boy: *Don't cheek your master.* Masters could do whatever they wanted to their apprentices, and no one would say a thing: not the clients, who preferred to look elsewhere; nor the other masters, who would just look on in approval; and certainly not any of the lads, who were usually grateful not to be on the receiving end themselves.

Nursing his bruised cheek, he began gathering the sheet together into a makeshift sack to collect the rest of the soot. It was long and tedious work, and Gerard stood over them to make sure they collected as much as possible: every gram was worth money to him, so to his way of thinking every speck wasted was coin stolen from his purse.

The other boys avoided eye contact with Billy; there was no word of thanks for his intervention, nor even a grateful look. Billy did not care. There was no friendship between him and those boys—he didn't know their names, and probably wouldn't bother to learn them unless they stayed with the gang for more than a year. The little 'uns were just a nameless mass of staring eyes, shrunken faces and hungry mouths to him, and so many of them ran off or wasted away from cold and hunger that Billy had stopped caring about them years ago.

Tosher was the only one who meant anything to Billy. He had been in Gerard's gang the longest, and had taken Billy under his wing when it became apparent that Billy wasn't about to expire or sneak off in the night. It was Tosher who had showed him the ropes and taught him the best way to climb without risking death or injury. It was due to Tosher alone that Billy had lasted as long as he did—Gerard certainly hadn't taught him anything, and if Billy died tomorrow he would hardly have batted an eyelid.

If only Tosher could bring himself to be sensible once in a while. He was forever larking around, joking about getting stuck and mimicking the panicked cries of a boy trapped in a flue. And now there was this business with whatever it was Tosher had found. Knowing him, it was something unremarkable, a shiny scrap that had caught his eye. But all the same, Billy couldn't help himself wondering, and the thought stayed in the back of his mind as he worked.

As they were cleaning the last of the ashes from the fireplace, the parlour door opened and a severe-looking woman in a cap and apron peered in.

"Nearly done, are you?" she demanded.

"Nearly there, madam, nearly there!" Gerard instantly adopted the writhing, fawning attitude he reserved for the clients, whipping his cap from his head and stretching his filthy mouth into what he considered to be a smile. "The boys do take their time, don't they? I 'ave to give them a good kicking now and again to learn 'em—worse than mules, ain't they? But they're only little 'uns, after all. They're learnin', they're learnin'!"

He chuckled, expecting the woman to join him, but she just sniffed and glared at the spots of soot on the walls and furniture.

"Not exactly clean, is it?" she remarked sharply.

Gerard's smile hardened, and Billy saw his fist clench around the cap. "Well, it's a messy job, madam," he said, his geniality suddenly forced. "Dirt is as dirt does, and what dirt does is make places dirty. I'm sure you'll find we does our best, as good as any other."

The woman sniffed again, her expression declaring louder than any words that she doubted this was the case—but she did not press the issue, and disappeared to leave them to it.

As soon as the door closed Gerard turned on them, his face dissolving into its usual snarl. "Get this cleared up!" he barked. "And if it costs me a penny I'll take it from your flesh!"

Fortunately the mess didn't cost them: Billy made sure the boys did their best, despite the one who had been kicked limping and moaning the whole time, and within twenty minutes the parlour was merely grubby rather than filthy. The housekeeper returned to inspect the damage, but even she had to admit (grudgingly) that the job was not half bad, and not as bad as some she had seen. A few minutes later coins changed hands, Gerard tugged his cap and bowed, "Thank 'ee, madam, very kind, very kind I'm sure!", then they were hustled downstairs, out the scullery door into the backyard, and through the gate to the alley that ran between the backs of the houses.

The wind in the alley cut through them instantly, seeking every tiny gap in their ragged clothes and burrowing through to the warm skin beneath. The little 'uns, bowed under the weight of their sacks of soot, shivered and looked fit to drop. Billy gritted his teeth, thankful for the woollen waistcoat he had managed to scavenge last winter, and tried to ignore the numbness already creeping into his bare feet.

"Come on," Gerard growled, shuffling off up the muddy

path. "There's work still to be done."

They spent the rest of the day tramping from house to house, agreeing an appointment here and going in to sweep a chimney there. Billy did his best to ignore the throbbing pain around his eye, but by the time they were finished for the day the area had blossomed into a handsome bruise.

He helped the other two boys tie up the last of the sheets in silence. Gerard took the money from the last client with his usual obsequious leer and much tugging of his cap, and they emerged from the house into the slowly gathering dusk.

At the junction at the top of the road they found Tosher's crew lounging on a low wall, watching the horses and carts rumble past. Tosher jumped up as they approached, digging out a purse from inside the dirty black jacket he wore. He also possessed a battered top hat, which he sometimes perched on top of his head, saying it gave him a distinguished air as befitted the lead apprentice. In reality it made him look ridiculous, with his hair sprouting out from under the brim in all directions like an orange explosion; but Billy never had the heart to tell him, and the rest of the lads were content to snigger at him behind his back.

"Two shillings and sixpence, guv," Tosher declared, dropping the purse into Gerard's blackened paw. "Mrs. Ellis at number six says can we come by Tuesday, and them at number twelve says come by in a fortnight."

Gerard emptied the coins into his palm and counted them carefully. While they waited Tosher shot a look at Billy's black eye, but he said nothing.

When Gerard was satisfied, he stuffed the coins into his jacket pocket, then jerked his head down the street. "All right," he growled. "Let's go."

The boys trailed after Gerard through the freezing London dusk, hurrying to keep up with his long stride. Tosher and Billy walked together, with the little 'uns trailing in a ragged line behind them.

Billy was dying to ask Tosher about the trinket he had flashed at him up on the rooftop, and he deliberately slowed down so that there was a gap between them and Gerard.

When he was sure they were out of earshot he gave Tosher a nudge.

"So?" he said.

Tosher looked at him blankly. "What?"

"That … thing you were showing me. Up top. 'All in good time,' you said. Well? Now's a good time. What was it?"

"Oh!" A look of delight crossed Tosher's long face. He glanced over his shoulder to make sure none of the little 'uns were watching, then darted his hand into his waistcoat pocket and drew something out, something that glinted in the light of the gas-lamps.

Billy's breath caught in his throat, and his chest tightened with a mixture of excitement and fear. A second later the object had disappeared back into Tosher's pocket, and Tosher was grinning all over his thin face—but there was no mistaking what Billy had seen.

It was a tiny, perfect, silver spoon.

3
The Devil's Lads

"TOSHER ..." BILLY SAID SLOWLY. "How did you—?"

"It were just lyin' there," Tosher whispered, still grinning. "Down beside the dresser. No one around. I just ..." He snapped his fingers. "Easy as that."

"Is it ..." Billy shot a look at Gerard's back, and lowered his voice. "Is it *real*?"

He could hardly believe what he had seen. This was insane—to steal from a client was outrageous; if the thought had ever crossed his mind, he had certainly never been tempted to follow it. If Gerard found out ... Well, it wouldn't matter how long he had been with the crew, he would be dead for sure. And now Tosher had gone and done the unthinkable, and Billy was involved, and they would most likely be dead together.

Tosher was nodding, his grin wider than ever. Billy wondered if he had any idea of the kind of trouble they could be in, or if he really was as simple as everyone said.

"How much d'you think I could get for it?" Tosher asked, oblivious to the stunned expression on Billy's face. "D'you think Aggie would take it?"

Aggie was an Irish pawnbroker, with a shock of red hair as fiery as Tosher's and a temper to match. Now and then Billy and Tosher picked up odds and ends and traded them in at Aggie's shop, a few streets from the House. Aggie short-changed them outrageously, of course, but the pennies and shillings were enough to buy a mug or two of beer, so the boys never complained.

"What d'you reckon?" Tosher was still talking, caught up in his own daring. "Must be worth a couple a' guineas at least!"

Billy finally shook himself out of his startled silence. "You'll never get that much for it," he hissed. There was still time to talk some sense into Tosher: if he could per-suade him that it wasn't worth the risk, then maybe Tosher would realise how stupid he was being and change his mind. Taking the spoon back was out of the question, but at least they could get rid of it. "Aggie won't buy it for more than a few shillings."

"A quid, then? A quid's still a lot of gin!"

Billy looked at his friend. It was true: Tosher really had no idea how crazy he was. He struggled to think of the words that would convince him. "Look, Tosher—don't you think it's a bit, well ... dangerous?"

Tosher frowned. "How?"

"What if Gerard finds out?"

"Gerard ain't gonna find out!" Tosher's voice rose. Billy thumped him on the arm in warning, and he lowered it again. "He won't find out. We'll go straight there. Hand it over, get the coin: job done! You and me, down the Eagle, couple a' halves of gin ... have a chat with Clara ..."

Tosher waggled his eyebrows suggestively. The Eagle and Child was the pub where they spent any money they managed to lay their hands on. Visits to the Eagle were rare, as neither of them were paid by Gerard, and the only time they saw any coin was if they managed to steal it or trade something in at Aggie's shop—but Billy looked forward to each one, because it meant a chance to see Clara. She was the barmaid, who, according to rumour, had come over from the West Indies as a stowaway, having made a daring escape from the plantations. She was slender and dark, about Tosher's age, tall and proud as a lord's daughter, and there was something about the way she smiled that made Billy's stomach churn. She had a pleasant manner and an easy way of making conversation, and if they were lucky she would take a few minutes to sit and talk with them.

Billy sighed in exasperation. "This is such a bad idea ..." he said, and Tosher's smile slipped an inch, "... but I suppose it's too late now." Tosher practically skipped with glee, and again Billy had to restrain him. "But you keep this quiet until it's done," he warned. "You hear me?"

"Oh, I hear you." Tosher gave an exaggerated wink. "Say no more, me old mate."

Billy rolled his eyes, but left it at that. Trying to reason with Tosher was like trying to fly up a chimney.

Soon the broad streets and tall houses of the city fell away before the gloomy spires of the Palace of Westminster, and they started across the newly-rebuilt Westminster Bridge. The choppy waters of the Thames sloshed beneath them, and behind them Big Ben tolled five times, its sonorous chimes hanging in the chill night air.

Halfway across the river Tosher nudged Billy again.

"Look out," he muttered, and this time there was no humour in his voice. "Here comes trouble."

A rabble of boys and young men was striding along the pavement towards them, spread out from the parapet to the kerb. Billy recognised them instantly: a notorious gang who called themselves the Devil's Lads, and who prided themselves on a fearsome reputation on both sides of the river. They were famed and feared in equal measure, especially amongst the streets and alleys of Lambeth town, from which they roamed when the sun went down in order to rob and burgle their way through the city.

Swaggering along at the head of the crew was their captain, Archie Miller. Archie was a fearsome sight: a beast of a man standing a full head taller than Gerard, with bulging muscles and a thick neck that made him look like a bull. Looking at him, it was easy to believe the tales that had grown up around him, from the claim that he once tore a man's arm from its socket to settle a debt, to the whispers that he could bend an iron bar without breaking a sweat. And Archie was not just ferociously strong: he had the sharpest mind and keenest wits of all the gang bosses in London, and he put them to good use. It was rumoured Archie had blackmailed police and politicians in order to keep them off his back, and he had eyes and ears in the darkest shadows of the deepest holes in the city.

The Devil's Lads slowed as they approached Gerard's crew, and Archie stepped out in front of them. A filthy pipe was clamped between his teeth, and he wore a cloth cap pulled low over his close-cropped hair. His hands, which were as large and flat as a pair of shovels, were jammed into the pockets of the long overcoat he wore, and Billy could not help noticing the suspicious red stain surrounding a newly-darned hole under one arm.

"Gerard, me old lad!" Archie drawled, drawing out his 'a's in the thick West Country accent that had never left him. "'Ow's business then?"

"Good enough," Gerard replied cautiously, eyeing the Devil's Lads as they spread out, blocking the pavement. Pedestrians coming up from behind crossed swiftly to the other side of the road and kept their heads down, avoiding trouble. The little 'uns hung back, their eyes wide with fear: Archie's name was a watchword for horror amongst them.

"Pay day tomorrow, Gerard," Archie said. "You ready?"

"You'll get yer money," Gerard growled. Archie was the only one who could set him on edge, and he didn't like it.

Archie smiled easily. "Tha's the way," he said, surveying the boys who had edged into a tight group behind Gerard's back. "This your crew, is it? 'Ow's life with this old sinner, lads? Treating you well, is he?" There was silence from the pack. Archie snorted. "Not right talkative, are they? I bet you likes it that way, though."

"Yeah, well, we'd best be gettin' home," Gerard said, making to pass. Archie stepped to the side, blocking him, and when Gerard tried to get around he blocked him again. The lads behind Archie sniggered, but Gerard kept his mouth shut and his eyes down, and after a moment Archie moved aside to allow them to pass.

Billy kept his eyes down as well as they cringed between the crowding bodies. All he could think about was the silver spoon inside Tosher's waistcoat. If Archie had known it was there they wouldn't have lasted ten seconds. He had probably killed men for less.

The Devil's Lads leered at them as they passed, and one or two put out their legs to try and trip the boys, but soon they were through the crowd and hurrying down the bridge to the far bank.

"Pay day!" Archie called, as they disappeared into the murk. "Don't forget!"

The south bank of the Thames was as poor and run-down as the north bank was majestic. Shabby houses teetered precariously over the scummy brown water, shored up by rotten timbers but looking as if they might tumble into the river at any moment; wharves and jetties littered the water's edge, their posts mired in green weed, backed by ramshackle sheds and workshops crowded together in a jumble of grimy brick and decaying wood.

The boys shuffled down Westminster Bridge Road, merging with the crowds of tradesmen returning home from a long day's work. Passing under the massive viaduct that carried the railway lines in and out of Waterloo, they turned off the thoroughfare into the maze of streets and alleys that huddled behind the station. Immediately they were plunged into darkness, punctuated only by the grubby flickering of candlelight from grime-smeared windows, or else the odd fire roaring in a brazier on a corner, around which shadowed figures huddled, desperate for warmth.

The boys stayed close to Gerard—they had all heard the stories of children being snatched from the street, never to be seen again—and followed him deeper into the maze, passing shuttered shops, looming tenement houses, and smoky pubs from which the noise of raucous laughter and frantic music mingled with fumes of whisky and gin. Street children scuttled in the shadows, their eyes wider and their bellies more shrunken than any of the boys who trailed after Gerard. Hard, suspicious faces glared out of doorways as they passed, men and women whose expressions were a mixture of defiance and creeping fear: fear of living, fear of dying, fear of cold, hunger, thirst and pain.

Gerard ducked through a narrow doorway off one of the darkest alleys, and the boys followed him up a steep flight of rickety wooden stairs in pitch blackness. At the top of the stairs Gerard paused while he fished out a ring of keys from inside his jacket, then fumbled around in the darkness for a minute; there was a rattle and a clunk, then the squeal of a door being shoved open, and the line of boys began to move again. They filed through the door into a freezing black void, and waited while Gerard muttered and cursed and looked for matches to light the lamp. When they were found he struck one, and a feeble light flickered into life, illuminating the squalid attic they called the House.

There was not much to see. The room was long and low, the roof sloping sharply down on either side and the whole space criss-crossed with heavy wooden beams. Shadows congregated in every corner; cobwebs hung thick from the rafters; dust and muck and filth carpeted the bare wooden boards, where old beer bottles and chicken bones lay scattered. In the farthest corner was the place where the boys slept, and in the opposite corner was Gerard's hay-stuffed mattress and his padlocked clothes trunk.

Gerard waved carelessly at the boys' corner. "Right, you useless wastrels," he grunted. "Get yerselves down, and not a word, yer hear?"

The little 'uns scrambled over to the corner, vying for

31

the filthy sheets to cover themselves against the cold. Billy and Tosher hung back. They had their own spot, halfway between Gerard and the little 'uns: one of the perks of being a senior apprentice. There was no need for them to kick and punch over a scrap of cloth.

Whilst they settled themselves, Gerard rooted around in his trunk, exchanging his stained work clothes for a tattered shirt and frayed jacket, which he shrugged on before extinguishing the lamp and returning to the doorway.

"I'm off out," he declared. "You keep yerselves quiet now, you hear? If I hears you been makin' a racket for Mrs. Grindle downstairs I'll break yer fingers."

"Can't you leave us a light?" one of the little 'uns piped up, but it was too late. The door slammed shut, the key turned in the lock, and they were left alone in the freezing darkness.

The darkness did not bother Billy or Tosher. They had known it every night since they had first joined Gerard's crew: stifling in summer and bone-achingly cold in winter. You got used to finding your way around by feel and by ear, and if you were lucky it would be a cloudless night with a full moon, and the silver light would make it practically as bright as day.

Tonight was not such a night. The moon was barricaded behind iron-grey clouds, and the city was smothered in the usual shroud of smog. Not a glimmer of light fell through the smashed window high up in the gable of the roof, just the sounds of revelry from the nearby pub, and the constant biting wind.

The little 'uns were settling down in their corner, but Billy and Tosher ignored their sobs and whimpers. Billy was counting silently in his head, picturing Gerard descending the stairs then striding down the street towards the King's Head on the corner: his nightly destination for a thrupenny ordinary of stew and bread, and glass after glass of gin. He would stagger back in a few hours' time, probably blind drunk, maybe with a pint or two of beer for the lads to pass around, maybe with a loaf of bread, and maybe with nothing. In the meantime there was no one to watch them, and they were free to do as they wished. For the little 'uns this meant a long evening of fitful slumber, punctuated by the cries of those who dreamed—for Billy and Tosher it meant a few precious hours of freedom.

Once Billy had counted to five hundred in his head he felt around in the gloom for Tosher's hand.

"That it?" Tosher murmured.

"Yeah," Billy replied. "Let's go."

Tosher led the way to the end of the attic and Billy followed, ducking under the beams. When they reached the gable end they shimmied up the rafters until they were level with the smashed window, then, careful to avoid the remaining shards of glass still clinging to the frame, they slipped through and out into the night air.

The roof of the house next door was lower than theirs; it was a simple matter to drop a couple of feet down on to the tiles, then pick their cautious way to where the drainpipe snaked down the side of the building. A minute or two later they were standing in the street, looking around to make sure no one had seen them.

"Come on," Tosher muttered, setting off through the murk. Billy followed him, and within a few seconds they had disappeared.

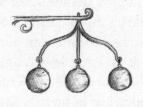

4
Aggie

TOSHER AND BILLY slipped down the twisted backstreets of Lambeth, a pair of shadows flitting against darker shadows. They ducked past the King's Head pub, its windows bright with orange light and the sound of drunken singing blaring from its open door, accompanied by an out-of-tune fiddle and pipe. Billy glimpsed Gerard standing at the bar, a pint of ale already in his hand, roaring with laughter at a joke being told by one of the other patrons.

As always, the sight of Gerard's bristling face made a barb of hatred twist in Billy's gut. The only thing that kept him with Gerard was the knowledge that he was no good for another kind of work, and that a life on the streets would be worse—if only slightly—than the life he had now. He silently repeated the promise he had made to himself many times before—that he would get away from Gerard one day, and make a life far from the cloying blackness of the chimneys—then he followed Tosher down the next street and away from the din.

After ten minutes they stopped in a square, overshadowed

on all sides by rickety tenement houses, their wooden balconies barely held up by woodworm-riddled posts. A tiny pawnshop sat huddled beneath one such balcony, its windows all but obscured by years of dirt and grime. The wooden balls above the door, once painted gold, were now stripped of all colour and dangled forlornly.

Glancing up, Billy saw yet more children crowded along the balconies above, their cheeks sunken and their bellies swollen, gazing silently down at him and Tosher. There were no adults to be seen anywhere.

He dropped his gaze, and followed Tosher through the narrow door into the shop. A bell jingled as the door closed behind them.

"Be wid ye in a minute!" a thick Irish voice growled from the dark recesses. The shop was narrow, but deceptively deep; Aggie's counter lay at the far end, through a dusty maze of ancient display cabinets. A gas-lamp burned in the depths, barely illuminating the cave. Aggie's voice dropped low and continued speaking, picking up the conversation from which it had been interrupted.

"What was it ye were sayin'? About this Act o' Parliament?"

"Aye," a second voice replied, and as soon as Billy heard it his insides turned to ice. The voice belonged to a man called Harry, a sweep whose crew worked the same area as Gerard, and who could be found most nights in the King's Head pub, drinking and laughing with Gerard and the other sweeps.

They had no idea what he was doing down at Aggie's shop this late—probably pawning some suit or other to pay for that evening's drinking—but they knew what would happen if he saw them: they would be hauled straight off to Gerard, who would find out that they had been escaping from the loft most evenings. Then he would want to know why they had come to Aggie's on that particular evening; and then he would find out about the spoon, and it wasn't a stretch to imagine what he would do to them after that.

Wordlessly, Billy pulled Tosher down behind a display case, where they crouched with beating hearts and listened to the conversation being held between the two men.

"Aye," Harry was saying. "Load o' claptrap, if you asks me. Them fancy lords with their fancy ideas, all sittin' up there in their fancy chamber and decidin' what the likes o' you and me can and can't do? Bah! What does they know, eh? Has they been down 'ere? Has they seen what it's like? Not likely! Wouldn' see one o' them muddyin' 'is shiny shoes down in the dirt o' Lambeth town now, would ye? Couldn' stand the smell, I'd say—'e'd tek one whiff and keel right over!" He gave a short, barking laugh that descended into a filthy cough.

"But I thought they'd already passed some Act or other, years back now?" Aggie said, while Harry cleared his passages. "Tha' didn't come to much now, did it?"

"Nah." Harry sniffed. "Folks knows what's good for 'em, doesn't they? Tryin' ter tell us we can't send the lads up the flues? Bah! Everyone knows it's best way ter clean a chimney—send 'em scurryin' up, they'll get it clear better 'n any brush. But I 'ear there's one o' them lords 'as taken a special int'rest, ain't 'e? Goin' around like, 'Oh, them poor little chiddlers, ain't they sufferin'!' Sufferin'? Pah! They knows what's good fer 'em, that's what I say!"

"Who is he, then? This lord?"

"Dunno. Shaft-something-or-other. Some toff."

"Shaftesbury, maybe?"

"Who knows? Somethin' fancy."

"Aye, I think it's Shaftesbury," Aggie repeated thoughtfully. "I know that one. Heard of him, anyway. Did some work wid the lunatics in Bedlam a while back, so I heard. Makin' trouble with the factories as well. Got a soft spot for little 'uns, they say."

"Hah!" Harry laughed derisively. "Can't say as I can see why. What good's a lad fer, if it's not fer workin', eh? Shut 'em up an' work 'em hard, that's my motto. And the devil tek any that says otherwise. Nasty, snot-nosed little rats—I'd as soon kill 'em meself."

"Were ye not a boy once yerself, Harry?" Aggie's voice carried a hint of mild amusement. "Or did ye spring full formed as the man ye are from the streets of London town?"

"Course I was a boy, yer daft Irish," Harry snarled. "But not like these 'uns. I grew up quick, I did. None o' this whingein' an' whinin', sobbin' an' screamin'. I did as I was bid, and I kept me 'ead down, and I made meself a man by the time I were five year old. Now all I get is, 'Please, mister, can I 'ave a crust o' bread?', 'Please, mister, can I 'ave a sup o' beer?', 'Please, mister, I don't want ter go up, I'm scared.' Scared? I'll give 'em scared! I put a fire under 'em, don't I? That sends 'em up quick!"

He roared with laughter, and Aggie chuckled with him— but it was forced, and Billy could tell he was tiring of Harry's ranting already.

"Well," Aggie said, his voice changing as he moved to another part of the shop. "It won't last much longer if men like this Shaftesbury have their way, will it? Got ter move wid the times, Harry. Got ter modernise!"

"They'll not modernise me," Harry grumbled. "Nor me lads. Like ter see 'em try ter tek me lads away."

"They'll only fine ye. Ten pound, I heard. Have ye ten pound, Harry?"

"I got a fist," Harry retorted. "They can 'ave ten from that if they likes!"

Aggie did not reply, and whatever he was doing must have signalled to Harry that the conversation was over, because he pocketed whatever coins he had managed to extract from Aggie and shuffled to the door. The boys flattened themselves against the back of the counter as he passed, still muttering and grumbling to himself, and only when the shop door had closed did they let out the breath they had been holding and get to their feet.

"That was a close one, eh, lads?" Aggie said. They turned to find him watching them from across the counter with a smile creasing his already lined face. "Right lucky he didn't see yez."

"What was all that about?" Billy asked, as he and Tosher crossed the dusty shop floor. "About this Act, and that lord?"

"Nothin' ye should be worryin' yerselves about," Aggie said, dismissing the question with a wave. "And nothin' that'll make any difference to ye. Now. What can I do for you fine gentlemen today? Got something for me, has ye?"

"'Old on." Tosher reached into his jacket, rummaged around for a moment, then pulled out the spoon and held it up triumphantly. "Look at that, eh? Pretty, innit?"

Aggie grunted, less impressed than Billy would have hoped, and held out a hand. "Give it here, then. Let's 'ave a look."

Tosher handed over the spoon with some reluctance,

and both boys crowded in while Aggie inspected it with narrowed eyes. He rubbed the spoon on his food-stained shirt, then held it up to the gas-lamp that hissed on the wall behind him.

"Pewter, is it?" he asked, casually.

"Not likely!" Tosher retorted. "That's silver, as well you know!"

"That so?" Aggie raised his eyebrows doubtfully. "And how would you know? Come from the silver spoon gutter, did it?"

Tosher opened his mouth to tell Aggie exactly where the spoon had come from, but Billy elbowed him in the ribs and he shut it again.

"It's silver," Billy said. "Pewter would've dented already."

"Hm." Aggie stared hard at Billy for a minute, then turned his gaze back to the spoon. "I'll give you a shilling," he said.

"A shilling?" Tosher exploded in indignation. "You're 'avin' a laugh! That's worth a good five pound at least."

"Really?" Aggie's eyebrows shot up. "Reckon you could get five pound for this somewhere else, do ye? Then I suggest ye go there." He tossed the spoon back down on the counter. "And the best o' luck to ye."

Tosher's face went as red as his hair. He was about to retort, probably with something filthy, but Billy put out a hand to silence him. Clearly this was going to take a little more thought than their usual transactions.

"All right," he said. "Fine. Maybe we couldn't take this anywhere else. But fact is, we brought it to you and we want to sell it. Wouldn't be any good to us otherwise. Silver spoons don't buy beer, am I right?"

Aggie looked at him with an expression of mingled

respect and amusement, much as he might regard a dog which had learned an impressive trick. "I'm listenin'," he said.

"We know this spoon's worth a lot more than you're going to pay us," Billy continued. "But that's not our concern. We're not lookin' for a fair price. All we want's a bit of coin to take down the Eagle and keep us in drink for a while. But a shilling won't cut it."

"Nor will a fiver," Aggie shot back.

"So let's meet in the middle, shall we?" Billy eyed Aggie, sizing him up. He decided to push his luck. "Three pound."

Aggie laughed. "One."

"Two, then. That's more than fair."

Aggie shook his head. "You lads wouldn't know what to do with two pound," he said. "Look. Here's what I'll do. One pound for the spoon, and—" he raised a hand against Tosher's protest, "—and another pound if I sells it on for more than a fiver. Like I said, there's not many would take it off ye, and not many more who'd take it from me. Ye got lucky today, I'd guess: don't push yer luck too far now."

Tosher and Billy looked at each other. A pound was more money than they had ever seen in their life, more than Gerard would take in some weeks. And it would be all theirs. Tosher nodded, and Billy turned back to Aggie.

"Done," he said, and put out his hand for the Irishman to shake. After a long pause Aggie clasped the hand in his own rough paw, his eyes narrowing and a wry smile creasing his craggy lips.

"And done," he said.

5

The Eagle and Child

THE TWO BOYS left Aggie's shop with their pockets heavy and their hearts light. They were both giddy at the thought of the deal they had just struck. There was no way they would be able to spend a whole pound in one night, but that was not a problem. Weeks and weeks of nights at the pub stretched out ahead of them, and for the moment they felt as rich as kings.

But even as they wound their way down the narrow streets towards the Eagle and Child, another thought was turning over in Billy's mind. He was thinking about the conversation he and Tosher had overheard in the shop, and all the talk of chimney sweeps and climbing boys, and lords, and Acts of Parliament. The idea that such things were being spoken of by such high and mighty men was quite frankly incredible, and Billy had a hard time believing it.

He had glimpsed lords before, usually in the streets around the Palace of Westminster, but they were always closeted in their carriages, looking over the heads of the people they passed, their faces as hard as those that glared out of the doorways and windows of Lambeth; except this hardness was born of greed and privilege rather than fear. Like Harry, there was no way Billy could imagine one of them descending to the filth and squalor in which most of the city lived, or even being aware of people like him.

This Lord Shaftesbury could not be much different. Any sympathy the man claimed to have was probably just fine words and fancy speeches, the same as the rest of them. All he really cared about was his riches and his comfortable life—he couldn't possibly care about what climbing boys were doing. If he did, he wouldn't be trying to stop them from working.

Climbing was all Billy knew, and all he had known for as long as he could remember. If he couldn't climb for a living, what then? He was too small for manual labour, too bent from years in the flues for factory work. If he had to stop climbing tomorrow he would probably end up on the street, begging or stealing, or worse. No. As bad as life was with Gerard, at least it was secure. That was what these lords didn't understand; if they had, they would have known to keep their noses well out of it.

They were nearing the Eagle and Child now. The pub stood on a typically dirty corner of a typically muddy street, its frosted windows leaking yellow light into the foggy darkness. The door was open, and from within came the usual sounds of laughter and music: working men doing their best to forget the toil of the day just gone and the day to come.

Tosher and Billy did not bother going through the front door: climbing boys were not welcome, and in any case there was always the chance that they would come across one of Gerard's associates. Instead they made their way around to the back of the building, where a dirt yard was surrounded on all sides by tall buildings with blank windows, and the sounds from the bar were muted.

The back door of the pub stood open as usual, revealing a tiny cave of a kitchen where the innkeeper's wife, an enormous woman called Mrs. Hallam, sweated over vats of stew bubbling on an iron range. She waved a stubby hand when she saw them.

"Here for Clara again?" she wheezed, mopping her brick-red brow with the back of a hairy forearm. "She'll be out in a mo. Not too busy tonight."

Billy felt himself blush, embarrassed that their interest was so apparent; but Tosher just tipped his cap with a cheeky wink, unaware or unconcerned what Mrs. Hallam thought.

"We'll wait out here," Tosher said. He fished in his pocket for a couple of farthings. "And while we're about it why don't you give us a couple of helpings of that fine stew you got there? Smells delicious!"

Mrs. Hallam laughed again, took the money, and dished out two enormous bowls of the greasy brown slop. It was mostly gravy, with the odd carrot and lump of potato bobbing to the surface, but it was hot and filling, and the boys shovelled it into their mouths as fast as they could.

They were almost finished when Mrs. Hallam glanced into the passageway and called, "They're out here!" and a moment later a girl appeared at the kitchen door. She was tall and slim, with a mass of tight black curls barely contained under the cap she wore on her head. Her face was round, and although her eyes were surrounded by deep shadows they still managed to sparkle with a mischievous glint. When she saw them her tiny mouth spread into a smile.

"All right, boys?" Clara said. "After beer again, are you?"

"After your company, more like," Tosher replied; all Billy could do was nod dumbly and wonder why he suddenly felt so warm. "And we're drinking gin tonight, if you don't mind."

"You sure?" Clara raised a delicate eyebrow. "Isn't gin a bit strong for you?"

Tosher puffed out his chest and drew himself up to his full height. "Nah," he said carelessly. "We always drink that stuff now. Beer's for kids."

"If you say so." Clara's smile broadened as her eyes flicked from Tosher to Billy, "All right there, Bill? Cat got your tongue, has it?"

Billy muttered something and shrugged, and Clara laughed with delight.

"Two halves of gin, then." She held out a hand. "Cough up."

Tosher counted out a couple of coins and placed them in her palm. Clara's eyes widened a fraction as she glimpsed the rest of it, but she said nothing.

"You going to join us?" Tosher blurted, as Clara turned to go back inside. She stopped and regarded him with her dark eyes before shrugging carelessly.

"All right then," she said. "Back in a mo."

As soon as Clara left, Billy's tongue came unstuck from the roof of his mouth. Tosher was gazing after her with a dazed expression, which Billy felt sure mirrored his own, and as he looked at Tosher's gormless face he felt a pang of jealousy.

Clara returned a few minutes later, bringing two brimming glasses of clear liquid for the boys and a tankard of beer for herself. They sat on the kitchen step as Mrs. Hallam bustled in and out behind them, and swapped tales and news of the week so far.

Clara was a natural raconteur, and she regaled them with stories of their patrons, including frighteningly accurate impressions of the regulars. There had been at least four fights in the last three days, including one in which a man had lost all but three of his teeth and another which had quickly turned into an all-out brawl to which the police had to be called.

"You should have seen 'em!" she chuckled. "These three bobbies turned up, and they didn't 'ave the first clue. There's about ten dockers all brawlin' in the street out there, blood all over the place, cussin' and yellin'; then the sergeant tries to lay 'ands on Mickey Tanner, and Mickey turns and belts 'im one in the face and lays 'im flat out, and the two other peelers—only lads they are—they turns tail and scarpers! You should'a seen the sergeant's face when it were all over and the boys got 'im inside and roused 'im with a whisky! Didn't know where 'e was or 'ow 'e'd got there!"

She laughed, a throaty sound Billy could have listened to all day. Tosher laughed with her, only his was a loud honking bray that sounded more like a goose being strangled. He had no problem joining in the talk: words came easily to Tosher, even if they didn't make much sense sometimes. Billy wished he had that gift, but all he could do was sit and nod, and sip the fiery gin.

"So what were it over?" Tosher asked, leaning forwards, his head bobbing on the end of his long neck like a ball on a stick.

"Ah, the usual," Clara said, shrugging. "Cards and money.

They makes bets, then they can't agree on the rules, so two of 'em think they've both got the winning hand, and before you know it they're outside in the mud and the blood. At least they've decency enough to spare Pa's shop."

Tosher drained the last of his gin and handed the glass to Clara.

"Get us another one, will yer?" he said, rising unsteadily to his feet. "Nature calls."

"You payin' or what?" Clara called after him.

"In a minute!"

Tosher disappeared round the corner. Clara snorted and shook her head, then looked down at Billy's glass, which was still half-full.

"You finishin' that?" she said with a wicked smile.

Billy flushed and hurriedly drained the glass. The liquid burned his throat, and fumes exploded in the back of his nose. He coughed and spluttered, and Clara roared with laughter and swept back inside, leaving him to recover.

By the time she returned bearing three more glasses, Billy had regained his breath, if not his pride. He took the drink from her with a nervous smile, and this time when it went down it did not burn quite so badly. In fact he was beginning to feel pleasantly warm; the sensation spread out from his chest, tendrils of heat creeping through his body and fending off the freezing air around him.

He realised he was staring at Clara, and she was staring back at him. She was still smiling, but now it was with a thoughtful air. She took a gulp of gin herself and wiped her mouth with the back of her hand.

"Nice shiner," she said.

Billy stared dumbly, wondering what she meant. His head

was warm now, right to the tips of his ears. He reckoned he must be bright red, but he didn't mind.

"Your eye," Clara prompted, pointing. "Gerard give that to you?"

Understanding dawned, and he nodded. He wanted to speak, but his nerves and the gin had conspired to seal his lips shut. He probably needed another glass to loosen them up again.

Clara leaned forwards on the step, reaching out for the side of his face. He flinched away, but she tutted and shushed him, and held his arm with one hand while she used the other to explore the place where Gerard's fist had left its mark. The touch of her fingers sent a tiny shock through his body, and he was surprised to find he felt no pain. He would gladly have let her keep her hands there forever, whether it hurt or not.

After looking at the bruise for a minute Clara made a noise of disgust in the back of her throat.

"I'd like to give 'im one an' all," she muttered. "Big drunk bully. Thinks 'e's a big man 'cause 'e hits kids." She sat back, looking hard at Billy, but he had the strange feeling that she was looking at something else, something beyond him or behind him.

"I've known plenty like him," she said after a moment. "Back home. They're all like that over there. All the men. Walking around like they own the earth and everyone on it. They knows they can do what they likes and there ain't no one gonna stop 'em. The women too an' all. Treating us like beasts. I *hates* 'em!"

She spat, and a wild fury flashed in her eyes. Billy had never admired her more than he did in that instant. He took another drink, steadying his nerves. His heart was hammering, the strength of it almost suffocating him. He could feel words building up inside him, clustering behind his lips. He trembled with the force of pent-up longing. He was ready. Now was the time. He was going to say something. He was going to tell Clara how he worshipped her and wanted to spend every day with her.

Then he saw Clara's eyes look past him, distracted, and she dropped her glass and leapt to her feet with an expression of mingled fury and terror. Billy turned too, and his insides turned to water as he saw what she had seen.

Tosher was standing at the end of the alley, his face white and his eyes wide. Behind him stood Gerard, one arm wrapped around Tosher's shoulders, the fist gripping a long knife with the blade resting against Tosher's cheek.

"All right, Bill?" Gerard slurred. "What we got 'ere, then?"

6
Stand-off

"YOU LET 'IM GO!" Clara yelled.

Gerard bellowed with laughter. The knife dug into Tosher's cheek as the hand that held it danced. "She's a little wildcat, ain't she?" Gerard sneered, still addressing Billy.

Billy couldn't reply. The warmth of the gin had evaporated, doused by a cold wave of fear. Whatever courage he had been summoning to speak to Clara had also been washed away.

"She got your tongue an' all?" Gerard chuckled. "Don't blame yer, mate. She's not a bad looker."

Clara's eyes flashed, and Billy saw her fists clench. She made as if to step towards Gerard, but he tightened his grip on Tosher's neck with a warning shake of the head.

"Ah!" he said. "You stay right there, miss. Can't 'ave yer making any mistakes now, can we?"

Gerard was drunk: Billy could tell by his drooping eyes and the slurred edge to his voice. He swayed unsteadily, half hanging on to Tosher to keep himself up. In any other circumstance it would have been a simple matter for Tosher to slither away, and the three of them could have outrun Gerard easily. But there was the knife, the blade resting against Tosher's ashen-white skin. The knife made all the difference.

"Right," Gerard said, with the air of a man about to make a speech. "I think we all know why I'm 'ere today!"

"I told yer, Gerry," Tosher piped up. "We don't know nuffin!" His voice was high with panic, his eyes bulging like a fish.

"Shurrup!" Gerard shook him hard and Tosher's legs buckled. With a flush of embarrassment Billy saw that he had been crying. "You'll speak when you're spoken ter," Gerard growled. "Understand? Now Bill. Me little Billy. You're a good lad, ain't yer? A Christian lad. You wouldn't lie to yer uncle Gerry, would yer? Naw. You're a good lad. Not like this'un 'ere."

He snarled and gave Tosher another shake, then focused on Billy as best he could.

"I know you done something, Billy," he said. "I know you been a naughty lad. But I'm a good soul, as God knows. I'll treat yer fair. Just tell us where it is, and we'll say no more about it."

Billy knew at once what Gerard meant, though he had no idea how Gerard had found out about the spoon. He looked at Tosher, who quickly shook his head.

"I dunno what you mean, Gerard," Billy managed to say. His voice was thin and pathetic; he cleared his throat and tried again. "I dunno what you're talking about. Why don't you tell us?"

"You know what I mean!" Gerard snarled, and Tosher gave a whimper as the knife slid down to his throat. "You took something, and now yer gonna give it back, yer filthy brat!"

"What's all this noise, then?"

They all turned. Mrs. Hallam was standing in the kitchen doorway, frowning at the scene playing out in her yard. She took it in at a glance: Clara and Billy frozen on the step; Tosher and Gerard wrapped in their deadly embrace, the knife glinting in the light from the kitchen. Her eyes widened, and she turned and bellowed: "Henry! Get the lads and get out 'ere!"

"Now then, ma'am," Gerard protested, doing his best to sound innocent despite all evidence to the contrary.

He raised the knife in a placating gesture, and in that instant Clara darted forward and jumped on him, her fingers grasping his knife-hand. Gerard went down with a roar; Tosher was knocked to the ground, wailing and scrambling to get out of the way; Clara hissed and bit at Gerard's face as they rolled over and over in the mud.

Henry Hallam appeared behind his wife, flanked by a couple of dockers with arms like steel cables.

"What's all this?" he said. He was old, and his bushy mustaches were flecked with grey, but he had been a corporal in the army and Billy had never known him to be bested in a fight.

Gerard and Clara were still squirming on the ground, and it was impossible to see who had the upper hand. Billy saw the knife flash, and he wished—oh, how he wished— that he was brave enough to leap into the fray and save her. But he wasn't. He was paralysed with fear, just like Tosher, who cowered against a pile of crates and whimpered.

Mr. Hallam nodded to the dockers, who stepped out into

the yard. But even as they spread out to the left and right, the two combatants fell still, and with a sinking heart Billy saw that it was Gerard who had gained the upper hand. Both he and Clara were smeared all over with stinking mud, and blood was dripping from a cut above Gerard's eye, but Gerard was gripping Clara's arm in one meaty fist, and the other was holding the knife to her throat.

"Right," Gerard panted. The fight had sobered him up; there was a dangerous glint in his eye now, and he looked around at them all like a cornered wolf. "You fellas just stay right where you are. I don't know this little lady, but I must say I'm curious to see if she's as dark on the inside as she is on the outside. I'll cut her if I have to—don't think I won't!"

Mr. Hallam made a motion, and the dockers fell still.

"What do you want?" Mr. Hallam demanded gruffly. "Is it money?"

"I want me boys," Gerard replied, jerking his head, first at Tosher then at Billy. "They took something, and they need to give it back. I'm not lookin' fer trouble, just a bit o' justice. Like the Good Book says."

"You never read a Bible in your life," Mrs. Hallam snapped. "I know you, Gerard Sloan. You're a wicked man. I know how you treats them boys. An' if these are yours I'm not surprised they took from you, you black-'earted sinner! Probably less'n they deserve!"

"Weren't me they took from," Gerard replied piously. "If it were I'm sure I'd find it in me 'eart to forgive 'em. But there's folk come a-lookin' for 'em, and it's my duty to see that these boys face up to their crimes."

Mr. Hallam drew himself up. "This true?" he said, glaring between Billy and Tosher.

Billy nodded miserably. He knew the landlord had little enough love for them; he tolerated their presence at his back door, and he didn't mind his wife feeding them, but Billy doubted he would go so far as to put himself at risk for their sake.

Tosher cowered silently against the crates, trying to make himself invisible. Clara was shooting daggers at Mr. Hallam, clearly more angry than afraid. Billy doubted she would have hesitated to use the knife on Gerard if the tables were turned. Mr. Hallam ignored her. He spoke to Gerard instead.

"All right," he said. "Mr. Sloan, is it? I can see we've got ourselves a bit of a situation 'ere. You want these two boys, and as I understand things they're yours by right, so not much I can say against that. But the girl's a different matter. She's mine, and I'd rather not see her harmed."

"I'd rather not 'arm 'er," Gerard said. "I'm a gentle soul, sir, as God is my witness. But I'm in a bit of a bind now, see? If I lets 'er go, what's to stop these two from scarperin'? Then I'm back where I started."

"You'll get nothing if you hurt her."

"I'll get nothing if I don't." Gerard turned to Billy. "Come on now, Bill. Be a good lad. You know it's only sense. Give it over, and we'll call the 'ole thing quits, eh? Nice bit o' beer for you back at the House."

Billy hadn't thought it possible for his spirits to sink any lower, but now they did. Gerard didn't know they had sold the spoon.

"We—we ain't got it no more," he said quietly.

Gerard's black bushy brows settled low over his blood-shot eyes. "What's that?"

"I said: we ain't got it. The spoon. That's what you're

looking for, ain't it?" Billy could hear his voice wavering, and he knew how weak and pathetic he sounded.

"Whatcha do with it, then?"

"Sold it. At Aggie's."

"You little—"

Gerard's attention had wandered for an instant; quick as a whip Clara twisted from his grasp, and as he tried to stab at her with the knife she caught his arm and drove the blade down into his own leg. Gerard howled with pain, then Clara was away and running, and before Billy knew what he was doing he was running too, darting after Clara with Tosher beside him as Gerard's snarls and curses echoed after them.

For a split second Billy's heart soared. He was dizzy with exultation and the thrill of escape, and he even gave a wild laugh of pure joy—but then a foot shot out from the shadows, and he tripped and fell face first to the ground, and the crushing weight of a knee was jammed into the small of his back. He heard a stream of swearing from Clara, and he knew she had been caught too, and when he twisted his head around he saw Tosher being held against a wall by a third figure.

"Hold still," a voice said in his ear. He ignored it and kicked and squirmed, trying to break free, but a mighty blow to the side of his head stilled him. "I said hold still," the lad repeated, quite calmly. "I'd rather not blow yer brains out, but I will if you make me."

There was movement in the alleyway behind them. Billy heard uneven footsteps dragging in the dirt, accompanied by a muttered stream of oaths in Gerard's voice.

"Those little rats," Gerard grumbled. "That one—'er over there. Look what she done!"

Someone laughed nearby, a harsh cruel sound. "Her?" a boy said. "*She* got the better o' *you*?"

The two other boys joined in with the laughter, as strong hands hauled Billy to his feet. Gerard was leaning against a nearby wall, clutching at the wound on his thigh where the knife had gone in. It was bleeding freely, and Billy could see sweat beading on Gerard's brow. Two boys stood by, one holding a terrified Tosher and the other struggling to hang on to Clara, who was writhing and snarling as she tried to escape. They could not have been more than two or three years older than any of them, but Gerard stood back and eyed them warily, as a man might eye a rabid dog.

The boy holding Clara dealt her a crushing blow to her ear, and she fell still and sagged in his arms. Gerard made a move towards her with fire in his eyes, but the boy held his hand out straight and Gerard halted at the sight of the heavy double-barrelled pistol clasped there.

"Now then," Clara's boy said calmly. "I think that's quite enough bother for one night, eh? Let's all just simmer down a bit, shall we?"

"I'm not makin' no trouble," Gerard muttered, raising his hands and backing down. "Just wanted—"

"I know what you wanted," Clara's boy said. "You'll have it soon enough. Just as soon as we get what we came for."

"Which one of 'em took it?" Billy's boy said. He gave Billy a shake. "Were it you?"

Billy clamped his lips tight shut and refused to answer. He tried to catch Tosher's eye, but Tosher was staring wide-eyed at the ground in front of him, plainly terrified. The boy holding Tosher glanced at him, then shook his head.

"This one ain't sayin' nuffin," he said.

"All right then." Clara's boy sighed, then turned the pistol and laid the muzzle against her temple. "We'll start with 'er and see if it loosens some tongues."

"No! Wait!" The words burst from Billy's mouth before he thought them. He started forwards, but the boy holding him tightened his grip painfully and jerked him back. "Please," Billy begged. "Wait. Don't hurt her."

"Better," Clara's boy said, though he kept the pistol where it was. He was handsome, with jet-black hair oiled and combed straight back from his forehead, and he was the best-dressed of the three, in a red waistcoat and black shirt. His narrow face was twisted in a wry smile: he looked as if he was enjoying the moment. "Something you care to share with us?"

"We don't have the spoon," Billy said. "We sold it. We can give you the money."

Clara's boy shook his head. "Not good enough," he said. "We got orders to get that spoon, or nothing. See, Archie Miller don't take kindly to folk holdin' out on him. You don't go thievin' under Archie's nose, boy, not if you live on his streets and breathe his air."

Billy didn't ask how Archie knew about the spoon—Archie knew of everything that went on in the city, or so it seemed; especially if it was something outside the law.

Clara's boy narrowed his eyes, thinking. Eventually he said: "Who'd you sell it to?"

"Aggie," Billy said.

The boy laughed. "That potato-eater? Well, he's a man who sees sense and won't cross Archie in a hurry, I'll wager."

He tightened his grip on Clara's arm and gestured with the pistol. "Let's go pay him a visit, shall we?"

7

Smoke and Flames

BILLY TRIPPED AND STUMBLED through the darkened streets, the boy's grip as firm as ever on his arm. He was trying to see a way out of the disaster into which they had fallen, but no matter how hard he thought he could see no solution.

He briefly considered calling for help, but one glance at the faces they passed told him that would be useless. No one looked twice at them: they were on Archie Miller's business, and no one in their right mind messed with Archie.

Escape, then? No. That would be equally useless. Billy could see the gun hanging casually from the hand of the black-haired boy who walked with Clara. He had seen guns used in street fights once or twice; they were terrifically loud, and gave off enormous clouds of smoke, and when the aim was true they could maim and kill easily. They depended on luck as much as the skill of the user; but how lucky were they likely to be, judging by the night so far?

Besides, even if they did manage to get away, it wouldn't take long for Archie to track them down. If they wanted to be safe they would have to leave the city entirely, and even then their safety wasn't a sure thing.

A smack around the head brought him back to the moment. They had emerged into the courtyard where Aggie's shop was situated. The same gaunt faces peered down at them from the shadowed balconies above. Gerard was nowhere to be seen: probably skulking back to the House, nursing his wounds.

The black-haired boy was looking at Billy. "Now you just watch your tongue in there, boy," he said. "Wouldn't want anything unfortunate to happen, would we?"

He waggled the pistol by Clara's head to emphasise the point, then turned and pushed her in front of him. The punch from earlier had subdued her; she walked with her head down and her shoulders sagging, barely lifting her feet. Billy could see a trickle of blood at the nape of her neck. Tosher shuffled along silently, giving as much resistance as a leaf in a thunderstorm.

"I'm near to closing!" Aggie shouted from the dim recesses of the shop as they entered. "This best be quick. I'm in no mood to bargain."

He emerged from the dusty darkness and stopped short, taking in the ragged group: the three older boys with their captives; the blood; the gun.

"And how can I help you fine gentlemen today?" he said, addressing them mildly.

The black-haired boy released Clara and stepped forwards, leaning on the counter with the pistol dangling from his hand, looking Aggie straight in the eye. He was much too close, but Aggie made no move away from him. There was a length of wood studded with nails and glass stowed just beneath the counter—Billy had seen it used once on a man who had tried to steal from the shop, and he knew Aggie was thinking about using it now.

"We're looking for an item," the black-haired boy said quietly. "A spoon. Sterling silver. It was sold to you by these fine young gentlemen today, only it wasn't theirs to sell."

"Stealin' from Archie, are they?" Aggie raised his eyebrows in mock surprise, then made a show of studying Billy and Tosher's faces. After a second he shrugged and shook his head. "Can't say as I've seen either of these two lads before. Sure it's my shop you want?"

The black-haired boy smiled and gave a little laugh. "Oh, quite sure," he said. "Now, are we going to get along over this matter?"

"Or?"

"Or … we kill you and find the spoon ourselves. It would take longer, but I'm sure we'd get there in the end. What do you say?"

There was an agonising moment of silence as the two faced each other, their eyes locked. Then Aggie's face broke into a broad smile, and he stepped back and held up his hands.

"All right. All right!" Aggie declared. "Just me sense o' humour! A silver spoon, you say? I think I know the one. Fine piece of work. Bought fer five pound, as I recall. So if you gentlemen could show me the colour of yer money, we can all part ways wid a smile and a handshake—what d'ye say?"

The black-haired boy's face hardened, and his smile dissolved. His fingers tightened around the stock of the pistol.

"Archie don't pay for what's rightfully his," he growled. "If you want your money, I suggest you make an arrangement with these gentlemen here."

He swept the pistol in a wide arc, taking in Billy, Tosher and Clara. The pistol came around to point straight at Aggie's placid face, and the boy calmly pulled back the hammer with a click that resounded in the sudden silence.

"Now," he said. "Are you going to hand it over or not, yer dumb Irish?"

Aggie looked down the barrel of the gun for a second, as if considering the boy's proposition. Then, with a sudden movement, he swung the nail-studded length of wood up from under the counter and brought it down on the boy's hand. An almighty bang split the air. Dense smoke filled the shop as everyone ducked and covered their ears, and the gas-lamp behind Aggie exploded into hungry flames that roared across the walls and ceiling. The pistol flew through the air as the black-haired boy roared with rage and clasped at his hand, but before he could make a move to retrieve his weapon, Aggie was leaping over the counter and bringing the wood down again on his upraised arm.

The boy holding Billy had let go of him at the sound of the gunshot. Billy darted away from him, making for Clara, who was cowering by the counter with her hands over her ears. Before he could reach her, a fist came from nowhere and knocked him sprawling on the floor; he twisted round to see a boot descending towards his face, and just managed to raise his hands to ward it off. The boy who stamped at him had not expected resistance, and Billy's deflecting hands toppled him off-balance so that he crashed to the floor himself, striking his head hard on the edge of the counter. He did not get up.

Billy scrambled to his feet. Smoke was everywhere. The

flames from the shattered gas-lamp were pouring across the ceiling, licking around the shelves and cabinets. Aggie and the black-haired boy were wrestling together on the ground; Aggie had dropped his club, and he and the boy were grappling for the pistol, grunting and swearing.

Tosher appeared at his elbow with a bleeding nose.

"Come *on!*" he shouted, tugging at Billy's sleeve. "Let's go!"

Billy shook him off. "We need to get Clara!"

He took a step towards Clara. Aggie and the boy were between them, a struggling mass of limbs on the floor.

"Clara!" Billy yelled to her, stretching out a hand. "Clara! Come on!"

She roused herself and looked up at him. Her eyes were wide with fear, but she nodded and rose unsteadily to her feet, and began to edge around the combatants. A boot lashed out and caught her on the shin; a glint of her usual wildness flashed in her eyes, and she returned the kick savagely before skipping past them and joining Billy and Tosher.

"You all right?" Tosher asked before Billy could say anything. Clara nodded wordlessly. "Come on then," Tosher said, wiping at his nose with a sleeve. "Let's get outta 'ere."

He reached past Billy and grabbed Clara's hand, and despite the fire and the terror and the two figures struggling in the middle of it all Billy felt a shard of jealousy stabbing at his heart. But he pushed it down and turned to follow them, even as another deafening shot rang out. Clara cried out in pain, and almost fell; Tosher gave a cry of panic and caught her, but there was no time to stop or think: the ceiling creaked and groaned, a long split appeared in the plaster, and Billy shoved Tosher and screamed at him to run as the timbers collapsed with a groan and a blossom of fire, and the shop disintegrated all around them.

They sprinted through the door, pursued by hungry flames, and ran blindly into the night. Behind them they could hear cries of alarm from the children in the upper storeys, but there was no going back, no way to help. They ran and ran, darting this way and that past startled faces, Tosher clinging to Clara, whose right arm dangled uselessly in a mess of blood, half-leading and half-carrying her, and Billy following behind, his mind full of fire and smoke and the ear-splitting crack of the gunshot. They did not know where they were going, and they did not care. Terror carried them along as they plunged through the twisting streets, deeper and deeper into the dark heart of the city, fleeing from the flames into the maw of the night.

8

The Gentleman

IN A DARKENED PARLOUR in a tatty house on the edge of the slums of Lambeth, two men sat at a table and waited.

The older of the two sported a great grey-streaked beard that touched his chest. He reclined in his chair, his head back and his eyes closed, trying to get some sleep in preparation for the long night ahead. His name was Daniel Tanner.

The younger man, whose name was Robert, fidgeted constantly, tapping his fingers on the table and ducking his head to look through the grimy window to the street outside.

"What time's he due?" Robert asked.

"Any time now," Daniel replied, without opening his eyes. "He's punctual. Doesn't keep others waiting on him, and he doesn't like to be kept waiting, neither."

"You've worked with him before?"

"Aye. Once or twice."

"What sort of a man is he?"

"Quiet." Daniel tried to make it a hint.

"I heard he's a grim sort of fellow. Unpleasant."

"Loud folk find quiet folk unpleasant," Daniel replied.

"Just as quiet folk find loud folk unpleasant."

Again, Robert missed the hint. "Why does he do it?" he said, squinting out of the window. "I mean, does he get anything from it?"

"Far as I know it's out of the kindness of his heart." Daniel sighed and opened his eyes, giving up on sleep. "He's a Christian gentleman, and a gentleman does his duty. Should do, elsewise. Visiting the widow and the fatherless—ain't that what it's all about?"

"Of course," Robert agreed absently. "But it's a rough business though, isn't it? Wouldn't have expected someone like him to be doing it. Plenty of other places he could be."

"Aye, but he's chosen this one, and we ain't here to change his mind. We're here to keep our mouths shut and our eyes open, and don't you forget it."

Robert nodded and looked around the room. There was a moment of silence, broken only by the nervous tapping of his fingers. Daniel shook his head to himself and settled back again with his eyes closed.

"How do you address an earl?" Robert piped up.

"You don't," Daniel replied sharply. "You let me do the talkin', and *if* he should address you then you call him 'my lord' and nothing else. You hear?" The way he said it suggested Daniel highly doubted any such exchange would take place.

A knock came on the door, loud and commanding. Robert leapt to his feet, and Daniel rose with only marginally less haste. He brushed himself down, ran a hand over his beard, then opened the door.

"Good evening, Tanner," a rich, deep voice said. "It's cold tonight."

"Aye, your lordship." Daniel nodded. He stood aside, allowing a tall man with a sallow face and hooded eyes to duck into the room. The man was dressed in a black frock coat, buttoned up against the winter chill, and he carried in his black-gloved hand a silk top hat. Between his stern expression and the severity of his dress he might have been an undertaker. He swept the room and his eyes lighted on Robert, who was standing by the table and fidgeting with his own battered bowler.

"Good evening," the guest greeted him, extending a hand. Robert shot Daniel a quick glance then took the hand and shook it once with a nervous half-bow. The guest smiled wryly. "Your first time, I take it?" he said. His voice rolled around the room, as if it was used to filling far larger spaces.

Robert nodded briefly and looked at his feet. The guest chuckled and turned to Daniel.

"Shall we pray?" he said.

They sat around the table and bowed their heads. There was a pause, then the guest raised his voice and began to speak:

"O Lord our Father," he intoned, slowly and with great solemnity. "Most high and holy God. We come before Thee in this hour, Thy humble servants, to implore Thy blessing and mercy as we go about Thy work in this place of iniquity. Send down, we pray, Thy Spirit from on high to go before us and prepare the way. Seek out such miserable creatures as Thou wilt have mercy on this night, and lead our footsteps that we may come upon them, the vessels of Thy grace, and be Thine angels unto them. Pour Thou the love of Thy Son, the Lord Jesus, into our hearts, and the words of Thy glorious Gospel into our mouths. Cleanse us from our sin, that we may be worthy servants about Thy business this night, and surround us with chariots of fire. In Jesus' name we ask these things…"

"Amen," the two other men murmured.

Immediately the guest rose to his feet. "Thank you, gentlemen," he said. "Shall we?"

They rose with him and buttoned up their coats, then followed him out of the door and into the bitter night.

The tall man walked swiftly and with determination, leading the way through the darkened streets as the others hurried to keep up. A few heads turned as he passed, and there were more than a few looks of interest at the finery of the gentleman's clothes and the nobility in his face—but one by one the expressions of greed turned to recognition, and one by one they turned away. No one bothered them—it seemed no one dared.

If Daniel was impressed by this he didn't show it, but Robert found it hard to contain his amazement.

"What's up with them?" he hissed to Daniel as they walked. "I'd have thought someone would at least give it a try."

"Respect," was Daniel's only reply.

They turned down a side street, then another, then another, until they found themselves approaching a hulking railway viaduct carried above the rooftops on a series of high brick arches. The viaduct was silent, the trains cold and asleep in their sidings for the night; but from beneath the arches came a low rustling sound like the leaves of a wood stirring in a constant breeze. As the men drew nearer, the murky wash of noise splintered into a thousand pieces: muttering, snoring, coughing, sneezing, sighing, weeping—the chorus of a hundred lives being painfully drawn out in the darkness.

In another minute they came upon the fringes of a curious settlement: rag-wrapped bodies lying discarded by the side of the path, some huddled together in twos or threes, others stretched out alone. Some stirred as they passed, white eyes peering up at them from filthy faces; others lay still—too still, to Robert's eyes, as if they might never move again. The gentleman slowed now, and picked his way carefully through the thickening crowds, his eyes sweeping this way and that like the beam of a lighthouse. Daniel fumbled in a deep pocket and took out two candles, which he lit with a flaring match before handing one to Robert and taking the other to light the gentleman's way.

By candlelight the ruin around them was even more evident: the sores on faces, the sewage lying in the open, the scuttling shapes that darted from shadow to shadow with beady eyes and yellow teeth. But still the gentleman passed through it without flinching or showing so much as a flicker of disgust. Indeed, when he turned, and the dancing light fell on his face, Robert could see that it was twisted into an expression of deepest sorrow and sympathy.

Presently they entered the dank darkness under the arch itself. Here the stench of human waste and sickness was almost overpowering, and Robert came to a halt and nearly turned back. The gentleman took a handkerchief from his pocket and held it over his nose and mouth, and continued without a pause. Daniel went with him, holding the candle aloft. Robert hesitated for a moment, then took a deep breath and followed them into the gloom.

He caught up with them by a huddled group of figures.

The gentleman was speaking to them, nodding occasionally; Robert glimpsed a person who might once have been a woman but was now little more than a scarecrow, clutching a ragged bundle in her arms and surrounded by smaller scarecrows. As he watched, the woman nodded towards two of her brood, and the gentleman looked at them and extended his hand. The tiny wraiths rose to their feet and went to him, and the gentleman stroked their hair tenderly before ushering them to stand beside Daniel.

A few more words were exchanged with the woman, then they moved on. Robert followed silently.

The encounter was repeated four more times: with another mother surrounded by shivering children; with a pair of boys who were only too eager to come with them; with a solitary girl who was barely more than a skeleton; with a squint-eyed man who grudgingly handed over three boys and a girl and demanded payment, which the gentleman eventually gave to him, along with some sharp words.

As they passed, Robert noticed a few figures scurrying away, glancing guiltily over their shoulders and only creeping back once it was evident they were not being sought. One or two spouted a stream of curses at them, and one woman leapt at the gentleman with clawed hands and had to be forced back by Daniel's broad arm. But by and large the inhabitants of the arch ignored them, too wrapped up in their own misery to care about three more strangers.

When the final exchange had been made, and the last of the children collected, they made their way back into the fresh air. Daniel had already thrust a group of children at Robert with a gruff command to make himself useful, and now they clustered around his legs and hung on to his arms, sniffing and whimpering and shivering.

"Duke Street?" the gentleman asked Daniel. Daniel nodded, and the gentleman turned without hesitation and led the way into the night.

Half an hour later they were knocking on the door of a tall building on a cobbled lane. The skeletal girl had collapsed soon after they left the arch, and the gentleman had immediately gathered her into his arms and carried her the rest of the way. She lay with her head on his shoulder now, her stick-like arms clasped around his neck, fast asleep.

A light appeared under the door, and a second later the bolts slid back and the door opened. An elderly lady in a nightcap and shawl peered out at them through the flame of a candle.

"Good evening, Mrs. Lucas," the gentleman said. "You were expecting us?"

"Of course, sir," the lady replied, bobbing a curtsey. "Please, come in. It's awful cold."

They shuffled inside, the children looking around nervously at the unfamiliar surroundings. Through the door a narrow hallway led to a cavernous kitchen where a fire slumbered in the grate. As they filed through the doorway the children rushed to the fire, pushing and shoving, greedy for warmth.

"All right, all right," Mrs. Lucas said, flapping her hands as she waded through the throng. "Let me build it up a bit, then you won't have to sit so close."

While she added wood to the embers and stoked up the flames, the men sat on rough wooden chairs around a huge table. The skeletal girl still clung to the gentleman, her breathing fast and shallow. He stroked her hair and held her tenderly as if she was his own daughter, and waited patiently for Mrs. Lucas to return.

When at last she did, she inspected the girl with much frowning and tutting, then took her gently from his arms. "She's in a bad way," she said. "I'll take her up and call Dr. Samuels, but I can't make any promises."

"Have someone read and pray with her," the gentleman said, in a tone of voice that was more command than suggestion. Robert suspected he was the kind of man who never suggested anything.

Mrs. Lucas nodded, and left them alone with the children.

"Please, sir," one of the older boys piped up after a minute. "But could we 'ave a bit o' bread? Only me an' me bruvver's ever so 'ungry. We ain't eaten since two days ago."

Daniel made to rise, but the gentleman pre-empted him, striding over to a large earthenware bin in the corner and reaching in for a hard brown loaf. At once every eye turned on him, and one of the littlest ones began to cry, partly from relief and partly from desperation, until he was comforted by his sister.

The gentleman knelt down by the fire and began to break up the bread, making sure every child had an equal share. There was some shoving, and someone cursed, but the gentleman shot them a stern look and they subsided and waited their turn. Soon they were each crouching and gnawing on a hunk of the loaf, and the kitchen was silent apart from the crackling of the fire.

Mrs. Lucas returned soon after, and smiled when she saw the children eating.

"Doctor's on his way," she said. "Mary's sitting up with

70

the poor creature and reading a psalm. She's in God's hands now."

"As are we all," the gentleman replied. "Do you need help getting these ones to bed?"

"Thank you kindly, but I've a couple of lads coming down presently. You've done more than enough tonight, your lordship."

"Then we shall trouble you no more." The gentleman stood and bowed, and Daniel and Robert did the same. "Good evening to you, Mrs. Lucas, and God bless you greatly for all the work you do."

"And God bless yer too, your lordship," she replied. "Lord only knows what these babes'd be facing tonight without the likes o' you and yer Christian charity."

"No more than my duty," the gentleman replied. "Good night."

As they left, Robert could hear the distant strains of a girl's singing drifting down from upstairs. It was a song he remembered from his youth, one his mother used to sing to him in his bed:

"Sleep, my child, and peace attend thee
All through the night.
Guardian angels God will lend thee
All through the night …"

The door closed behind them, cutting off the voice. They stood in the cold wind on the bare street. Robert buttoned up his coat and shivered, thinking of the hundreds of others lying in dark arches and forgotten corners all over the city, with no fire and no bread, and no prospect of any in the days or weeks to come. When Daniel had invited him on the mission tonight he had been curious, even excited at the thought of venturing into the unknown—but now he was just cold, and tired, and exhausted from the assault on his eyes and ears. He wanted nothing more than to return to his own bed, with his own fire and his wife and children, and to be secure in the knowledge that there would be tea and eggs waiting for him in the morning.

"Thank you again, both of you," the gentleman was saying. He shook both their hands again, gripping them with firm earnestness. "God is pleased with what we have done tonight."

"As you said, your lordship: no more'n our duty," Daniel said gruffly. "God bless you."

The gentleman nodded, his face a picture of stern satisfaction, then he turned and strode away into the night.

9
Silver Shillings

BILLY WATCHED THE MEN retreat and let out the breath he had been holding. When he had first seen them enter the archway he had panicked, but the longer he watched the more he felt sure they were not Archie Miller's men, and they were not looking for him. Still, he could not help feeling a rush of relief when they turned and went, taking the rabble of children with him. The less chance of being seen by anyone, the better.

"They gone?" Tosher hissed from the shadows behind him.

"Yeah," Billy replied. He watched the men as they picked their way through the mass of bodies towards the lighter patch of darkness at the far end of the archway. Two of them were unremarkable—the kind of men he saw every day, if slightly better dressed—but the third was different: tall, thin, but with a tremendous presence, as if an aura of power surrounded him. Billy wondered briefly who they were, and what they wanted with the kids—bound for the work-houses, maybe, or else for the mines in the west or the mills far away in the grey north. But it didn't matter. They were not looking for him, and that was all that counted.

He turned back to where Tosher knelt by Clara, in a dark alcove in the brickwork. They had taken the space from another boy who had hardly put up a fight, though they found it stinking and filthy. They had laid Clara down on a bit of wood to keep her out of the worst of it, and she had flinched and cried out every time they touched her arm.

It was the arm they both studied now, Tosher with a face that looked like it had been dusted with chalk. Just above the elbow was where she had taken the shot, and the flesh was blasted away almost beyond recognition. Clara had passed out, and she lay shivering, sweat gleaming on her brow despite the cold.

"What d'you think?" Tosher asked, his voice trembling. "She—she gonna die?"

"I dunno, Tosh," Billy said. He knew he shouldn't, but he found Tosher's naked concern irritating. Tosher was the one who had been about to leave Clara behind, yet here he was acting like the only person in the world who cared about her. "You just got to let me think."

"I saw Jimmy Bolton get run over by a cart once," Tosher continued, his words running together. "An' that messed his leg up, an' they got the sawbones in, an' they took it off an' all, but it got all stinky and he got real sick, and then a while later 'e jus' went ter sleep an' never got up again, and—"

"Will you just be *quiet*?" Billy snapped.

Tosher flinched like a kicked dog and fell silent.

"Look," Billy said, forcing down his temper, "Isn't no good worrying about what *might* happen. Right now we need to look after Clara as best we can, and make sure no

74

one's followed us. We need to be *safe*—understand?"

Tosher sniffed and nodded. "Can we at least get her some brandy?" he said. "Mrs. 'Allam always swore by brandy."

"I'll see if we can get some brandy," Billy agreed. He felt in his pocket for the coins Aggie had paid them. There were fewer than he remembered—with a pang he supposed some had fallen out during the chaos last night—but still enough for a good few glasses of brandy, and food for weeks besides.

He cautioned Tosher to keep an eye out for trouble-makers (though he doubted Tosher would be much good in a fight), and with a last long look at Clara's prone form he turned and scuttled away.

Curiosity drew him back to Aggie's shop, winning out over common sense. He knew the better thing to do was to stay as far away as possible, but he couldn't help wondering what had happened: whether Aggie had escaped, and what had become of Archie's boys. After all, he told himself, wasn't it better to know whether or not they had to keep watching their backs?

A crowd had gathered by the time he arrived. He kept to the shadows and peered over their heads at the scene.

The shopfront was gone, reduced to a smouldering black hole. A long, charred streak ran up the front of the building above, where windows had shattered and balconies had burned away. A group of soot-blackened men was milling about, having managed to put out the fire before it could spread too far; but the long row of sheet-draped bodies laid out in the courtyard dampened any sense of triumph. Most of the bodies were small, and Billy felt a twist of guilt as he remembered the faces of the children who had crowded along the balconies above, and the panicked cries that had followed them as they fled the blaze.

But there were no adult corpses, and for a moment Billy allowed himself to hope that Aggie had survived.

A heavy hand fell on his shoulder. Billy whipped round, fully expecting it to be one of Archie's boys, but when he saw who it was he wished it had been.

"Aw'right?" Archie Miller drawled, beaming down at him. "I knows you, don't I?"

Billy immediately looked for a way of escape, but the rest of the Devil's Lads were spreading out behind Archie, and with a sinking heart he realised he was cornered.

"Aye," Archie continued, nodding thoughtfully. "You're one 'o Gerard's lads, aren't ye? One of 'is pipsqueaks. Just the feller I were looking for."

"Gerard isn't here," Billy managed to say.

"I know 'e ain't 'ere," Archie said. "I got eyes, ain't I? But 'e ain't at 'ome, neither—and word is up in town that one of 'is boys got itchin' fingers." He leaned down, resting his hands on his knees, and brought his face right up to Billy's. "That set me to wonderin' if ol' Gerry ain't got somethin' else goin' on—somethin' I should be knowin' about. So I comes down to me patch, and what do I find? All this commotion, and three o' my lads dead. What does yer make o' that, eh?"

Billy kept silent, clinging on to the slender hope that if he just stayed quiet maybe Archie would get bored and leave him alone, and turn his attention to Gerard instead.

Archie held Billy's terrified gaze for a moment, then he straightened up with a sudden movement that made Billy flinch. Archie bellowed with laughter.

"I ain't gonna hurt you, boy!" he guffawed. "Ain't no good ter me that way, are ye? Naw—what I want to know is what Gerry's got goin' on the side. Can't 'ave him 'oldin' out on me, can I?"

"There isn't nothing," Billy managed to say. "It weren't him. I swear, Archie."

"Then 'oo were it?"

Billy hesitated, and Archie's eyes narrowed. He reached out and grabbed the front of Billy's jacket with a meaty hand, his eyes suddenly dead and flat. "Gerry's got summat going on," he growled. "Now are you gonna tell me about it, or do I 'ave ter persuade yer?"

"I swear I don't know, Archie," Billy managed to stammer. "I swear to God in heaven an' all the angels. I'll swear by anything you want—just please don't hurt me."

Archie roared with laughter again, and turned to look at the gang surrounding him.

"You 'ear that, lads?" he drawled, then raised his voice into a squeaky falsetto. "'Don't 'urt me, Archie! I'll do whatever you wants, just please don't gut me like a pig!'"

As the rest of the gang joined in with his laughter, Billy cursed himself for his foolishness. Why had he come back? Why couldn't he have just left well enough alone?

Abruptly Archie released him and shoved him backwards, sending him sprawling in the mud.

"It's aw'right," Archie chuckled. "I'm not gonna 'urt you, boy. But when you see ol' Gerry you tell 'im Archie's got an eye on 'im. An' if he's 'olding out on me—well, I'll come round 'is place and gut 'im from stem to stern, and you and all yer little friends too. Got that?"

Billy nodded, too full of shame and fear to speak. Archie

grunted and turned to go—but just when Billy thought the ordeal was over Archie's eye flickered downwards, and what he saw made him stop.

"Well now!" he exclaimed. "And what exactly do we 'ave 'ere?"

He crouched down and picked something out of the mud, and with a feeling like the bottom had dropped out of his stomach, Billy saw him raise up a shiny silver coin.

"A shilling?" Archie wiped the mud away and studied the coin. "Gerard trusting you with 'is takin's now, is 'e?"

"There's another one, Arch," a dark-skinned boy said, pointing into the mud at Billy's feet. He darted forward and picked it up, then another, and another, and another, and when he had picked up eight of the coins he dropped them into Archie's outstretched hand.

Billy watched in silence. That was all the money he had been carrying, and now it was gone. But there was no use crying over it. He had other things to worry about, such as what Archie was going to do to him now. It was an odd sensation. The fear had grown to such a pitch that he almost didn't feel it anymore. It was like the smell of soot, or the pain of the scrapes on his elbows and knees: something so constant it faded into the background.

"Now then," Archie breathed, studying the coins. "Where does a smoke-monkey like you get coin like this?"

"It ain't mine," Billy managed. "I didn't know it was there."

"Course you didn't. We all knows coin just springs out o' the ground for the takin'. Right lads?"

Another round of laughter, but this time with a threatening edge to it. The gang crowded in, sensing an encore to

78

the night's amusement. Billy saw a couple of them silently drawing knives from sleeves and belts.

"Now, I don't know if ol' Gerry's been 'oldin' out on me," Archie continued in his slow drawl. He was still studying the coins, and spoke almost to himself. "But I can see you 'ave, boy. And you know what 'appens to those who 'old out on me, right? Leastways, I bet you 'eard a few stories in your time."

That was enough for Billy. Even as Archie pocketed the coins, Billy scrambled to his feet and sprinted away across the courtyard. A howl went up behind him, and he put his head down and pumped his legs as fast as they would go, his lungs already burning and the bruise on his face throbbing as he darted down a dark alleyway. He hardly cared where he was going. He only knew he had to keep running, because the moment he slowed or stopped he was dead.

The alleyway opened out onto a street. Billy turned left, his bare feet slapping on cobbles, and when he heard the clatter of boots he darted right again, down a narrower turning this time, tripping over broken boxes and barrels and ignoring the pain in his feet. The alley split; he turned left, and immediately regretted the choice. He had turned into a dead end, surrounded on three sides by vertical walls of brick. There was a doorway at the end of the alley, and above it the dark hole of a loft with the wooden arm of a crane jutting out; but the door was padlocked and in good repair, and the loft too high to reach.

He skidded to a halt. There was no escape. He was trapped.

10
Leap of Faith

"YOU GOT GUTS, BOY!"

Billy turned, panting hard, to see Archie advancing down the alleyway towards him. The Devil's Lads crowded in behind, craning their necks, eager to see what their leader would do with his prey.

"Ain't many would try an' run," Archie continued. He was holding something in his hand, something that glinted wickedly. "Most would give up there an' then. But you—you got somethin' in yer. Guess in a minute we're all gonna find out what it is."

Billy backed away, looking all around for a way out, but the walls loomed on three sides, windowless and dispassionate. There would be no witnesses to his death apart from Archie and his gang. It almost made him sob to think that their cruel laughter was the last thing he would hear.

His back came up against the rough wood of the door, and he stopped. Archie stopped too. He could see the desperation in Billy's eyes, and he was savouring it. A smile tugged at one corner of his mouth, but it did not touch his eyes: they were as dead and cold as the stars above.

"Any prayers yer want to say?" he asked softly. "There's many things a man can say afore he dies. Some ask for mercy; some ask forgiveness; some curse me and God, and spit the devil in the eye. What's yer prayer, boy? Where's yer soul bound? Someplace warm, I'll bet. Well, ye can send greetin's to all them I sent afore ye, and tell 'em I'll be seein' 'em all again afore the final trump."

His smile widened—but Billy didn't notice. He had barely heard a word. A sudden wild hope had seized him, so strong he could barely breathe.

He had thought of a way out.

It was a desperate idea. He would only get one shot at it, and if he failed he would be dead faster than he could blink. But it was his only chance now, and all he could do was take it.

He watched Archie approach, a knife held low in his massive paw. For a second Billy thought his legs might give way, but he swallowed down the fear and steeled himself. It was all or nothing now. Fear would not help him.

Without a word Archie lunged, but even as he struck, Billy leapt towards him, onto him, scrambling up his arm to his shoulder, his light frame and wiry strength propelling him into a mighty leap as he pushed up and back, twisting through the air, his arm reaching for the dark opening above the door …

His fingers caught on brick, and his body slammed into the wall below the mouth of the loft. He was dangling from one arm, his feet kicking against the upper lintel of the door. His arm burned, and he felt like he had expended the last of his strength making the jump—but he was alive.

Below him, Archie had stumbled to a halt, and now he was looking up in mingled fury and surprise. The Devil's Lads had fallen into stunned silence. None of them had seen anything like it before. Billy knew the silence would not last long. He swung the other arm up and scrabbled with his feet for purchase on the lintel. He wasn't dead yet, but unless he could make good his escape he soon would be.

He almost couldn't pull himself up. He was weak and weary from the events of the evening, and his head was still pounding from the bruise. All he wanted was to collapse somewhere warm and dry and sleep the night away.

But then Archie recovered his senses enough to shout, "You're dead, boy!" and the shout sent a jolt through Billy, galvanising him into action. His feet found purchase on the crumbling stone; he pushed with his trembling legs and hauled with his feeble arms. Ignoring the swelling chorus of shouts and curses rising from below, he scrambled over the lip and into the dank loft. Something struck the stone by his head with a metallic *whang* and spun off into the darkness: in a last fit of rage Archie had thrown the knife after him.

"I'll get yer!" Archie's shout echoed from below. "You just wait! I'll gut yer with me bare 'ands if I 'ave to!"

Billy lay with his face against the boards, ignoring Archie's threats and curses. There were a few thuds against the wall outside as some of the gang tried their luck at jumping to reach the loft—but they were all bigger and heavier than Billy, and one by one they fell short, until eventually they gave up, and retreated with a final stream of filthy oaths.

When they were gone, Billy hauled himself to his feet with a groan and set off to find a way out. He desperately wished he could lie there and sleep, but for all he knew the Devil's Lads were heading around to find the entrance to the building. He had to get out before they did, and get back to the archway, and Clara.

It took far too long stumbling around in the darkness, but eventually he found a side door which opened out onto a deserted street. After a quick glance to make sure the Devil's Lads were not waiting for him, he slipped through it and away.

At first he ran, feet slapping on the cobbles and the cold night air tearing at his lungs; but before long the aches and pains throughout his body forced him to slow down, and he staggered into a doorway to catch his breath.

He could still hardly believe that he had managed to escape Archie Miller and the Devil's Lads. The thought was as exhilarating as the memory of the escape was terrifying, and Billy almost laughed aloud. Then he remembered the coins shining in Archie's palm, and the laugh died. Eight whole shillings—money they desperately needed for food and drink—gone, in a few seconds, never to be seen again.

He sighed and levered himself out of the doorway. What was done was done. There was no going back. He had to get back to Clara and Tosher, and decide what to do next.

By the time he found his way back to the archway Big Ben was tolling five, and the barest smudge of navy blue was creeping into the night sky to the east. With the creeping dawn came clouds, hanging low and heavy, and as Billy eyed them he prayed they would not hold rain.

He picked his way back through the crowds, trying his best to avoid stepping on the arms and legs flung every which way. When he finally approached the alcove where he had left Tosher and Clara, he found Tosher waiting for him, twisting his fingers and biting his lip.

"Where you been?" Tosher demanded, scanning Billy's empty hands. "And where's the brandy? Why didn't you get it?"

"Just give me a minute," Billy said, fending off Tosher's questions with an impatient hand. The thought of having to admit what had happened, especially to Tosher, made him ashamed, and the shame made him angry.

He knelt down beside Clara and studied her face. She was pale, her dark complexion waxy and glistening with sweat, the collar of her blouse soaked through. He reached out to wipe some of the moisture from her forehead, and drew back his hand with a start. She was boiling hot.

"What is it?" Tosher loomed over him, wide eyes goggling in the darkness. "What's the matter?"

"I don't know," Billy snapped. "Everything. She's … she's really hot. Too hot, I think."

"But that's good, right? We don't want 'er to be cold, do we?"

"I don't know." Billy frowned. "What happened to your friend? The one who got run over? Did he go hot or cold?"

"He went cold, in the end," Tosher said. "But only 'cause he was dead."

Billy bit back a sharp retort. As usual, Tosher was no help at all, but there was no point saying anything. Tosher wouldn't understand. "Well, Clara ain't going to die," he said firmly. "She's going to be fine. We're going to get help."

The declaration prompted a thought in Tosher's mind. "So where's that brandy?" he said. "Did yer get something to eat as well? I'm starved."

"I didn't get it," Billy said, still studying Clara's face.

"What? Why?"

"Because I ran into Archie Miller," Billy said, "and he took all the money."

"What, all of it?"

"Yes, Tosh!" Billy stood up and rounded on him. "It was *Archie Miller*, for Pete's sake! What did you think? That he might ask me for a few coppers and leave the rest out of the kindness of his heart? I was lucky to get away alive! You heard those lads: he knows about the spoon, Tosh! He knows someone stole it from one of Gerard's clients, and he thinks Gerard's holding out on him! That's why he took the money. That, and the fact that he generally takes what he wants anyway. I was lucky he didn't gut me!"

Tosher was staring slack-jawed at Billy, startled by the outburst, and the sight of his gormless face made Billy's temper flare. He pressed on, unable to stop now, unloading every ounce of his frustration onto Tosher's bony face and ridiculous red hair.

"Why'd you do it, Tosh?" he demanded. "Why'd you take it in the first place? For a laugh? Because you thought it'd be a good joke? No—I know why you took it: because it was there, and because it was shiny, and you *didn't* think about what might happen because you *never* think about what might happen! You *never* think about other people, Tosh! You go through life just doing what you want, and you don't *think*!" Billy shook his head. "We had a good thing going for us, and you just went and ruined it all. And for what? What we got to show for it? What's Clara got to show for it?"

"But …" Tosher looked down at Clara, then back up at Billy, his eyes wide and bewildered. "But Gerard was mean to us, Bill," he said. "You always said you hated him. You always said you'd get away one day—"

"But not like this!" Billy threw up his hands. "Yes, it was bad with Gerard, but it was better than this, wasn't it? Better than sitting in the mud waiting for Clara to die, with Archie Miller after us, and no one to help and nowhere to go!" He trailed off and shook his head, suddenly exhausted. "Why am I even talkin' to you? You don't get it. You never do."

He turned his back on Tosher and sat down beside Clara, bringing his knees up to his chin and holding back the furious tears that brimmed in his eyes. He could feel Tosher staring at him, probably with his usual blank expression, still not understanding just how bad a situation they were in. The only upside, as far as Billy could see, was that there was no way it could get any worse.

An hour later, it began to snow.

11
The Blind Leading the Blind

BY THE TIME Big Ben tolled six, the mouth of the archway had turned to a brilliant white curtain as fat flakes poured from the sky. As the snow fell thicker, so the crowds who had lain outside began to make their way into the arch, pushing and scuffling for space.

Billy stood guard over Clara, a length of wood in his hands, glaring at the newcomers who eyed their space and occasionally shoving away a particularly daring interloper. Tosher sat uselessly beside him, mouth turned down, eyes gazing at the ground; Clara lay motionless on the plank, her chest rising and falling in uneven movements. Occasionally a low moan escaped from between her lips, and once or twice her face tightened in a spasm of pain, but apart from these meagre signs she might as well have been dead. Billy longed to reach out to her, to give her some comfort or at least let her know he was there—but Tosher sat between them, holding tightly to her good hand.

As the dawning light strengthened, the archway grew more and more crowded, bodies pressing in on all sides.

Billy was forced to lash out more than once to keep from being crushed.

They needed to get out of here, that was plain: but to where? Not to Gerard, and certainly not back to Aggie. Billy considered briefly returning to the Eagle and Child and asking the Hallams for help, but he quickly discarded that idea. There would be no welcome there, not after the commotion he and Tosher had brought to their door. Besides, taking them in now would mean going against Archie Miller, and there was no one in the whole of Lambeth foolish enough to do that.

There was nowhere to go, and no one who would help. They were alone and friendless, and Clara was slipping away from them minute by minute.

The crowds were so thick now there was barely room to move. Billy glared at a drunk with a peg leg, and elbowed a girl who began to shuffle onto Clara's plank. Tosher was oblivious, and only when a particularly large woman trod on his foot did he finally look up, blinking as if waking from a dream.

"It's gettin' awful crowded, Bill," he said.

"You think?" Billy replied, shouldering the woman to one side and ignoring her snarled curses.

"What we gonna do?"

"If you got any ideas I'd love to hear 'em."

A couple of men had crept up behind them, and were about to roll Clara off the plank to take it for themselves. Billy turned and rapped one of them on the knuckles, and after exchanging insults the pair of them slunk away.

"Can't we just go?" Tosher asked.

"Go where?"

"I dunno. A church, maybe? There's good people in churches, ain't there?"

Billy considered this. It was an idea, but he hadn't had much experience with church people. Did they take in strays from the streets? He pictured the churchmen he had seen before, getting in and out of carriages around Westminster Abbey in all their finery, treading lightly to avoid getting mud on their pristine robes—those men didn't seem the type to welcome in three urchins, and one whose life was slipping steadily away.

"I s'pose it depends on the church," he replied. He glanced down at Clara. He didn't have any better ideas, and they were running out of time. "Is there a church around here, though?"

He didn't expect a reply from Tosher, and he didn't get one. Tosher just shrugged, and turned his attention back to Clara. He fully expected Billy to take care of everything.

Billy wasn't so sure he could. He had no idea where to begin. He tried to recall passing a church on his way back here last night, but he had been so caught up with his brush with Archie Miller that he hadn't noticed anything. He sighed. It was no good expecting Tosher to take action. He would have to ask around and see what he could find.

"Here," he said, handing the length of wood to Tosher. "Just keep anyone away from Clara. I'll be back as soon as I can."

He left Tosher standing by Clara, fiddling nervously with the makeshift club, and began to pick his way through the crowds, looking for the most alert face he could find. A mother sitting in the middle of a crowd of children returned his glance with a touch less animosity than anyone else, so he decided to start with her.

"Sorry to bother you, ma'am," he said. "Only I'm looking for some help with a friend of mine—"

"No help here," the woman snapped, cutting him off. Her brood all turned on him with suspicious eyes, a collection of boys and girls aged from about seven all the way down to the tiny baby lying blue-lipped in her arms, swathed in filthy rags. "Well?" she added. "You 'eard me—no help here, not for you nor me. Now shove off!"

Billy stumbled away with a muttered apology, and the woman glared as he went.

The next person he tried was a young man in a grubby suit, who stood looking around as if he wasn't sure how he had ended up in this place. The man hardly heard him at first, and when he finally registered that someone was speaking to him he just looked down at Billy with empty eyes for a moment, before shrugging and mumbling incoherently under his breath.

After that Billy approached an old lady so wrapped up in shawls and blankets as to be hardly recognisable as a human being at all. She simply shrieked with laughter when he asked her where the nearest church was, and continued to wail and cackle long after he had left her.

The more Billy looked, and the more he saw of the inhabitants of the archway, the more it dawned on him how few of them were capable of helping him, much less willing. He was standing in the very middle of the crowd, gazing around helplessly and wondering what to do next, when a filthy chuckle came from somewhere in the region of his knees, and he looked down to see the dark face of an old man grinning up at him through broken teeth.

"You lookin' for 'elp," he said, in an accent so thick and unfamiliar Billy could barely understand him. "You won' find it roun' 'ere."

Billy didn't reply. Clearly the man was a lunatic, and only wanted to take delight in his misery.

"No, none o' them gonna 'elp you, boy," the man continued. "They can' 'elp themselves, so 'ow's they gonna 'elp you? They's blind, an' you's blind, and we's all blind down 'ere. How's a blind man gonna 'elp another blind man? We's all 'eaded into the dark, down 'ere in de pit. All blind men leadin' blind men, and we's all goin' down to de pit."

He paused, and raised himself up on one elbow. Billy was about to turn away when a sinewy hand shot out and grabbed his bare ankle. The man's flesh was ice-cold; it was like being touched by a corpse.

"You needs a man who ain't blind, don'cha?" The dark-faced man's smile widened, and he pointed with a long finger to somewhere behind Billy. "You needs a man 'oo can *see*."

Despite himself, Billy could not help turning to see what the man was pointing to, and what he saw made his chest tighten. It was the men from yesterday—not the tall man, the gentleman, but his companions, one older and one younger. They were picking their way through the crowds again, looking this time more than talking, as if they were searching for something or someone in particular. Now Billy had a chance to look at them more carefully, he could see that they were not Archie's people. They were too well-dressed, and their movements were gentle and courteous. Archie's boys would have shoved their way through the crowd, expecting people to make way for them.

So who were they, then? And why had they been taking all those children away? They must be from the factories, or the workhouse, he decided; or (and this was what made his heart rise with a flutter of hope) maybe they were from a church, or one of the ragged schools that had begun to pop up here and there throughout the city. He had seen the lines of children from these schools before, marching to and fro in the dirty streets, shepherded about by harassed-looking women in severe bonnets and stern men in tight collars. He had always wondered how the children came to be there, and what misery it must be to be shut up in such places from morning until night without the freedom, however brief, that he and Tosher had enjoyed—but now the prospect didn't seem quite so bad, especially if it involved anything approaching a bed or a hot meal.

"They's got eyes, all right." The dark man's words broke into his thoughts, and Billy looked down to see him nodding sagely, his smile as wide as ever. "They's got eyes to see. Not like us. Not like you an' me, boy."

With a final throaty chuckle the man released Billy and lay back, staring up at the curved brickwork high above them, and Billy stumbled away from him in the direction of the two men.

He caught up with them as they were exchanging quiet words with a scrawny woman who huddled on a broken door. The older of the pair, whose cheeks and chin bristled with a magnificent beard, was crouching beside her, spreading his hands in explanation; the younger man stood just behind, his shoulders hunched and his fingers laced, clearly deeply uncomfortable.

Billy waited while they spoke, and noted the quiet

tenderness in the bearded man's murmured words, the way he reached out, unflinching, to take the woman's grimy hand in his own, then moved the hand to her shoulder when she broke down in exhausted sobs.

"I'm sorry," he heard the man say, more than once. "I really am very sorry. We did all we could but …"

It was then that Billy made up his mind. No workhouse foreman would be so tender; no factory boss would come to see a grieving mother about the state of the child he had taken from her. If these men weren't from a church, they at least had some kind of Christian charity about them. And besides, what other hope did he have right now?

He took a deep breath, stepped forward, and tapped the younger man's elbow.

"Excuse me sir, I—"

The young man wheeled round, fists clenched and raised, his jaw set and his eyes flashing.

"What is it, you young ruffian?" he demanded. "Eh? Go on! Get away now! Mind your own business!"

Billy started back in alarm, and almost turned and fled, but in another second the bearded man appeared at his companion's side, gently pushing down his fists.

"All right, Rob," he said. "I doubt this one's armed."

The man called Rob reluctantly subsided, and only then did Billy see that the look in his eyes was one of fear. He was as startled as Billy had been.

The older man placed his hands easily on his hips and regarded Billy with a level gaze.

"Now then," he said, his voice soft but commanding. "What is it that ye want?"

"It's my friend," Billy said. "She's sick, and we don't know what to do. That's me and Tosher—he's my friend as well, but she's a girl: her name's Clara …"

He continued, telling as much of the story as he felt comfortable with, and patching over the rest with hasty lies; and as he spoke he found the words coming easier, and his trepidation melting away. There was something in this man's gaze that reassured him, some deep current of strength flowing beneath the kindness in his eyes; he was stern, but in the way Billy had hoped his father might be stern. His gaze said, *Don't worry. I'll lead. All you have to do is follow.* He almost felt bad about not telling the man the whole truth.

When he was finished the man sighed and looked around.

"Where is she, then?" he said. "This friend of yours?"

Billy pointed. "Over that way. Tosher's watchin' over her, but I don't think she'll last long. Can you help her? Only, I saw you takin' those other kids last night, and I thought …"

He trailed off. In truth he didn't know what he thought. That this man would sweep Clara up in his strong arms and carry her away to be healed? That he would take him and Tosher along as well, and feed and clothe them? That all their problems would be solved at a stroke? Yes—all these things; but it was more a desperate hope than anything else, and a slim hope at that.

The man took a long, hard look at him. Billy had the sensation that he was being weighed and measured, and the guilty feeling that his lies were shrivelling beneath that gaze like paper in a flame. But in the end maybe the truth didn't matter, or else the man was satisfied that he had heard enough of it to make up his mind. Either way, he grunted and nodded.

"Show me," he said.

12
Rescue

BY THE TIME Billy returned with the two men to where he had left Tosher and Clara, they were nearly overrun in the press. Tosher was crouching beside Clara with the piece of wood hanging limply from his fingers, his eyes wide in fear and confusion. But as soon as the two men arrived they took charge. The bearded man—whose name, Billy learned, was Daniel—started by ushering the closest bodies aside, then began to issue orders in a gruff bark:

"Rob, get some rope, or rags, or whatever you can find. Anything to get this girl tied to this board. We're going to have to lift her out. You." He pointed at Tosher as Rob darted away. "Clear us a path so we can carry her out. And you," he looked at Billy, "hold her down. There. By her shoulders."

Hesitantly, Billy placed his hands on Clara's shuddering shoulders while Daniel bent over her and inspected the wound. He grunted.

"This was no accident," he said. "This girl's been shot. You didn't mention that."

Billy kept his mouth closed in shamed silence, and

avoided Daniel's eyes.

"You ready?" Daniel said. "No. Hold her tighter. *Tighter*, boy! This is going to hurt, but it might save her life."

Billy nodded and gripped Clara's shoulders as hard as he dared, bearing all his weight down on to her limp form. She winced and stirred, muttering in her fevered sleep. Daniel had torn a strip of material from the hem of her skirt and was threading it around her injured arm, above the wound near the shoulder. When he was satisfied that Billy was holding Clara firmly enough he doubled the material over and swiftly pulled it tight.

Clara let out a ragged scream and arched her back in pain.

"*Hold her!*" Daniel bellowed as Billy's hand slipped; Billy closed his own eyes and gripped as hard as he could, forcing Clara down while Daniel did something with the material that jerked Clara's arm twice, each time eliciting a fresh scream from her.

"There!" Daniel said eventually. "Let her go. That's all I can do."

Billy opened his eyes. The material had been wrapped and tied tightly around Clara's arm, so tightly that the skin was pinched and the flesh of her lower arm had turned pale. She had fallen back into unconsciousness, her face nearly grey and her forehead beaded with sweat.

"Will she be all right now?" he asked.

"Not yet." Daniel dusted his hands and stood up. "She's caught a fever, and if we don't do something about this arm it'll eat her up from the inside. Where's that Rob?"

He cast around, and spied the younger man picking his way back through the crowds. Tosher was stuttering and mumbling his way around the nearest groups; Billy doubted he knew where he was any more, much less what he was doing. He had a glazed expression on his face, and his eyes looked through the people he was trying to move along. In any case they ignored him; Billy suspected Daniel had given him the job just to get him out of the way.

"Here," Rob panted, holding out a dirty blanket. "Will this do?"

"Well enough," Daniel grunted. "Help me. If we're quick we might be able to save her. I'll not lose another one today."

Between them the two men tore the blanket into strips, wound them round the board on which the boys had laid Clara, and tied the strips tightly across her body. The wounded arm was grey-white now; Daniel tied it as gently as he could down the side of Clara's body, then nodded in satisfaction.

"That'll do," he said. "Right. Rob. You get that end. I'll get this. Boy, see if you can make a space."

Billy nodded and immediately darted over to the nearest group of vagrants sitting between them and the exit. Tosher was standing over them, twisting his hands together and mumbling an apologetic explanation as to why he would like them to move, thank you very much, if it wasn't too much trouble. Billy shoved him aside and glared down at the group, three boys and a girl a few years older than him.

"Right," he snapped. "You best get out of the way, 'cause these fellers are comin' through here, and if you don't move I'm sure they'll be happy to give yer a kickin' as they come— and if they don't I will, and I'll enjoy it a sight more'n them."

"Shut yer pie 'ole," one of the boys growled. "We're stayin' 'ere, and you can't move us."

Something in the boy's tone touched a nerve deep inside Billy. He had been as calm as he could, given everything that had happened that night, but this was the last straw. As the boy turned away disdainfully, Billy raised his bare foot and drove it into the back of the boy's head, sending him sprawling on the floor.

"I told yer!" Billy snarled, as the boy's friends scrambled to get out of the way. "I told yer I'd give you a kickin'!"

The boy shot Billy a dirty look, but he kept his mouth shut. Billy looked around. Dozens of pairs of eyes had turned in his direction. He pointed towards the snowy entrance to the archway.

"We're goin' that way," he said, raising his voice for the benefit of the crowd. "Anyone else want to argue?"

Grudgingly the crowds parted, and Billy stepped through them with Tosher mutely at his side, and the two men, Rob and Daniel, carrying Clara on the makeshift stretcher behind them. People looked up as they passed, some with a laugh and a wink of congratulation for Billy; others with a tut and a disapproving shake of the head. But most turned aside with blank indifference. Fights were a common enough occurrence, as were sick and dying children. Nothing about the procession was remarkable to them.

Billy could not help feeling a swell of pride and satisfaction every time he caught a wink or a nod. He had done something. He had helped Clara. But when he glanced back at Daniel for his reaction, he was disappointed—and strangely ashamed—to find the bearded man's brows lowered and his mouth grimly set. There would be no words of congratulation from him—and for some reason this bothered Billy far more than he thought it should.

Once they were clear of the archway the two men moved in front, leading the way through the snow-blanketed streets. The morning's flurry had died down to a few solitary flakes drifting from the flat grey clouds, and in the crowded alleyways the smooth drifts were undisturbed save for cats' pawprints here and there. The two men ploughed their way through, the snow piling up and spilling around their legs and ankles, and Billy and Tosher followed in their wake.

"Not far," Daniel grunted, glancing down at the boys' bare feet and thin shirts. "We'll get you inside and get something hot down yer. But don't get comfy," he warned. "We'll do what we can for her, as there's a bed just become free, but I can't promise either of you two anything. Understood?"

Billy nodded; and though Tosher just looked down at his feet and kept walking, Daniel took his silence for understanding and said no more.

Billy didn't mind. It didn't matter what happened to them—they could survive on the streets if they had to, maybe even find a new master in another part of the city, take up sweeping again, get their lives back together. As long as Clara was safe, that was all that mattered.

"You all right, Tosh?" he said, putting a hand on Tosher's shoulder. "Don't worry about Clara, eh? She'll be all right now. You'll see."

Tosher nodded, but he did not take his eyes off their path through the snow. Billy let him be. It had been a long night, after all.

Soon they turned on to a wider street, where the snow had been churned into a brown-black slush that banked up on either side of the road. The odd horse and carriage rattled past, throwing up more of the freezing mud as they passed. The two men raised Clara's stretcher up high every time this happened, not caring for the fact that their boots and trousers were soon soaked through and filthy.

"Not far," Daniel kept saying, as if they needed the encouragement. In truth both boys were far too cold and tired out to do anything but put one foot in front of the other. They would have kept walking until they dropped if Daniel had not finally brought them to a halt.

"Here," he said. "Knock for us, boy."

Billy looked up. They had stopped in front of a narrow door set between two shopfronts, on a street where the upper storeys of the buildings leaned in sharply. Billy stepped up to the door and rapped on it.

After a moment, a noise of shuffling and grumbling came from within:

"… on a day like today? Can't they give us a moment's peace? Bones weren't made for this cold, no sir … not as old as I am … what with my rheumatitis and all … Lord have mercy on us …"

A bolt was pulled back, and the door swung open to reveal an elderly lady wrapped in about seven shawls, with a cloth cap tied tightly over her head. Her eyes narrowed when they lighted on Billy, and she was about to say something; but then she glanced up at Daniel and Rob standing behind him, and her face softened a fraction.

"You're back, then," she said, sniffing. She peered at their burden. "Got a few more, I see. And the other one not yet cold. Well, you'd best bring them in."

She shuffled aside and held the door open while Daniel and Rob gingerly lowered Clara's stretcher down and eased it through the doorway.

"Take her down to the kitchen," the old lady said. "Warmest place for her."

The two men continued down the long passageway that ran from the front door to the back of the building. Tosher and Billy followed, under the watchful eye of the woman, who scowled at them and almost trod on their heels in her determination not to let them out of her sight.

There was a single door along the right-hand side of the passageway, shut fast. As they passed the door it opened a crack, and Billy caught sight of an eye peering out at them, and heard a muffled giggle from within; but the old woman quickly pulled it to again.

"Go on," she said. "Never you mind about them."

The kitchen was a large room with a range along one wall and a flickering fire burning in the grate. Billy's eyes went to the fireplace immediately: it was spacious, designed for cooking on rather than simply warming the room, easy to get into without too much fuss. But that was not why he was here. He turned his attention back to Clara. The two men had laid her stretcher down on the floor beside the enormous table that took up most of the rest of the room, and they were now untying the strips of blanket from around her.

The old lady tutted and fussed as they worked, shaking her head and pursing her lips—in disapproval, Billy thought at first, until he saw the look in her eyes and realised she was as worried as the rest of them.

"Get her up on the table," Daniel said. He and Rob lifted Clara's limp body and laid her out as gently as they could. She was completely still now, not even shivering. Billy watched her, hardly knowing what to think. Surely they hadn't been too late. It couldn't have happened that quickly, could it?

Daniel bent over her face, turning his cheek towards her mouth and squinting. "No good," he said. "Bring us a glass or something, Mrs. Lucas."

The old woman turned and grasped a polished copper saucepan from a shelf.

"Will this do?" she said.

Daniel nodded and grunted a word of thanks as he took it and held it over Clara's face, nearly touching her skin. A fine mist appeared on the gleaming surface, then faded almost immediately. A second later it returned, then vanished, then returned again, pulsing in a steady rhythm.

"Well she's alive," Daniel said, straightening up. "Not sure for how long, though. Rob, you mind fetching Dr. Samuels? He won't be abed yet, I suspect. Tell him it's urgent, will you?"

The younger man nodded silently and disappeared down the passageway. A moment later the door opened and closed, and then there was silence.

13
Amputation

"Now then," Mrs. Lucas said, when Rob had left. "What's all this about, Daniel? I wasn't expecting you back so soon, and with three? You know we can't—"

Daniel held up a hand. "I know," he said. "I know. This wasn't my idea, believe me. I only went back to see that girl's mother and break the news, but I was waylaid by this young gentleman here, and … well … you know me. I can't pass by on the other side, as it were."

Mrs. Lucas tutted, though there was a smile at the corner of her mouth. "A regular Samaritan, you are," she said. She gazed down at Clara, taking in her ruined arm and the hastily-tied bandage. "What happened to her?"

"Shot, as likely as not," Daniel replied. He glanced at Billy, who looked away in shame. "This young man would have me think it were an accident of some kind, but I've seen enough in my time to know. What were it over?"

Billy looked up to find both adults staring at him.

"Nothing," he said defensively. "Least … not any more. It's over, if that's what you're worrying about. No one's going

103

to come looking for her." He looked between them. "God's truth. I'll swear on anything you want."

"There's no need to be swearing," Mrs. Lucas said primly. "Let your yea be yea and your nay be nay. Leave swearing out of it."

Billy nodded silently, though he wasn't entirely sure what she meant.

"Now I suppose you'll be wanting something to sup on?" Mrs. Lucas continued. "The both of you look like you haven't hardly eaten."

Tosher's head came up at that, and he nodded emphatically, though his eyes retained their faraway look.

"We had something last night," Billy admitted. "But it wasn't much. We can pay," he added hastily.

"Oh, tush." Mrs. Lucas shook a hand at him. "We won't take your money. Just wait there a minute."

She busied herself around the kitchen while the boys stood by. Daniel lowered himself into a nearby chair and produced a pipe from somewhere. He proceeded to clean it with much ceremony, before filling the bowl with tobacco and borrowing a glowing ember from the fire to light it. Then he sat back and began to take long draws on the pipe, staring hard at Billy and Tosher through the thickening cloud of smoke slowly forming around his head.

Billy tried not to pay him much heed. He had the distinct feeling Daniel didn't much like him, probably because of what he had done to that boy in the archway—though he couldn't see any reason why that was anything to be disapproved of. It had worked, hadn't it? And it was more than Tosher had done. If it had been left to Tosher no one would have moved.

He glanced over at Tosher, who had edged nearer to the fire and stood with his shoulders hunched and his gaze fixed on the floor. Now the immediate danger was past, Billy was able to relax a little and take stock of the situation. As soon as they knew what was happening with Clara, Billy decided he was going to have to take Tosher in hand and knock some sense into him, one way or another. He forgave him, of course, for stealing the spoon and bringing all this about in the first place. Tosher hadn't meant to get them into trouble, and now it looked like things might be working out—but if they were about to start a new life on the streets together it was probably time to lay down some rules. He couldn't have Tosher going off and doing whatever he wanted, not any more. He would have to get his head screwed on right, or else they wouldn't last a week.

"There you go, now." Mrs. Lucas bustled over, bearing two steaming bowls of something hot and brown. "Get that down you, the pair of you."

Billy remembered to thank her before tucking in; Tosher said nothing, but practically submerged his face in the bowl. Mrs. Lucas sniffed, but she no doubt had low expectations of them anyway, and she left it at that. Daniel sat and watched them in stony silence, still puffing on his pipe.

The boys had just finished, and Billy was running his finger round the edge of the bowl and relishing the feeling of having a full belly twice in two days, when a knock came on the front door. Mrs. Lucas went to answer it, and returned with Rob and a short, round gentleman in a black frock coat with a black leather bag.

Daniel raised a hand to his forehead as the gentleman entered. "Doctor," he said, "good of ye to come."

"I couldn't very well refuse," the man replied. He peered at Clara over the top of his half-moon spectacles. "Is this the girl?"

"That's right," Mrs. Lucas said. "Can you help her?"

"Give me some room," the doctor said. He shrugged off his coat and handed it to Rob, then proceeded to roll up his shirtsleeves, all the while running his eyes up and down Clara's unmoving form.

"Gunshot wound?" he said at last. Daniel nodded, and the doctor shook his head. "Nasty business. Some kind of blunderbuss, by the look of it. Who tied the tourniquet?"

Daniel raised his hand.

"Well, you probably saved her life, if not the arm." The doctor opened the clasp on his black bag and took out a long black tube with branching metal prongs on one end and a metal cup on the other. He inserted the prongs into his ears and placed the cup against Clara's chest, then he stood and listened with a tiny frown of concentration on his face.

Billy craned his head to look. He had never seen such a thing before, and he couldn't for the life of him see what good it could do, when the problem was plainly not anywhere near her chest. The doctor saw him looking.

"I'm listening to her lungs and her heart," he explained. "This instrument is called a stethoscope: it amplifies the sound to enable me to detect any irregularities, so that I may determine the extent of the infection that has taken hold through this wound."

Billy nodded, despite having lost the thread at 'instrument'. The doctor turned his full attention to Clara, and after a few moments he straightened up with a sigh.

"The best recommendation I can make is to have the

limb amputated," he said. "The child may survive, but she is in the hands of the Almighty now."

Billy looked between the doctor and the three other adults in the room, all of whom were nodding grimly. Rob's face had lost most of its colour.

"What's that?" Billy demanded. There was something in their expressions that told him this was definitely not good news at all. "What's 'amperated'? What you going to do to her?"

"It means he needs to take the arm off," Daniel said grimly. "There's nothing else to be done. Take the arm, and pray that God holds her in His."

Billy's chest tightened. He looked down at Clara, lying still and pale on the table. This couldn't be right. There had to be another way.

"You can't," he said, shaking his head. "You can't just … cut her up, like a butcher. You got to do something!" He turned to the doctor, who was packing the stethoscope into his bag. "You got something in that bag o' yours, right? You got something to help her?"

"The only thing that will help her now is the saw," the old man said sadly. "If we don't, the infection will spread to her heart, and she will die."

"All right then," Daniel said, rising to his feet with an air of finality. "You boys have done all you can for the lass. Let the doctor take over now. Go on. It's time."

Billy shook his head stubbornly. "I'm not going any-where," he retorted, balling his fists. "Not while you lot carves up Clara."

"Don't be a fool." Daniel's eyebrows lowered. "I won't have your kind making trouble in this house."

"What d'yer mean, my kind? What kind is that, eh?"

"I know you, boy," Daniel growled. "I seen too many like you. Think with yer fists afore yer head. I won't have you stayin' 'ere. She's better off without you. Don't make me ask you again. You knew the deal when you came 'ere—you've eaten your fill, now get along with you."

Rob was on his feet as well, edging slowly around the table. Billy knew he could take either of them in a fight, if he had to.

He turned and glared at Daniel. "What's your problem?" he demanded. "Why d'yer want to get rid of us? Eh? We're not causing no trouble!"

"You're causing trouble now," Daniel replied. "This is a decent place, for decent folk, and—"

"Decent folk?" Billy cut across him incredulously. "What kind o' decent folk cuts up girls and chucks starving boys out on the street? And how d'yer know *we* ain't decent? You don't know us! You jus' met us!"

"I know your type," Daniel shot back. "Rude, ignorant, violent, un-Christian … I saw what you did to that boy back at the archway. What's wrong with words, eh?"

"Words doesn't get things done!"

"There's more done with words for the likes of you than you know, boy!" Daniel drew himself up, seeming to fill the room with his presence. "There's men I know stands up in Parliament, and speaks mighty words on behalf of the poor and those with no means to help themselves! Words is what makes this world turn, boy! The words of the law, and the words of the Bible! It was with a word that the Lord Almighty made the heavens and the earth, and it was His Word He sent down to die for our sins! And you think you can accomplish anything with those fists o' yours, with blood an' violence?"

He fell silent, and the kitchen fell silent with him. Rob and the doctor were looking at him in mingled admiration and fear; Mrs. Lucas was nodding determinedly from her place by the fire; and Tosher was looking at the ground harder than ever and clenching his fists so that his knuckles turned white.

Billy could feel himself trembling with pent-up rage at the sheer, unrelenting *unfairness* of it all—at Daniel, for refusing to think that he could be anything other than a grubby street rat—at Archie Miller, for taking his money and trying to kill him—at God in heaven, for looking down dispassionately without caring whether he lived or died— and lastly at Tosher, for setting this whole miserable chain of events in motion.

"Do yourself and your friend a favour," Daniel said softly, still gazing steadily at Billy with his cold blue eyes. "Leave her with us now, and forget you ever knew her. There's a better life waiting here, but she won't have it if you try to make yourself a part of it."

Billy did not know what to do or say. His eyes darted over to Clara, then back at Daniel again. It wasn't true, he told himself. The man was lying just to get him to go away. They *could* have a life, all of them, all together, fending for themselves in the wide world. He and Tosher could work at sweeping chimneys, maybe even go into business together, get their own gang and make their own money; and Clara could work in a bar, and slip them free gin and beer whenever they wanted it, and they could live without a care.

But then his eyes lighted on the dark hole of the gunshot

wound on her arm, and he knew it would not be so. Clara needed to live, and to do that she needed these people's help—and the only way to get their help was if he and Tosher left her with them.

"All right," he said at last. The words barely made it past his lips, and he had to clear his throat and try again. "All right," he repeated. "We'll go. But you make sure you save her, you hear? If we leave her, and she dies ..."

He trailed off, unable to find the words to articulate the horrors he would wreak upon them if they did not keep Clara alive. But Daniel understood what he meant, and he nodded.

"We'll do our best, son," he said. "But only God can save her now."

Billy nodded and turned away, angry and ashamed to feel tears pricking at his eyes.

"Come on Tosh," he said. "Let's go."

He brushed past Rob, who stepped aside to make way. It was only when Billy reached the door that he realised Tosher had not followed him, and he turned to find Tosher still standing in his place by the fire, still clenching his fists, still staring at the floor.

And crying. Two glistening trails ran down his cheeks, white against the dirt and grime. His shoulders gave a great heave as a silent sob wracked him, and he squeezed his eyes tight shut and shook his head.

"Please," he said, his voice little more than a husky whisper. "Please sir. I can't go. I can't. I'm sorry."

"I'm sorry too," Daniel said, with none of the sharpness he had reserved for Billy. "But rules are rules, son. We just can't take in everyone. There's other places you'll find help, never you worry. Go on, now."

But Tosher did not move. He stood stubbornly by the fire, shaking his head and muttering to himself:

"No …" he said. "No … no … no … I can't … I can't …"

Mrs. Lucas started forward, her face creased in sympathy, but Daniel raised a hand to stop her.

"You can, and you must," he said. "Go on. Be like your friend. See reason."

Still Tosher shook his head, and now a gulping sob escaped his lips, echoing around the stone kitchen. "I can't …" he repeated. "I can't … I can't … please … I can't …"

"Boy," Daniel said, and now a note of iron crept into his voice. "There's nothing for you here. No food we can give you, no bed."

"Don't want a bed. Don't want food."

Daniel frowned. "Then what is it that you want?"

In reply Tosher raised a trembling finger and pointed it at Clara. "I want … her," he said, between shuddering breaths. "I can't … can't leave her … she … needs me …"

"Daniel," Mrs. Lucas said, looking at the older man with pleading eyes. "It's too much to leave this poor babe all on her own. Think of the other girl—the one who passed with no one and nothing to give her comfort save for strangers. Can't we take at least one …?"

For a moment Daniel hesitated, caught between his own determination and Mrs. Lucas' pleading eyes. Then he threw up his hands in resignation.

"Fine!" he said. He pointed a thick finger at Tosher. "You can stay. For tonight, mind! But you—" and here he turned to fix Billy with his fiercest stare yet, "—I'll not have you stay here a moment more. I've a bad feeling about you, my boy.

111

There's violence in your eyes."

Billy gaped. He could not believe what was happening. He looked at Tosher, but he would not meet his gaze.

"Tosh …" he said. "What're you doin'?"

"I can't do it, Bill," Tosher said miserably, still staring at his feet. "I'm not like you. I can't go back out there. I'll die. But you … you'll be all right Bill. You know?"

Billy shook his head, still caught in the shock of the moment.

"But Tosh—"

"That's enough, now," Daniel interrupted, barging over and turning Billy around by the shoulder. "Go on. Out."

Billy stumbled down the passageway in a daze. He heard muffled giggles from behind the door as they passed, then the front door was opening and Daniel was nudging him gently but firmly into the freezing street.

The door closed, but Billy hardly heard it. All he could think of was Clara lying still and pale, and Tosher standing in the corner and crying—and with a sudden leaden weight in his heart he realised that they were lost to him forever, and now he was utterly alone.

14
Christian Charity

ANTHONY ASHLEY COOPER, the Seventh Earl of Shaftesbury, poured a modest glass of brandy and handed it to the large, well-dressed man sitting in the high-backed chair by the fire. The chair was one of a pair set close to the large fireplace, in which a small pile of coals glowed. Gas-lamps hissed softly in brass brackets around the walls of the study, lending a warm glow to the bookshelves that surrounded the two men.

The man in the chair, whose name was Lord Dungannon, peered at the glass and gave a loud sniff.

"You know, I appreciate your piety, Shaftesbury," he drawled, in the rounded vowels of a man accustomed to the very finest things in life. "But must you really foist your asceticism on the rest of us?"

Shaftesbury did not reply. He crossed to the far side of the fireplace and rested a hand on the mantel, gazing deep into the glowing coals. The ruddy light cast deep shadows across his high cheekbones, the deep-set eyes half hidden behind their lids, the strong Roman nose, the long jaw framed by greying whiskers, and the mouth set in a stern line from which it rarely broke.

"A little temperance will do you good," Shaftesbury said eventually, his soft voice rolling effortlessly around the small room. "Abstinence would do you better."

"Oh come," Dungannon chuckled. "Does the Good Book not command us to take a little wine, for our stomach's sake? And did not Jesus Himself turn water into wine? Eh?"

"The Good Book also commands us not to be drunk with wine, wherein is excess," Shaftesbury replied, politely but firmly. "And I fail to recall our Lord ever turning water into anything so foul as brandy, gin, or beer."

"You're a grey rain cloud and no mistake." Dungannon chuckled, then took a sip of the amber liquid and sighed. "But your vintage is excellent, and so I forgive you."

Shaftesbury ignored the dig. "You have business here," he said briskly. "Kindly state it."

"Ah." Dungannon smiled and gazed down into his glass, swirling the drink gently. "Well if you're so determined to be unsociable, I shall tell you: I've come to reason with you, Shaftesbury."

"On what point?"

"On a point of charity, my good fellow." Dungannon spotted the slight furrow in Shaftesbury's brow, and raised a finger. "Hear me out. I know you feel I'm ill-disposed to speak of such things, but I am a Christian after all, the same as you. We were both baptised into the church, were we not? And are we not entreated to speak to a brother overtaken in a fault?"

This time the eyebrows rose, though Shaftesbury's dark eyes did not move. "And to what fault would you hold me?" he asked.

"To the sin of pride, my dear fellow."

"Pride?" Shaftesbury stood up straight, and for the first time turned the full force of his gaze on Dungannon, who quickly looked away.

"Oh, not presumptuously, of course," he said. "And I see how you might believe that you are honouring our Lord—but I feel it my solemn duty to point out to you the error in your judgement."

Shaftesbury gave a heavy sigh and lowered himself into the chair opposite Dungannon. He crossed one long leg over the other and regarded the other man over the tops of his steepled fingers.

"Society and honour demand that I hear you out," he said after a long pause. "Pray enlighten me."

"To be frank, it's this business with the schools," Dungannon said. "'Ragged schools'—is that what they're called? Now, I understand you have a great heart—I've never met a fellow so disposed towards helping his fellow man. But opening up every hayloft and meeting-hall in the city for a gang of urchins to descend upon? Presenting the holy Scriptures to vagabonds and street Arabs? This is casting pearls before swine—and for what? What earthly good can be achieved by trying to educate such creatures? A colossal waste of time and resources! The campaigns for the lunatics and the working hours I understand, but this? What good can possibly come of it?"

"What would you have me do with them?" Shaftesbury asked.

"Send them to the places already prepared for them, of course! To the workhouses! The factories! The mines! There are plenty of places crying out for labourers, and we all know what good workers they can be, given the right incentives! I know your heart lies in that direction—I've followed your little crusades with great interest over the years, and we all applaud the good you have done. But teaching children such as this to read and write? What earthly good will that do them? And these Bible lessons ... Come now, you don't presume to be a man of the cloth! Leave the matters of the soul to the clergy, and concentrate instead on getting these children into employment!"

Shaftesbury regarded Dungannon steadily over the tips of his fingers. Silence descended over the room, gradually stretching out until it became uncomfortable. Dungannon took a nervous gulp of brandy.

"Look," he said. "You must know the degradatory effect these establishments have upon the neighbourhoods in which they are situated. Gather a troop of petty criminals together in one place, and there's no telling the evil that will ensue. Theft, vandalism ... not to mention the poor influence of the strong-willed upon the weak. Why, we might as well call them colleges of crime!"

"So rather than providing places of education," Shaftesbury said quietly; "rather than shedding light into darkness, and giving such creatures the opportunity to rise above their station and attain to some measure of respectability; rather than gathering the chicks beneath our wings, nurturing them, clothing them, feeding them in body, soul and mind—rather than all these benefits and blessings, you would shut the doors on them and drive them to the mines and the factories?"

"In pursuit of an honest wage and an honest day's labour!"

"And have you been to such places?" Shaftesbury demanded, rising suddenly to his feet. "Have you witnessed the misery in which these children—*children*, sir!—expend every ounce of strength, through every hour of the day that the law permits their masters to chain them there? Have you looked into the face of a boy forced to squeeze his starving body up a chimney inches wide, terrified to go on and terrified to go back lest his master thrashes him for indolence? Have you walked the streets of Lambeth or Soho, and witnessed for yourself the hell on earth these children call home? Because I have, sir! I have! And I tell you, there is nothing honest about it!"

Shaftesbury towered over Dungannon, his eyes flashing in the light of the fire, and the other man appeared to shrink into his seat.

"My 'little crusades', as you call them, are no more and no less than every Christian man's duty to preach the Gospel to the widows and the fatherless! Christ himself summoned children to come to Him when others would turn them away. And here you sit, insisting that I hold my peace and leave this business to other men, and condemn these little ones to a life of slavery in the service of men whose only love is money. Shame on you, sir! And all those like you! You should be ashamed to call yourself a Christian!"

Dungannon hastily downed the last of the brandy and rose to his feet, shying away from Shaftesbury's fierce glare.

"It's clear you can't be reasoned with," he declared, edging towards the door. "And if you won't hear me in private then rest assured I will call you out in public, if I have to."

"Do," Shaftesbury replied, turning to watch him as he went. "And you shall have my reply in public too."

Dungannon had reached the door by now. He gave a stiff, reluctant bow, then turned and fumbled with the door handle before making his escape without another word.

When he had gone Shaftesbury subsided. He seemed to shrink into himself, his eyes lowering and his shoulders stooping. He lowered himself back into his chair and stretched his long legs out in front of him, gazing pensively into the fire.

After a few minutes a knock came on the door; when he gave no reply the door creaked open, and a middle-aged woman with a soft face and dark eyes entered.

"Anthony?" she called softly. "Are you still in here?"

"Here, Emily," Shaftesbury replied, raising a hand above the back of the chair for her to see.

The woman—Lady Emily Ashley Cooper—crossed the room and took the hand in hers, squeezing it gently as she gazed down at him.

"A difficult interview?"

Shaftesbury nodded. "Exceedingly. Why must I be surrounded by such men? They use religion as a cloak for their own hypocrisy, speaking the name of Christ with the same breath they use to deny His mercy and grace to the very creatures who need it most. It is an evil age, my love, in which the name of God rests upon every man's lips alongside a multitude of lies—such an evil age, that I doubt we will see its like again. I would express no hint of surprise were Christ to appear in the skies this very night."

"Well, if He does indeed return, let Him be the judge," Lady Emily replied. "You cannot be answerable for their lack of charity." She moved around to take the seat opposite Shaftesbury, regarding him steadily. He felt her gaze and glanced over, and his face softened a touch.

"You're right, of course," he said. "I know I feel these things too deeply. Perhaps I fear for the work of the Gospel, when it is men such as Dungannon who occupy the highest seats in the church. How are the poor to hear the name of Christ, when such men would deny it to them on account of their attire? And what am I to do to stand with them?"

"'My grace is sufficient for thee'," Lady Emily quoted, "'For my strength is made perfect in weakness.'"

"And a weaker specimen of the human race you never did see as the wretch who sits before you," Shaftesbury replied, smiling. "I could not do without you, my love."

Lady Emily's eyes narrowed shrewdly. "Something's wrong," she said. "Tell me. What's brought this on all of a sudden? It can't just be Dungannon."

"I received word from Daniel Tanner, of the Duke Street Ragged School," Shaftesbury admitted, "just before this meeting. The death of a girl, from the archway we visited on Wednesday night. He assures me they prayed with her before she passed, and she made some motions in response to the Gospel as they presented it to her—but for every one we find I wonder how many others pass away without ever hearing the name of Christ. Hundreds ... thousands, I should think. And more and more every day."

"You do feel it too keenly," Lady Emily agreed. "But that is no bad thing. I would rather my husband suffered in his fellow feeling for the poor of this world, and did all within his earthly power to ease their plight and bring them to Christ, than to have him be a clown with a smile painted on his face. Tears that are shed for lost sinners are not shed in vain—did our Lord not weep for Jerusalem?"

"He did indeed," Shaftesbury replied. He yawned and stretched, then rose to his feet and extended a hand to his wife.

"Shall we go to bed? I have much to pray for tonight."

PART II
THE RED NECKERCHIEF

"Blessed is the man that walketh not in the counsel of the
ungodly, nor standeth in the way of sinners,
nor sitteth in the seat of the scornful."
Psalm 1.1

15
Old Sal

A BRASS POCKET WATCH with a scratched face. Two pocket handkerchiefs. A battered cigarette case. A monocle.

One by one Billy placed the items on the dirty table, trying to keep his hands from shaking. Across the table sat a girl who could have been no more than eighteen years old, but who had a lifetime's worth of experience written across her hard features. Her blonde hair, streaked with dirt and grease, was pulled tight back across her skull and secured with a leather thong. The remains of some child-hood disease puckered her right cheek, pulling the lip back in a permanent leer. Her eyes were quick and bright, and her nose was long and fine. In a respectable house in a fine dress she might have been beautiful; in the crowded kitchen of the filthy boarding house she was simply cruel. Her name was Old Sal, and she surveyed the items with an expert eye before sitting back and fixing Billy with a piercing look.

"Two and six," she said.

Billy's heart sank. "I was thinking six shillings," he said, indicating one of the handkerchiefs, which was embroidered with a delicate pattern of flowers. "That's a kingsman, that is. I could get at least—"

"I know what it is." Old Sal's eyes drifted up towards the ceiling in an affectation of boredom. "Two and six is my price, for the lot. Take it or leave it."

Billy nodded miserably. This was Old Sal's kingdom, and her word was law. Arguing with her was about as much use as trying to hold back the Thames.

Two silver coins clattered onto the tabletop along with a shower of copper, but as Billy reached out to take the money, Old Sal's dirty hand shot out and drew the silver coins back.

"That'll cover what you owe for food and board," she said with a leer. "Nice doin' business as always, Master Sweep."

Billy silently took the remaining pennies and stuffed them into the bag he wore inside his trouser leg. Then he rose and pushed his way back through the crowded kitchen to the equally crowded hallway. He did not look back, but he could feel Old Sal's predatory smile following him.

Master Sweep. That was what she had called him from the first time they met. He had no idea how she knew about his past, and he hadn't asked. Old Sal knew everything—you learned that soon enough. Nothing was stolen, robbed, bought or sold in the maze of streets around her Soho boarding house without her knowing about it. And if you worked on her patch you dealt with her, or you found yourself facing a couple of her lads in a dark alleyway before the day was out.

Billy had very nearly met with Old Sal's judgement once already. On his fourth day after leaving Tosher and Clara, starving and frozen half to death, he had snatched a hot pie from a street vendor's stall while the man looked the other way. The man had been too fat and slow to catch Billy, but the two boys who cornered him in a nearby alleyway were not, and Billy had been too weak to escape from them the way he had from Archie Miller.

As he was new to the neighbourhood they had gone easy on him, and left him with only a few bruises before explaining the rules: mainly, that Old Sal owned everything and everyone, and everyone paid their dues to her. If you wanted to beg, pick pockets, rob or steal, that was fine by Old Sal—as long as you paid, promptly and regularly. They had told him the address of the boarding house, and advised him to pay her a visit sooner rather than later.

That was how they had met, when Billy had presented himself in the boarding house kitchen that evening, tired, shivering, and desperate for food. Old Sal had given him bread and stew, and watched with barely-veiled amusement as he wolfed it down; then she had called him 'Master Sweep', and offered him a job.

The proposition was simple: learn a street trade, be it begging or pickpocketing, and bring the proceeds to Old Sal in return for food and a place to sleep. Billy had hesitated to shake her hand, but only for half a second. There was no other choice, unless he wanted to starve to death.

Over the next two weeks he had learned—if not mastered—the art of picking pockets and petty thievery. One of the lads who hung around the kitchen showed him the ropes: how to move through a crowded street, looking for an open pocket or an unattended bag; then how to dart in quickly with two stiff fingers and get away with whatever you touched first: handkerchief, purse, spectacles—Old Sal would take them all, though the price depended on her mood that day and how much she liked you.

As Billy climbed the narrow stairs towards the top of the house, he jingled the few coins in the purse down his trouser leg. He wasn't exactly thriving. Today's haul was the most he had ever taken, and what did he have to show for it? Sixpence, and that was as likely to be spent on lodgings as on food or clothes.

His room was little more than a wooden box at the very top of the house, right under the eaves. It was completely bare, save for a pair of pallets with a couple of hay-stuffed sacks flung across them; a chill breeze blew unceasingly along the floor, bringing with it a constant supply of dead leaves and pigeon feathers which collected in a drift against the far wall. Old Sal charged sixpence a night for rooms like this. It was a steep price, but better—if only slightly—than spending another night on the streets.

Billy collapsed on one of the mattresses. It was cold and damp, and smelled of mould, but if he was lucky he would be able to catch a few hours' sleep before his room-mates returned. There were two of them, both older than him, and though technically the beds were available to whoever got there first, the other boys usually turfed him out whenever they wanted one. Most nights found him curled on the narrow strip of floor between the beds, shifting every few minutes as the wind changed direction and found new ways to creep in under his pitifully thin clothes.

He closed his eyes, but sleep was slow in coming. As always when he found himself in a quiet moment, the faces of Tosher and Clara rose in his mind: Tosher red-eyed and weeping, and Clara pale-faced and still. For the first week he had cried himself to sleep with the injustice of everything that had happened, and he had spent hours wondering what they were doing, and if Clara had survived. In those days the memory of their faces might have kept him awake, as the events of that night played over and over in his head.

But since he had started boarding at Old Sal's his tears had dried and his heart had hardened. Now when he thought of them it was with cold bitterness, and the memory of Tosher's betrayal was a constant reminder: it was no good making friends and caring about other people, because friends would either hold you back or turn on you.

He rolled over, pushing the memory away. Tomorrow, he told himself. Tomorrow would be the day he found his feet.

He rose at five the next morning, bleary-eyed and aching. His room-mates had returned just after midnight and tipped him out of bed, and sleep had proven almost impossible. He had tossed and turned for hours, until finally he gave up and decided he might as well get a head start on the day.

Pulling on a pair of soft-soled shoes—bought from one of the other boarders for a couple of pence—Billy slipped from the room, leaving his snoring companions behind him.

The staircase was pitch dark and nearly vertical, and more than once he slipped and cursed, almost pitching himself down to break his neck. He kept his hands firmly against the walls and took his time, and eventually arrived at the ground floor, where he padded down to the kitchen on his way out of the boarding house.

The kitchen was deserted for once. The fire had burned down to no more than a handful of ashes, and its heat had all but died away; once the day began, it would be built up again, but for now the cold from outside was creeping in through every crack it could find.

Still, the room was warmer than the dead black night, and Billy stood for a moment by the fire, drawing on its remaining heat as he prepared to leave.

"Goin' out early, are yer?"

He jumped, and turned to see who had spoken. A shadow moved in the corner by the fire, leaning into the light, and revealed itself as Old Sal, who had moved from her table to a bench in the corner.

Billy nodded cautiously to her. "Mornin' Sal."

She grinned. "Rich pickin's out there. Feelin' lucky?"

Billy shrugged. "Ain't down to luck, is it?"

"Luck's all yer got right now. Best give yerself up to it." Old Sal held up a withered, leathery strip of what might have once been fur: some kind of charm or talisman. "I keeps me luck close by. You'd best do the same."

"Don't need it," Billy said. "I make my own way."

"Then you're a braver man than most, Master Sweep."

The door banged open and a person swept in, bringing with him a blast of the chill morning air. He looked at the two of them and smiled.

"Mornin' all," he said. "Yer up early, Sal. Or is it late?"

"Neither," she said. "Or both. Either way, you won't catch me nappin'."

Billy recognised the newcomer: his name was Flash Jim and he was one of Old Sal's lads, the heavies who policed the boarding house and threw out those who couldn't or wouldn't pay their way.

Billy avoided Old Sal's lads, and they didn't generally talk to him. He was small fry to them—they had other jobs they did for Old Sal, jobs that involved fists and knives, and

127

midnight excursions into the City. There was something empty about their eyes, something that made the back of his neck prickle—but at the same time there was no denying they had a dashing air about them, and secretly Billy had looked on them with admiration.

Flash Jim was one of the best. He had earned his nickname from his habit of dressing like a young gentleman, complete with frock coat and cravat, and shoes he kept black by the regular application of soot mixed with pig fat. But a gentleman he most certainly was not. His weapon of choice was a set of brass knuckles, which he wielded with ruthless efficiency; he had a habit of whistling as he fought, a high-pitched off-key melody which he forced through his large front teeth.

Those teeth showed now, brown-white in the glow of the fire, as Flash Jim smiled at him.

"Who's this, then?" he asked.

"My name's Billy," Billy said, with as much bravado as he could muster.

"And what's your trade, Billy?"

"I pick pockets."

"He's a sweep," Old Sal chimed in from her corner. "Out o' work fer the moment."

"A sweep?" Flash Jim raised his eyebrows. "Bet you're quite the climber, ain't you?"

Billy shrugged cagily and said nothing. The less that was known about him around here, the better.

Flash Jim laughed. "No mind," he said. He dug in a pocket and pulled out a small bag, which clinked when he tossed it over to Old Sal. "There's what was owed," he said. "Plus interest. That lot won't be 'oldin' out on you no more."

"You didn't do no lastin' damage, I 'ope?"

"Come on, Sal." Flash Jim spread his arms wide, and in the ruddy light of the fire Billy could see his shirtsleeves were stained. "I ain't no animal."

"You're a dog," Old Sal snapped. "You bark when I says so, and you bite when I says so. Don't you forget it."

Flash Jim's smile tightened, and the humour died in his eyes. "It's your house, Sal," he said, and without another word he swept from the room.

Billy hovered in the doorway for a moment. Old Sal was staring into the fire, and she seemed to have forgotten about him; he left her to her ruminations and ducked out into the freezing dawn.

16
Flash Jim

NINE O'CLOCK FOUND BILLY hunched in an alleyway, looking out on a busy high street. The city had been awake for hours, but so far he had found no opportunities for pockets to be picked. The backstreets were too quiet, and those who walked them were too cautious to be taken advantage of.

The high street was another matter: now that the day was underway it was a crawling, heaving, swelling mass of life. Horse-drawn omnibus carriages rumbled constantly to and fro, overflowing with passengers, advertisements in bold letters plastered over every available surface. Ladies in black dresses and lace bonnets hurried along arm in arm, ignoring the cries and bellows of the street traders hawking their wares: pies, matches, muffins, buttons, shoe-shining, knife-sharpening, and every other conceivable item or service under the sun. Dogs barked, bells rang, men cursed and horses neighed. It was chaos, and it was perfect.

Several other boys were sauntering up and down the street, most of them one or two years older than Billy. He made sure he stayed well out of their way—they belonged to the Unpardonables, the gang who controlled the streets east of here. They were led by a Scotsman named the Bouger, who Billy had seen once or twice, sitting outside a pub at the upper end of the high street with his face all but hidden behind a vast red beard from which an enormous pipe drooped, clamped between yellow teeth. He had recognised Billy as one of Old Sal's pickpockets, and had saluted him with a raised glass. Billy hadn't known what to do, so he had touched his forehead in reply, at which the Bouger had roared with laughter.

Every inch of London was divided up in this way: each gang had its own territory, which its members defended vigorously, and within which they carried out their particular brand of crime. Some, such as Old Sal's lads, preferred petty thievery and pickpocketing; the Unpardonables went in for blackmail and extortion; others engaged in old-fashioned robbery and murder; and then there was burglary, forgery, arson, fraud, and all the other dark arts for which they were feared throughout the city.

By and large the gangs kept to their territory. Boundaries were respected, and a tentative peace was maintained. If you happened to wander into a rival gang's neighbourhood it was your own fault, and the consequences were on your own head.

Billy wasn't exactly sure whether he was allowed to work this street, it being the boundary between the two gangs, but he was desperate. Other streets had thinner pickings, and they had already been claimed by other inhabitants of the boarding house. If he was going to stand any chance of making any kind of a living he was going to have to take risks.

His eyes lighted on a potential candidate: a young man, foppishly dressed in a top hat and tails, who was sauntering along with a hand in one pocket and a cane in the other. His tailcoat was pushed back, revealing a silver watch-chain dangling from his waistcoat, and he was observing the shops and stalls with a barely-interested eye.

Billy glanced around. As far as he could tell, no one else was interested. This could be it. Old Sal would have to give him a fair few shillings for that watch. If he was quick enough, he could be away before the young man realised what was happening.

He rose and sidled out on to the street, weaving through the crowds with his eyes on the man, who was sauntering along with the unconcerned pace of someone with nowhere to go and nothing to do. Billy rolled up his sleeve and wiped his hand on his trouser leg. The young man slowed, inspecting a display of flowers; Billy hesitated, watching as the young man bent low to smell the blooms. His eyes were fixed on the watch chain, his heart was hammering ...

He darted forwards, his hand shooting out—but at the last second it was knocked away as another hand snatched the chain. Before Billy could see who had beaten him to it, the young man was turning with a look of shock and surprise on his face, which quickly turned to anger when he saw Billy standing before him.

"Here!" he demanded in a braying voice. "What's your game, eh?" He looked down at his now-bare waistcoat, and his eyes widened. "You thieving rat! Hand it back!"

Billy froze, but only for a second. Then he turned and sprinted away, pursued by the young man's cries of "Stop! Thief!"

Suddenly the crowds were thicker than before, blocking his way; Billy stumbled and barged his way through them, never seeming to get a clear run. The young man's cries were not fading, and with a lurch Billy realised he was being pursued. Heads were turning at the commotion; eyes were following him; someone reached out to grab him, and Billy only just managed to dodge away.

"Stop! Hey! Stop that thief!"

A hand clasped Billy's arm, spinning him around and sending him tumbling to the floor.

"Not so fast," someone growled, as two or three men closed in on him. Billy looked around in desperation. He had landed in a doorway, but the door behind him was locked and bolted. A crowd had quickly formed, fencing him in. There was no way out, no way to escape the hands reaching for him, except …

He looked up. It had worked before. Why not now? It was too late to think. All he could do was act.

He scrambled to his feet as someone made a grab for him, then took a running leap and clawed his way up on to broad shoulders, and jumped for the door frame. There was a gasp from the crowd, then a ripple of laughter, as Billy's feet found purchase and his hands found fingerholds, and he lifted himself up and tumbled in through a first-floor window.

There was no time to stop, no time to look back. Billy barged through an empty room into a dusty corridor, flung open the first door he came to, and hauled open the window. Outside was an overgrown yard full of rubbish, with a dark alleyway on the other side. Billy didn't think twice. He climbed through the window, dropped down into the rubbish below, and tripped and stumbled his way into the darkness, cursing himself for his foolishness.

Half an hour later, Billy stumbled back into the yard at the back of Old Sal's boarding house, tired, cold, and hungry.

He slumped against one of the wooden posts that supported a thatched awning along one side of the yard, and cursed himself yet again for being such a fool. *Better to snatch a handkerchief and get away with it, than to go for a watch and get caught.* Well, he had gone for the watch, and he had almost been caught for his trouble. All it would have taken was one slip, one mistake, and those strong arms would have clasped him and not let go until the police arrived. Never again, he swore to himself. Even if he had to steal pocket handkerchiefs for the rest of his life.

He rested for a minute, catching his breath. Tall buildings rose all around him, their windows thick with grime. Across the yard was the kitchen door, from which the smell of stew and the sound of a drunken fiddle drifted over to him. Soon enough he would have to go in and face Old Sal, and admit he had nothing to bring her today. She might take pity on him, and let him stay on credit; or she might throw him out until he had earned his keep. There was no way of knowing.

He was just about to haul himself reluctantly inside when he was interrupted by the sound of tuneless whistling coming from the entrance to the yard, and a moment later Flash Jim sauntered in. He stopped when he saw Billy, and gave him a nod. Then, instead of going into the kitchen, he leaned up against an empty crate, took a pipe from his pocket, and began picking at the bowl with a fingernail.

"Blasted thing won't draw," he said after a minute. It took

Billy a second to realise he was being addressed. Flash Jim tossed the pipe into the mud, then produced another from his waistcoat pocket.

"I go through pipes like an Irishman goes through potatoes," he said cheerfully, placing the new pipe between his teeth and fishing around for a bag of tobacco. "P'raps I'm smoking 'em wrong."

He tamped down a wedge of the frayed tobacco leaves, then started patting his pockets. "Blasted matches …" he muttered. "There's never any when you need 'em …"

Billy hesitated for a second, then took a tiny matchbox from his pocket and held it out. Flash Jim's eyes lit up, and he sauntered over to take it.

"Cheers," he said. He struck a match and applied it to the bowl, then sucked in a deep breath and expelled a cloud of bittersweet smoke. "Lovely," he declared, with a contented sigh. "Want a puff?"

He held out the pipe. After a pause Billy took it and examined it. He had never smoked a pipe before, but it didn't look all that difficult. He clenched the stem between his front teeth, pursed his lips, and sucked in a deep breath.

Fire filled his lungs. He coughed, his throat burning, and doubled over as Flash Jim snatched back the pipe with a roar of laughter.

"First time, eh? It gets easier."

Billy cleared his throat and spat into the mud. The inside of his chest felt like it had been rubbed with sandpaper. When he looked up, Flash Jim was holding out the match box.

"Thanks for those," he said, as Billy took back the box and thrust it into his pocket. Flash Jim took another draw on the pipe. He held the smoke in for a second, then gently released it in a pale grey-blue circle which drifted across the yard.

"Nice performance today," he said. "In the circus, was you?"

Billy looked up sharply, and Flash Jim laughed out loud.

"Yeah," he said. "I saw you. I were curious. Wanted ter see what you was made of."

He reached into his pocket again, and this time he drew out a silver pocket watch on a long silver chain, which he swung round a couple of times before catching it with nimble fingers. Billy flushed, recognising the watch he had failed to steal that morning, and Flash Jim smiled as he saw the colour rise in his cheeks.

"Caught me eye just as it caught yours," he said. He twirled it another couple of times, then tossed it over to Billy, who caught it with a look of surprise.

"There," Flash Jim said. "You're a miserable pickpocket, but most lads are. You'd be amazed how many go out and don't come back. At least you didn't get felt by the law, eh?"

He pushed himself away from the crate and slipped an arm around Billy's shoulders. Billy flinched, but he didn't resist. Flash Jim's breath reeked of alcohol as he leaned in close.

"You ain't a pocket-snatch, Billy," he said. "That ain't where your talent lies, is it?"

Billy didn't answer. Flash Jim already knew the truth— that he was struggling to adapt to this new life on the streets; that, in all probability, he would not last another week in here. Admitting to it would only make him appear more feeble than he already was.

In any case, Flash Jim didn't appear interested in a reply. "I seen you today," he said. "I seen 'ow you scampered up that wall like a little monkey. That's quite a skill, that is. Not many lads can do that. They can beg, steal and rob, but you ... You're not like them, are yer?"

Still Billy said nothing. He could tell Flash Jim was building up to something, and he wanted to hear what it was.

Flash Jim lowered his voice still further, until it was a conspiratorial murmur. "There's a little jaunt being organised tonight," he said. "Me and a few of the lads. We could use someone of your talents. I've a feeling it'd make our lives a lot easier. If you meet me and the lads downstairs at closing time tonight, you'd be welcome to tag along. You help me, and who says I couldn't help you, when the time came?"

Billy fingered the watch. There were ten shillings right there: two weeks' rent at least. It was the break he had been dying for, a way out of the constant grinding cycle of thieving and debt to Old Sal.

But still he said nothing. Flash Jim and his lads were a different breed altogether from the petty crooks and ne'er-do-wells he had come to know so far: their work was darker and more violent, and the thought of participating in it made him afraid.

Sensing his hesitation, Flash Jim gave a throaty chuckle and released him.

"You take a while ter think about it," he said. "You want in, you be in the kitchen at kickin'-out time. I'll make it worth yer while."

And with that, he strode out of the yard into the grubby snow.

17
Bad Company

OLD SAL SAID NOTHING when Billy presented her with the watch, but counted out eight silver shillings and slid them across the table. Billy took them without arguing: it was the best and only deal he was going to get.

He didn't fancy the idea of going out and trying to steal something else, and the weight of coins in his pocket was reassuring, so he spent the rest of the day in and around the house, losing a few pence at cards and listening to the idle chatter of the other boarders. In the afternoon he made his way up to the room at the top of the house, where he managed a few hours' sleep before waking with a start to find that it was dark. For a moment he thought he had overslept, and missed Flash Jim's deadline; but then he heard the distant sounds of singing and laughter drifting up from the kitchen. Kicking-out time had yet to arrive. He had plenty of time.

He rose from the mattress, peering around in the gloom. He could see nothing, but he could hear the soft rasp of snoring coming from the other bed. Only one of the boys was back, then. He wondered if the other had not managed to pay that day, and had been thrown out. He hoped so. It would serve him right, whichever one it was.

He pulled on his shoes, then felt his way to the door and descended the almost vertical staircase to the landing.

There was light here, leaking up from the lower floors through the boards. Around him dark doorways opened into musty rooms, where shadowed forms stirred restlessly and whispered voices engaged in clandestine conversation. A sickly-sweet smell hung in the air, which made him dizzy if he breathed too deeply. Billy moved to the top of the stairs, where the air was fresher, and listened to the voices floating up to him from below, trying to make out who was speaking. He soon picked out Flash Jim's braying laugh, followed by a chorus of cheers and groans—the lads were playing cards again, and by the sounds of it Flash Jim was winning.

For a second he hesitated. This was it. If he went down now, he was committing himself. There would be no turning back. He thought of the silver shillings, and Flash Jim's words: *You help me, and I'll help you.*

He took a deep breath, then started down the stairs.

There were two more flights to the ground floor, where Billy found the dark hallway crowded with bodies. He picked his way through, treading on a foot or a hand here and there and eliciting the occasional barked curse, and ducked through another doorway into the kitchen.

The room was packed, hot, and noisy. The fire burned brightly, and the air was thick with tobacco smoke, the smell of ale and the clatter of voices. Someone was playing a pipe in a corner, and someone else was singing along to the tune, twisting a folk song into a lewd parody. Bodies were crammed everywhere: shoulder to shoulder along the benches that lined the walls, or crowded around the warped table in the middle of the room. Old Sal sat by the fire, watching everything with her sharp eyes and dragging on a black cigar; Flash Jim was dealing another hand to his cronies, and one or two others who fancied their luck that night. They would lose, of course, because Flash Jim cheated outrageously, tipping winks to his friends and palming cards, and at the end of the night they would doubtless be thrown out into the snow for their trouble.

Billy sidled over to the fire, where Young Sal, the cook, sat on a low stool. No one knew exactly how or when Young Sal got her name, only that it was a running joke in the boarding house, as she was as ancient and shrivelled as the carrots that went into her bubbling pot. Every day she cooked up a mess of something hot and brown and not altogether identifiable, and for tuppence served up one bowl per lodger per day; for an extra penny she would fish you out a lump that was more meat than gristle. She was chewing on a scrag-end of meat with her two remaining teeth now, glaring at the room in general with her one good eye.

Billy had already had his bowl earlier that day, but Young Sal had a soft spot for him, and sometimes she scraped him up an extra portion from the residue at the bottom of the pot. It was thick, and bitter, and mostly burned flour, but it was food.

She glanced up at him now, cracked her withered lips in a smile, and set to work with her spoon. When she was done she handed him the bowl, then turned her head to the side and tapped her cheek. Billy bent down and gave her a quick peck, and she cackled with delight as she turned away.

"She likes you."

Billy turned to find Old Sal regarding him steadily from her place at her table.

"I can see why," she continued. "You're a nice lad, Master Sweep. Likeable. Not like most of us. Anyone can see you don't belong 'ere. Makes me wonder what drove you from the life you had."

"Nothin'," Billy muttered. "I'm jus' making my way is all."

Old Sal smiled sadly. "Ain't we all, Master Sweep? Ain't we all? But somethin' tells me your way's been made for you more than once recently. It's in your face: you're on the run. Away from somethin', towards somethin' … don't really matter. All that matters is you're gonna keep runnin' till you find what you want. But I don't think you knows what that is yet. Does you?"

Billy shrugged. He didn't know what Old Sal was talking about, and he didn't much care. All he wanted was to be left to eat in peace.

"Let me give you a word of advice," Old Sal said, beckoning him close. Billy hesitated, but you didn't refuse Old Sal. He shuffled over until he could smell the grease in her hair.

"*Be careful in the company you keep,*" she hissed. "There's more than one devil walks these streets in fine clothing."

Her eyes drifted past Billy, and he turned to see Flash Jim crow with laughter as he won yet another hand. A shiver went through him, but when he turned back to Old Sal her head was bent low over her accounts, for all the world as if they had never spoken, and after waiting for a second to see if she wanted anything else Billy retreated.

He had just managed to gulp down the burnt scraps of stew when a bell rang out through the kitchen. Immediately

Flash Jim threw down his hand and scooped his winnings from the tabletop.

"That's it!" he yelled, rising and striding around the kitchen, kicking shins and slapping heads as he roused the assembled rabble. "Time's up, ladies and gentlemen! Anyone who hasn't paid yet today, it was lovely to have the pleasure of your company, but regrettably the time of our parting has come!" He paused and turned slowly with a wicked smile, surveying the puzzled faces that surrounded him. "That means *get out!*" he finished, upending a glass of ale over the nearest man. The dregs splashed in his hair, and the crowd roared with laughter as the man spluttered and swore.

Slowly the patrons began to disperse, groaning and muttering, some stumbling towards the stairs and others—reluctantly—out into the yard.

As always there were a few who tried their luck, hoping for a free bed. But Old Sal's lads stood at the door, checking faces and taking payment, and they turned away anyone who wasn't in credit and didn't have the money.

One old man in particular kicked up an almighty fuss, insisting that his account was good until the end of the week.

"Ask Sal!" he shouted, in a voice cracked with drink. "She'll tell yer! Sal! Sal! Tell yer boys ter let me up!"

But Old Sal did not even glance at him. She sat with her face turned to the fire, gazing deep into the flames, as her lads seized the man by his arms and legs and carried him, still kicking and swearing, to be dumped in the yard.

"What a loon!" Flash Jim declared, dusting off his hands and laughing. "Cart 'im off to Bedlam, I say."

The lads sniggered in agreement. Billy kept silent and watched from the corner as Flash Jim sauntered over to Old

Sal and stuck his thumbs into his waistband.

"All done, Sal," he said. "You all right?"

She nodded, but did not reply. Flash Jim cleared his throat extravagantly.

"We'll be off in a bit," he continued. "Any last words from our fearless leader?"

A shake of her head this time, and still no reply.

"All right then." Flash Jim looked around at the rest of the lads. "Go get ready," he said. "Meet back here in twenty minutes."

The room emptied, apart from Old Sal, Flash Jim, and Billy. Silence fell. Billy could not help feeling that he should leave, that this was a private moment between the two by the fire; but they seemed to have forgotten about him, and he was curious to see what would happen.

Flash Jim pushed back his coat and sat on the table in front of Old Sal, leaning in close to speak to her.

"You ain't happy," he said, so softly Billy had to strain to hear. "You think it ain't right."

"It *ain't* right, Jim," Old Sal replied huskily. To Billy's surprise he realised she was crying. It was so unexpected he thought he must be mistaken, but when she looked up he saw her cheeks wet with tears. "This weren't what we signed up for," she said. "Protectin' our own is one thing, but this …" She shook her head. "It's evil, Jim. Plain and simple."

"We're all evil here," Flash Jim said with a shrug. "None of us is goin' anywhere but the fire when we dies—might as well make the most of what we got while we got it."

Old Sal looked up at him in disbelief. "You got no conscience, Jim?"

He shrugged again. "Never found a use for it."

"So that's it then?"

"That's it. It's a choice we're all goin' to have to make—eat or be eaten, kill or be killed."

"What happened to turnin' the other cheek?"

Flash Jim barked with laughter. "You turn the other cheek, all you're gonna get is two slapped cheeks," he said. "Me, I'd rather have coin in me pocket, food and ale in me belly, and all me enemies in the ground. Then I'll be happy."

"Unless you're dead."

Flash Jim rose from the table. "Unless I'm dead," he agreed. "In which case you're welcome to say you told me so."

He turned suddenly and fixed Billy with a piercing stare, his mouth stretched wide in a manic grin.

"'Eard enough, 'ave you?" he said, and chuckled. "Ready for the fray?"

Billy didn't know what the fray was, and there was something in Flash Jim's eyes that made him pause. He glanced at Old Sal, but her eyes were turned down. He hesitated, thinking first of his draughty attic room with its damp mattresses, then of his own bed and an undisturbed night's sleep. He nodded.

"All right, then." Flash Jim jabbed a thumb towards the stairs. "Get the lads down, and we'll get goin'. It's gonna be a fun night tonight."

18
The Window

WHEN THE LADS CAME DOWN they were dressed all in black. One by one they crossed to the fire and spat into the embers to make a black paste, which they smeared all over their faces. Then they loitered in the kitchen, grim-faced and silent. Old Sal sat huddled in her corner, face turned towards the fire, ignoring them.

Only Flash Jim did not wear a serious expression. He wandered among them, whistling through his teeth and flexing his fingers through the guard of his brass knuckles. This set had wicked spikes jutting out all along the top; Billy shuddered to think of the damage they could do.

The rest of the lads were similarly armed with a collection of knives, clubs and other light weapons. There were about twenty of them, as far as Billy could count, and all of them ready for a fight. Two of the lads were winding lengths of rope over their shoulders; others were tucking wooden pegs into their boots and belts. Billy wondered what they were for, but he didn't dare ask.

"That everyone?" Flash Jim said, looking over their

heads. "Right. Let's go. And remember what I said: no noise, and no lights. We go in quick and quiet, and we get out just the same. Understand?"

He turned towards Old Sal, ready to bid her farewell, but her gaze remained fixed on the fire, and after a moment he snorted and ducked through the doorway into the darkness of the yard. The lads followed him, the kitchen gradually emptying until it was just Billy and Old Sal left. Billy was about to leave when Old Sal's head swivelled round, and her fierce eyes fixed on him.

"You've made your choice, then," she said.

It was a question, not a statement. Billy nodded, his heart thudding in his chest.

"Like angels tumblin' out o' paradise after the devil," she murmured, then she turned her attention back to the fire and said no more. Billy hurried after the lads, and when he glanced back the last thing he saw was Old Sal's shadow framed in the doorway, black against the orange fire.

The lads walked in silence, the only sounds the rustling of their clothes and the crunch and slush of their footsteps in the snow. Flash Jim led them through a maze of back-streets, then across a wide road which Billy recognised as the scene of his bungled robbery earlier that day. Now it was deserted, the omnibuses back at their sheds, the house-keepers at home, the shopkeepers behind their shutters. The grubby snow was cast in eerie yellow light by the public gas-lamps that burned on their tall iron posts.

None of the lads hesitated. One by one they slipped across the road into the shadows of an alleyway, their bodies instantly swallowed up by the darkness.

Only Billy slowed as he approached that opening. There

was an uneasiness in his stomach, which was slowly spreading into his chest. This road marked the boundary of the Bouger's territory; and if straying into another gang's patch by day was bad form, an armed invasion in the dead of night was an act of war. He had taken up Flash Jim's offer in the hope of becoming one of the lads, but stepping into that alleyway felt like stepping into the mouth of hell, and once he was through there was no going back.

But if he turned away now, what would happen to him? It would be the end of his time at Old Sal's for sure, and there was no guarantee that anyone else would take him in. Could he go back on the streets, freezing and starving in the cold and snow?

No. He had made his choice, and there was no going back. It was just the same as climbing chimneys: into the hole, where Death waited with his scythe and his hourglass and his ivory grin, and where he could at least battle for his own survival; or out to face certain punishment, at the mercy of a cruel world.

He took a deep breath and plunged into the darkness.

For a second Billy was blind. He tripped over a timber lying on the ground and almost fell flat on his face, but strong arms caught him.

"Mind yer step, now," Flash Jim whispered in his ear as he lifted Billy to his feet. "Can't have you gettin' lost, can we?" He tapped Billy on the arm. "This way," he hissed. "Not far now."

Billy followed him through the darkness, tripping and stumbling until his eyes became accustomed to the gloom. This alleyway opened into another, just wide enough for two to walk abreast. Flash Jim led him right, then turned left almost immediately, squeezing into an impossibly narrow gap between two buildings. Flash Jim barely fitted, but it was not so bad for Billy, who, besides being naturally small, was now malnourished almost to the point of being a skeleton. He sidled crabwise, his face brushing against brick, with Flash Jim puffing and swearing ahead of him, until at last they slipped out of the far end into a square void between the buildings. Crumbling brick walls loomed up on all sides, hemming them in.

The rest of the lads had already crowded into the space, though there was only just room. Still they kept silent, though they jostled and squirmed in their confined surroundings. Flash Jim turned to Billy.

"You're up, Bill," he said, his voice barely loud enough to hear. He pointed up one wall, to where a dark window looked out over the void. "See if you can't shinny up there and have a look-see, eh?"

Billy looked up. The window seemed impossibly high, more than four times the height of a man. But the wall was cracked and broken, and even as he looked he could see dark fissures in the brickwork where hands and feet could find purchase.

"Can you do it?" Flash Jim asked, sensing his hesitation.

Billy nodded. This was his moment. The least he could do was try.

Flash Jim gave him a thump on the back. "That's my man. Get on with you, then."

The crowd of lads parted to allow Billy to get to the wall. As he passed them he could feel their eyes boring into him. They didn't know him, and they didn't trust him. He ignored them, and tried to concentrate on the wall.

He had not done any climbing like this before—on a flat wall, without the sides of the flue to brace against—but as he studied the wall he thought he could see a way up. The method came to him much as it had done when he had faced Archie Miller in the dead end, all those weeks ago, or when he had scrambled up and away from the crowd on the high street yesterday: like a light dawning in his mind, filling him with quiet confidence; except this time the understanding dawned slowly, rather than all at once.

He reached up and slid his fingers into a jagged crack above his head, then searched for a toehold. When he found it he pushed up, extending his hands again, quickly settling into a rhythm: push, reach, hold, search, grip, push, reach, hold, search, grip … He was surprised by how easily it came to him, how natural it felt to slowly work his way upwards.

At first he was alarmed by the lack of anything solid behind him, but soon he found the sense of space freeing. There was just him and the wall, and nothing in-between. If he fell there would be nothing to catch him—but equally there would be no getting stuck. He felt as if he could really breathe, and by the time he reached the window he was actually enjoying himself.

His last push took him up to the sill of the window, where he sat for a moment to catch his breath. Below him was a vague mass of dark faces upturned to watch his progress. He could not make out which one was Flash Jim, but he was sure he would be watching him extra closely.

Billy turned instead to the grimy panes of the window beside him. He peered through the murk, but the interior of the building was pitch dark and he could not make out anything.

He examined the window frame. It was old, the paint long since flaked away by the heat and cold of the passing years; the wood crumbled to the touch. As an experiment, he prodded one of the panes. It wobbled in its setting, then came away in his hand. Billy stared at it for a second, then peeled the rectangle of glass from its precarious hold, put his face to the dark space where it had been, and peered through.

The room beyond was large: some kind of a loft, or storeroom, filled with bodies lying scattered around in attitudes of deep slumber. Soft sounds of breathing filled the air, punctuated by the odd rasping snore and the occasional cough. The room smelled stale and warm, the odour of unwashed skin and greasy hair. It reminded Billy of Gerard's loft, and for a moment the memory came back to him with startling clarity: the low rafters, the little 'uns in their pile in the corner, the hole near the gable where he and Tosher had slipped out on their way to Aggie's shop. How much had changed since then. His old life was almost like a dream.

There was a hiss from below, and he turned his head to see a hand beckoning him down. He rested the pane of glass on the window sill and lowered himself carefully down, making his way back down the wall to the ground.

As soon as his feet touched the frozen earth Flash Jim was there, a hand resting casually on the back of Billy's neck.

"What did yer see?" Flash Jim breathed. "A room o' lads, right?"

Billy nodded, and a ripple of approval went through the crowd.

"Quiet!" Flash Jim hissed. He turned back to Billy. "How

many?"

Billy thought hard. He hadn't counted, but he took a guess. "Maybe … thirty? Forty?"

"Well, which one? Thirty or forty?" Flash Jim's expression was unusually urgent.

"Say forty, then."

"All right." Flash Jim nodded and addressed the lads around them. "That's two each. Think you can manage it?" Heads nodded in reply, and Flash Jim smiled grimly. "Then let's do this."

He gestured to the two boys who had carried the rope, and they began unwinding it, while others drew the pegs from their boots and belts and held them ready. The pegs, Billy saw, had deep notches cut into both ends, while the rope was knotted at regular intervals; as soon as a good length was available the lads seized it and began to fix the pegs to the ropes just above the knots, tugging them to make sure they were securely fastened. Slowly but surely a primitive ladder began to form, the pegs forming the footholds between the two ropes.

When it was finished, Flash Jim tied the ends of the ropes together through a metal lanyard, leaving about nine or ten feet free at the end. This he handed to Billy.

"Take that up and tie it off somewhere firm," he said. "When you're ready, swing the ladder twice. Then get out of the way. We'll do the rest."

Billy obeyed silently, tying the rope around his waist to keep his hands free.

Going up was harder this time, as the ladder grew heavier and heavier as more of it uncoiled from the ground, and by the time he reached the sill his hands were trembling. He rested for a second to recover his breath, then began to lever the rest of the panes out of the window one by one, resting them on the sill with the first.

The frame crumbled beneath his fingers, and soon the window was just an empty hole in the wall. Billy eased himself through into the room beyond. The panes of glass clinked gently as his foot nudged them, and he froze, expecting to hear a shout of challenge. When none came he straightened up and looked around for somewhere to tie the ladder.

There was a thick post connecting the floor and the rafters, not far from the window. Billy dragged the rope over to it, wincing as the pegs clattered softly against the window frame. He tied it off as best he could, then returned to the window and swung the ladder back and forth a couple of times to signal the lads.

The ladder shuddered, then went taut as the first climber rested his whole weight on it. It continued to vibrate as the climber ascended, until at last Flash Jim's face appeared in the darkened window frame. He nodded when he saw Billy, then turned and beckoned the rest to follow him. They came one at a time, the whole process seeming to stretch on for hours while nearby the darkened shapes slumbered and snored.

When all the lads were assembled Flash Jim gestured for them to spread out, holding a finger to his lips for silence.

The lads melted away into the darkness, making no noise as they slipped between the sleeping bodies.

Billy sank into a crouch by the window, watching as they took up positions all around the room. The sleepers did not stir, blissfully unaware of what was about to take place.

But Billy knew. It was clear now, and he should have known from the minute they crossed into enemy territory. What other reason could there be for creeping into another gang's headquarters in the dead of night? That's where they were, after all: in the house of the Unpardonables. And Flash Jim had not come to make peace.

He turned and eased himself over the windowsill into the cold night air. He could not stay and watch. It made him feel sick just thinking about it.

He was halfway down the ladder when a piercing whistle from Flash Jim rent the air, followed by a patter of soft thuds like fists hitting a mattress. Billy scrambled the last few rungs down the ladder, desperate now to get away from whatever was happening up there, and fell to his knees in the yard. A hidden stone cut his knee, but he ignored the pain and scrambled away down the narrow gap between the buildings, trying not to imagine what was taking place behind him.

He did not stop running until he staggered into the boarding house yard and slumped against a post, panting and sweating despite the cold. He was trembling all over, and his heart was racing. The image of the sleeping bodies kept running through his mind, with Flash Jim's Lads spreading out around them. He squeezed his eyes tight shut, trying to drive it out, trying to forget what he knew had happened in that darkened room.

"Nasty business, isn't it?"

His head snapped up. Someone was standing in the kitchen doorway, framed by the flickering light of the dying fire. He was tall, and broad, and with a plummeting feeling in his chest Billy recognised his West Country drawl.

Archie Miller stepped into the yard, shaking his head and chuckling in disbelief.

"Well, well, well," he said. "It's been a while, boy."

19
Partners

BILLY KNEW WHAT HE wanted to do: he wanted to run, as fast and as far as possible. But he could not move. He was paralysed, rooted to the ground with the shock of hearing that voice and seeing that face. He could still remember Archie's last words to him, the threat of what he would do if they ever met again. And now here they were, alone in the yard, with no one around to help or to see.

Archie Miller chuckled again. He was still shaking his head, unable to believe what he was seeing.

"Who would'a thought it?" he said, strolling towards Billy. "Out of all the filthy dens in this 'ere filthy city, this is the one we both come to on this night. What d'yer call that, eh? Luck? Providence? Fate?"

He was almost on top of Billy now. His hands were tucked nonchalantly into the pockets of the long overcoat he wore, but he still managed to exude an air of menace with his exaggerated swagger and enormous frame.

"Whatever it is, I like it," he finished. He looked Billy up and down. "I seem to remember a certain promise I made when las' we parted. Somethin' I were goin' ter do ter you. You remember what it was, boy?"

He drew his hands slowly out of his pockets and flexed fingers as thick as iron cables.

"I don't deny I'm gonna enjoy this," he growled, raising his hands with a terrible light in his eyes ...

A sudden commotion made him halt: Flash Jim and his lads were pouring into the yard, laughing and slapping each other on the back. One or two were limping, and a couple nursed injuries to hands and arms, but every one of them wore a smile on his face.

At the front of the group strode Flash Jim, his usual swagger ratcheted up a few notches. From his lips hung an enormous drooping pipe, which Billy immediately recognised as the Bouger's. So that was it, then. The Unpardonables were finished, and Old Sal's Lads were victorious.

When Flash Jim saw Archie he stopped short, and the lads clattered to a halt behind him. The yard fell silent. The two of them eyed each other up, and for one wild moment Billy thought there was going to be a fight—but then Flash Jim extended a hand, and a moment later Archie took it, and the two of them shook hands with a laugh.

"Archie!" Flash Jim cried, patting him on the arm. "Didn't expect you here so soon."

"Well, word reached me ears about yer little expedition tonight," Archie replied. "Thought I'd come down and see fer meself. Did it go well?"

Flash Jim raised the pipe. "The king is dead," he grinned. "Long live the king!"

Archie roared with laughter, and in the next instant Flash

156

Jim and the lads had joined in, and they were all laughing and shaking hands and congratulating each other on a job well done and a battle well fought.

"I must admit I 'ad me doubts," Archie said over the racket. "Didn't know if a flower like you'd be up to the task."

A flicker of anger passed across Flash Jim's face, but then it was gone, and he was smiling and shrugging. "What can I say? I've a good bunch o' lads."

"That you do!" Archie looked around approvingly. "A finer bunch I've never seen—excepting me own, of course!"

"And this one!" Flash Jim's hand darted out and caught Billy around the shoulders, pulling him close. "A gem, 'e is. First time out with the lads, but we couldn't 'a done it without him!"

"That so?"

Flash Jim must have caught the sudden change in Archie's tone, because he frowned and tightened his grip on Billy.

"What's up, Archie?" he said. "Something wrong?"

"No, no. Nothing wrong. Except ..." Archie shrugged, and raised his hands helplessly. "I 'ad a small bone to pick with the boy, tha's all."

"And what bone would that be?"

"A disagreement. A point of honour, let's call it. I'd expected certain ... satisfaction."

"From our Bill? What's 'e done, then?"

Archie did not answer right away. His eyes were fixed on Billy, and the force of his stare was like the blast from a furnace. All around them the lads were still shouting and talking, but to Billy it seemed that he, Archie, and Flash Jim were in their own silent world, cut off from the rest. If Archie decided he wanted him, there would be no stopping him, not even by twenty strong young men. There was a wildness in his eyes, a primal urge that did not know conscience or reason. When Archie Miller wanted something he took it, and it did not matter how much blood was spilt along the way.

Then Archie laughed, and the spell was broken.

"Ah, it's nothin'" he said. "Nothin' that can't be bygones. What d'yer say … Bill, was it?"

Billy nodded, unable to speak. Archie thrust a massive hand at him.

"Shall we shake on it like men?"

Billy hesitated, then cautiously slipped his hand into Archie's. Archie smiled at him—then, with astonishing speed for someone so big, he brought his other hand around, grabbed Billy's wrist in an iron grip, and snapped Billy's little finger.

Pain flooded through Billy's hand, burning cold then hot, and he collapsed to the ground with a strangled cry of shock as Archie released him. The pain blossomed into an all-consuming halo, through which Billy could dimly hear Flash Jim give a shout of protest, and Archie's dismissive reply:

"He'll be fine! Give him a couple of days to heal. I broke more'n my fair share o' fingers in the past. Won't be no lasting damage, long as he gets it set."

"And how's he gonna climb with a busted hand, eh?" That was Flash Jim. "Why'd yer think I wanted him in the first place? Now what am I gonna do when I needs a window jimmied?"

"He'll heal just fine," Archie growled dismissively. "And maybe he'll remember what happens to those who cross Archie Miller—and maybe you should too."

"You threatenin' me?"

The yard had fallen silent again. Billy looked up, and through the fog of pain he saw that Flash Jim's Lads had closed in a semicircle around them. One or two had drawn their knives, their faces grim.

"Threaten? Me?" Archie placed a hand on his chest with a look of mock surprise. "No, lad. I don't threaten."

He whistled sharply, and with a clatter a dozen first-floor windows were thrown open all around the yard. In each window a dark shape crouched, clutching a long rifle, the polished barrels glinting in the moonlight.

The lads fell silent, their faces white and their eyes wide as they gazed up at the death surrounding them.

"Now," Archie said, turning to Flash Jim, who was quivering with barely-suppressed rage. "Let's 'ave a little chat about how things are goin'a be from now on, shall we? First off, I'm right grateful to ye for services rendered this night. The old Bouger was a stubborn sort, wouldn't see sense, and you done me a great favour by dealin' with 'im. I'll sleep easy in me bed knowin' he's in the ground. And with 'im gone, I see an openin' in these parts for a young man with a sharp mind and a thirst fer greatness. Do you 'ave a thirst, Jimmy boy?"

Flash Jim moved his head in a barely perceptible nod. His eyes were turned upwards to the windows, counting and assessing.

"Don' even think about it," Archie said with a chuckle. "I've a man on every corner from 'ere to Whitechapel. You wouldn't get ten paces. Come on. Let's be reasonable, eh? Young man like you. Big future, big plans. You could be top dog in these parts, 'specially with me on your side. Look at the Bouger, now: there's a man who weren't on my side, and see what 'appened to him. Don't make the mistake of thinking you're immortal, Jimmy boy: if you ever cross me you can be sure I'll rain down on you with fire and brimstone. But you stick with me, and I'd say your future's looking bright enough already. What d'yer say? Partners?"

Flash Jim's eyes travelled down to meet Archie's. He nodded slowly, and extended his hand.

"Partners," he said.

Archie bellowed with laughter. "It's a brave man, or a foolish one, who shakes me 'and after tonight." He reached out and enveloped Flash Jim's hand in his own massive paw. "But brave or foolish, that's a man I can respect."

He whistled again, and the rifles disappeared from the windows. The lads relaxed, though the fear remained in their eyes. Archie glanced down at Billy, who was still lying on the floor, clutching his injured hand.

"See to the boy," he said. "I'll be in touch. In the meantime, you've a kingdom to rule. Enjoy it while you can."

He turned and made his way through the crowded yard to the street, and the lads parted before him like the sea before a prophet.

When he was gone there was a moment of complete silence. Every eye turned to Flash Jim, who was staring at the ground. He must have felt their gaze on him, because he raised his head and glared back at them.

"Well, what are you waitin' for?" he snapped. "Go get yourselves cleaned up. Jack, Fletcher, Skinner—I want your eyes on the street. Any sign of Archie's boys, you get me word. I want to know where he is and what he's doin'." He glanced down at Billy. "And someone help Billy boy here."

He strode away grim-faced, as a couple of lads hauled Billy to his feet and dragged him into the kitchen, where they dumped him on a bench beside the fire.

Billy's hand felt like it had been stuffed with hot sand, and his head was beginning to pound. He lay back, his eyes drifting around the kitchen as he tried to escape the pain. That was when he noticed Old Sal's table: it was lying on its side, papers and ink strewn across the floor. Her chair had toppled back into the fire, where it lay and smouldered, black smoke curling up the chimney and bright flames licking lazily around the wood. The kitchen door hung off its hinges, and in the corridor outside Billy could see smashed furniture and scattered belongings.

The only thing he could think was that he would never see Old Sal again.

20
The Red Neckerchief

THE NEXT MORNING, the residents of the boarding house woke to find Flash Jim sitting at Old Sal's table, with no sign of Old Sal anywhere. When asked, he simply muttered something about her 'moving on', but beyond that he refused to be drawn.

At ten o'clock everyone was herded into the yard outside, where Flash Jim announced that rents were to be doubled immediately, and that anyone unable to front the money for the next five days would be sent out on to the street in order to earn it by sunset. This resulted in a general uproar, and more than a few arguments, all of which were swiftly resolved by Flash Jim's Lads setting on the protesters and leaving them bruised and bloody. In the end they slunk away, muttering under their breath but offering no more resistance.

Billy knew nothing of this. After having his hand bandaged up by one of the girls from upstairs, and a quantity of gin poured down his throat, he had been bundled up to a first floor room and left on a bed to recover. He spent most of the night in a nightmarish cycle of sleeping and waking, through which he was never entirely sure which state he was in. His hand throbbed deeply, even in his dreams.

He dreamed that Clara came to see him, her arm bandaged up to the shoulder. She didn't say anything, just stood and looked down at him with a beatific smile, and yet he writhed under her gaze, consumed with an awful feeling of deep black guilt.

Then he dreamed that he was wandering through deserted streets blanketed with snow, looking for somewhere he needed to be. He was late, and the more he wandered the later it grew, and the more lost he was, and the more panicked he became, until at last he woke with a frantic gasp and found the sheets drenched with sweat.

Gradually, however, the pain faded, and with it the dreams. At some point he managed to slip into blissful unconsciousness, black and empty, and he woke late the next morning to find himself in a proper bed, clean and dry, in an unfamiliar room. The house was quiet: no voices came from downstairs, no screech of a fiddle or trill of a pipe. When he pulled back the sheets, he found himself dressed in a clean pair of drawers and a new flannel shirt. His hand was freshly bandaged, and when he sniffed at the dressing he smelled the sharp scent of liniment.

The doorknob rattled. A girl a few years older than him burst into the room, carrying an armful of bandages and clean bedsheets. She stopped short when she saw him, and said: "Oh. You're up then." Then without another word she turned and left, taking the sheets and bandages with her.

Billy barely had time to wonder what was happening before the door opened again; this time his visitor was one

163

of Flash Jim's Lads, a lanky boy with greasy black hair called Long Paul. He sported a bright red scrap of cloth tied at his neck like a cowboy or a bandit, and he stopped in the doorway and examined Billy with a cursory glance.

"You all right then?" he said.

Billy nodded.

"You'd best come with me," Long Paul said. "Flash Jim wanted to know when you were up. Here. Put this on."

He threw something red at Billy: it was a red neckerchief, the same as the one he wore.

"It's what we wear now," Long Paul explained. "So's folk know who we are."

Billy picked up the neckerchief and frowned at it.

"Who's 'we'?" he asked.

Long Paul laughed. "Flash Jim's Lads, o' course," he said. "Come on now. Don't want to keep the boss waiting."

Billy had never seen the kitchen so empty. The only occupants were Young Sal, sitting on her stool by the fire and humming gently to herself as she rocked back and forth, and Flash Jim, whose head was bent low over a table overflowing with books and papers. He looked up when Long Paul coughed, and his face broke into a wan smile. He waved a hand at a nearby chair.

"Have a seat, Bill," he said. "I'll be with you in a moment."

Long Paul gave Billy a wink and left, and Billy sat down. The kitchen fell silent save for Young Sal's humming and the scratch of Flash Jim's pen. After only a few minutes Flash Jim sat back and threw the pen to the floor with a clatter.

"These numbers will be the death of me," he declared, then yawned hugely and rubbed his hands over his face.

"Sal, fetch us something to drink, will yer?"

Young Sal nodded and levered herself to her feet, still humming as she shuffled out of the room. When she was gone Flash Jim stretched out his legs and looked hard at Billy.

"How you doing, then?" he asked. "How's the hand?"

"It's all right." Billy held it up. "Still hurts."

"That gibface Archie." Flash Jim spat into the fire. "He's a right meater and no mistake. Doin' that to a kid."

Billy shrugged. "He's tried to do worse before," he said. "Nearly gutted me once."

"And you got away?" Flash Jim's eyebrows crept up his head. "There's more to you than meets the eye, ain't there? That why Archie was so mad at you? Cause you got away from 'im?"

Billy nodded, and Flash Jim gave a snort of laughter.

"Well, then you done more than most," he said. "Can't say as I heard of many who faced down Archie Miller and lived."

Billy wasn't sure what to say to that. He was curious to see what Flash Jim wanted with him, so he kept quiet and waited.

"You got your kerchief?" Flash Jim asked.

Billy held up the piece of red cloth.

"That's a mark of honour, that is." Flash Jim pulled down the collar of his shirt to reveal a flash of red beneath. "One for each o' the lads who was there that night, the night this all began. That kerchief affords you certain rights in this place, so you wear it with pride, you hear?"

He paused, gazing pointedly at the neckerchief. Billy hurriedly tied it around his neck, and Flash Jim nodded.

"You're one of us now, Billy," he said. "That means you're

family, and family look after each other. That means you never have to worry about paying your way here again. Anything you want, you got it, you hear? Anything you need, you take it. Food, drink … anything you fancy. You done me a great favour that night, and I won't forget it in a hurry. You understand what I'm saying?"

Billy nodded wordlessly. He could not help noticing that Flash Jim's hand had sidled casually over to the brass knuckle lying on the table, his little finger idly rubbing the stained metal.

"I understand," Billy said.

Flash Jim smiled. His hand left the brass knuckles and stretched over the table; Billy hesitated for a moment before he took it, and they shook once before parting.

"Welcome to the family," Flash Jim said. "Brother."

Of those boarders who had been thrown out in the morning, many did not return. Those who did found that their proceeds did not fetch nearly as much as they had under Old Sal. Again, some tried to argue, but they were dealt with quickly and brutally. The rest kept silent and took the money, thankful to have a place to escape from the cold.

Over the following days the character of the boarding house began to change. Where previously folk had treated each other with cautious respect, now it was a place of fear and suspicion. Flash Jim's Lads took to bursting into rooms and demanding to know who was there and what their business was. Nowhere was private, and no time of day or night was sacred; the knock could come at any hour, and when it did, those deemed unprofitable, or anyone staying on a friend's coin, were hustled down the stairs and out of the door without another word.

The nature of the guests changed too, from petty thieves and beggars to more hardened criminals: burglars, house-breakers, thieves and murderers. Dour men, dead-eyed and dangerous, slow to speak and quick to fight, who stayed in bed all day and went to work at night, and came back with blood on their hands and money in their pockets. Those of the old crew who stayed on made sure to keep out of the way of the new guests, and more often than not they were found out on the streets rather than in the warmth of the kitchen, fearful of being singled out as a target.

The only ones not affected by the new regime were the lads—who kept their rooms without having to pay a penny—and Young Sal, who turned up to cook the day's meals as usual without batting an eyelid. She served anyone, regardless of creed, colour or profession, and the new men noted this and left her alone.

On the Friday of the week of the coup (for that, people were slowly realising, was what it was) one of Archie Miller's lieutenants arrived at the kitchen with a ledger and a purse, and sat for a long time with Flash Jim at his table in deep discussion. The gist of the agreement, it gradually emerged, was that Flash Jim be permitted jurisdiction over all the territory formerly owned by Old Sal and the Bouger, as long as he paid a tithe of his earnings to the Devil's Lads, who in return would leave him to his own devices.

For the Devil's Lads were gradually extending their influence over the city's grubby underbelly, both north and south of the Thames. Rather than trying to hold sway by his own power, Archie Miller was instead encouraging insurrection amongst the local gangs, supporting various upstart lieutenants and commanders with their eye on the leadership, and once the dust had settled he came in to present the bill for his support: namely, a handsome cut of their profits. He made sure to back candidates who would not present him with too much of a problem once they were in power, and dealt swiftly and gruesomely with any who tried to go back on their word.

And so, slowly but surely, the long fingers of the Devil's Lads wormed their way into the filth and muck of the criminal community, and once they found purchase they began to tighten.

21
Flash Jim's Lads

TRUE TO FLASH JIM'S WORD, Billy found that being a part of his family came with its rewards.

To begin with there was his new room. Located on the first floor just above the kitchen, it was warm and dry, and, most importantly, it was his alone. At first this startled him; he had fully expected to be joined by one of the other lads, but when he asked about it he was met with an incredulous laugh from Long Paul, who had taken Billy under his wing.

"Bless your soul!" Long Paul declared. "Flash Jim's Lads bunk up together? You've a lot to learn, Billy boy!"

That was how Billy learned exactly what the gift of the red neckerchief meant. Flash Jim's Lads never wanted for anything: food, drink, clothes, entertainment—whatever they desired, they got, and it didn't matter how they got it. Wherever he walked through the boarding house, people moved out of the way. Even the most hardened of criminals who took to lurking in the hallways touched their foreheads in respect when Billy passed by.

The respect was not confined to the boarding house,

either. The week after his initiation Billy took a walk up to the high street, more for a breath of fresh air than out of any need. He wore the red neckerchief, and to his surprise the first beggar he passed nodded in greeting. He nodded back automatically, wondering if he knew the man; but then a shopkeeper standing in his doorway touched his head and bade him good morning; and after that a group of girls crossed to the other side of the street and hurried past with their heads down; and soon Billy realised that everyone he passed acknowledged him in some way, either out of respect or fear, and sometimes both.

By the time he reached the high street he understood: it was not him they feared, but the neckerchief. That splash of red at his throat marked him out as one of Flash Jim's Lads, and Flash Jim's Lads were not to be trifled with.

Billy did not stay out for long. The nods and salutes and hastily-averted eyes felt out of place to him. All his life he had been used to making himself small and quiet, to keeping his mouth shut and staying out of the way. Under Gerard it had been the only way to get through the day unbruised, and not even then. The experience of having people acknowledge his existence was gratifying, but at the same time disturbing.

He made his way back to the boarding house, clutching at his bandaged hand, which had begun to throb again. As he walked he knocked into an errand boy who was not quick enough to get out of the way. The boy spun away from him, a curse springing to his lips; but then he saw the flash of red, and the colour drained from his face.

"S-sorry sir!" the boy stammered. "I didn't see you there, honest! I'm awful sorry, really, I am!"

Billy stared at him. The boy was only a year or two

younger than himself, spotty-faced and scrawny. His eyes were wide, his face blanched, his lips trembling. It was a look Billy had never seen directed at himself before: the same expression the little 'uns had always worn whenever Gerard was around.

The boy stumbled away, and Billy resumed his journey back to the house, his mind a riot of confusion.

One of Archie Miller's lieutenants was in the kitchen with Flash Jim when Billy returned. Long Paul warned Billy against going in, with a dark look.

"Bound to be trouble soon," he said. "Archie's asking for more money already. Seems we've been doing a bit too well. Should'a kept our heads down, kept quiet." He heaved a great sigh. "Not Jim's style, unfortunately."

Instead, Billy went up to his room, where he found a stack of books on the dressing table. One of the girls had taken to bringing him the odd book now and then, all of them lurid adventures full of murder and mayhem—at least, as far as Billy could tell from looking at the illustrations. He had never learned to read (Gerard having considered it a waste of time for climbing boys) but he had been too embarrassed to tell the girl the first time she had turned up, and she hadn't asked him. He contented himself instead with studying the engravings, which usually showed the aftermath of a massacre, or a spectre prowling through a graveyard.

These latest books all appeared to be Westerns: stories about the frontier territories in America. The illustrations showed scenes of travellers huddled behind upturned coaches, desperately firing as a howling Indian horde closed in; a gunfight in an American bar, with pistols going off left and right and men rolling on the floor in the blood and the whisky; two cowboys facing off against each other in a dusty street surrounded by rickety wooden buildings, their guns held low at their hips as they both fired at the same time. One of the cowboys in this last illustration had been hit, and was frozen mid-fall, his hat tumbling from his head as his face twisted in an agonised grimace. Billy turned the page quickly. It reminded him too much of Clara.

The next illustration was of a man dressed in a fine suit and a long coat, with boots on his feet and two pistols slung at his waist. He wore a wide-brimmed hat pulled low over his brow, and a neckerchief drawn up to cover his nose and mouth. Only his eyes were visible, staring defiantly out at the reader; a third pistol hung limply from the fingers of his right hand, relaxed, but ready to raise and fire at a moment's notice.

Billy sat and stared at this illustration for a long time. He did not know why this particular image so arrested his attention. Perhaps it was the careless way the man stood, the nonchalant way he held the gun, almost as if he had forgotten it was there.

Without thinking, he pulled his own neckerchief up so that it rested across his nose and covered the lower half of his face, and he stayed staring at the picture while the light died outside his window.

Over the following weeks the snow finally began to thaw. Instead of white streets piled high with grey snowdrifts, there were grey streets gouged with deep brown ruts. Instead of freezing snow, freezing rain fell in driving sheets that stung cheeks and drenched overcoats.

Within the boarding house life had settled down to a steady routine. Flash Jim had stopped coming down to sit at Old Sal's table, and now mostly kept to his room, smoking impressive quantities of tobacco and drinking endless glasses of whisky and gin. Sometimes a sickly-sweet odour crept out from under the door, and if one of the lads ventured in they found him slumped half out of his bed with a blackened ball of opium lying in a saucer on the table. If he ate at all, it was the odd crust of bread here and there; he said the taste of meat made him sick.

Not that this affected the rest of the residents. They kept mostly to the kitchen, where they played cards and engaged in muttered conversation. The only interruption to the relative peace was the increased presence of the Devil's Lads. They seemed to treat the boarding house as a waystation, a place to duck out of the rain and find something hot to eat, and they never bothered to pay. Occasionally they summoned Flash Jim down from his room, and he brought a bag of coins and reluctantly counted them out across the table, his jaw working silently and his eyes glaring at the floor; but he never said anything, and the Devil's Lads always pocketed the money with a wink and a tip of their hats.

Billy had also settled into a routine. His finger had healed, and he was able to remove the bandages without shooting pains travelling up his arm. The little finger on his right hand was now nestled snugly up against its neighbour, and the only way to move it was by moving the two of them together; but at least the swelling had gone down, and some colour was beginning to return to it.

When he held up his two hands side by side he could see how they matched now, the finger on his left bent in by

Gerard, and the one on the right by Archie: two wounds from the two men he hated most in the world.

There was nothing to be done about it, of course. The idea of revenge had flitted briefly across his mind, but he had let it go. Getting back at Archie was an impossibility, and planning it about as much use as planning to walk to the moon; and Gerard … well, who knew where Gerard was now, and what he was doing? Probably still sending boys up chimneys, though maybe with a limp where Clara had driven his knife into his leg.

Billy rarely thought about Clara or Tosher these days. He was too busy running errands for Flash Jim (though it was Long Paul he reported to), collecting rents, taking messages, delivering packages and generally making himself useful. Everywhere he went people nodded in greeting, touched their caps or avoided him with eyes full of fear, and slowly Billy became used to the treatment. It no longer bothered him when people crossed the street to avoid him: it was his right, after all, as one of Flash Jim's Lads.

Evenings were spent in the kitchen, drinking ale and gin with the other lads and playing cards for shillings. He struggled at first, and built up quite a debt; but soon he learned the tricks and cheats the other lads used, and managed to claw his way back again. The lads laughed and clapped him on the back, and called him Billy Sweep, and for the first time in a long time he felt like he belonged.

Then Archie Miller came to call, and everything changed again.

22
An Unexpected Visit

IT WAS A DRAB AFTERNOON of driving rain when Archie Miller arrived. Billy was sitting in the kitchen, nursing a bowl of Young Sal's slop and hunting in vain for a scrap of meat amongst the claggy broth and sparse vegetables. The benches were lined with the usual undesirables, none of whom fancied venturing out into the teeth of the weather. But there was none of the talk or games there had once been; men sat stony-faced, nursing mugs of ale or stirring bowls of stew, lost in their own private thoughts.

Billy had just given up hope of finding anything more in his bowl than a shrivelled end of carrot, when the door burst open and Archie strode in, shaking the rain from his coat in a shower of droplets. He whipped the cap from his head and threw it in the general direction of a body by the fire.

"Hang that up ter dry," he commanded carelessly, then peered around through the smoky gloom. The assembled patrons returned his look with carefully blank expressions of their own, or else became suddenly fascinated with the palms of their hands.

175

"Flash Jim around, is 'e?" Archie growled. He smacked the arm of the man nearest to him, a housebreaker called Slim Alf, who clenched his fist but remained silent.

"Anyone?" Archie raised his voice. "What's the matter, eh? Cat got yer tongues?"

"He's upstairs."

Archie turned. It was Long Paul who had spoken. He stood by the kitchen door, hands behind his back, avoiding Archie's gaze.

Archie scoffed. "What's 'e doin' upstairs, then? 'Avin' a nap?"

Long Paul shrugged, and Archie swaggered over to him and looked him up and down.

"D'yer wanna fetch 'im fer me, then?"

Long Paul nodded and disappeared. Archie watched him go, then snorted and shook his head.

"Useless," he proclaimed to the room in general. "Tha's useless, that is. What kind of a leader stays up in 'is room while the rest of 'is men goes out and does all the work, eh? I'll tell yer what, if this were my place you wouldn't catch me abed at this hour. A general leads 'is troops from the front, not from 'is pillow."

No one replied. Archie's eyes travelled around the room, sweeping over the assembled faces. Billy put his head down and tried to be as inconspicuous as possible, but a moment later he heard a barking laugh.

"Little Sweep!"

Billy looked up. Archie was looking at him over the heads of the crowd.

"Well, I'll be blessed," Archie declared. "You just pops right back up, don'tcher?"

He swayed through the room, barging bodies aside until he towered over Billy. "'Ow's the finger?" he asked, bending down so that his face was inches from Billy's and his foul breath wafted in Billy's nostrils. "Bet it smarts. I 'ope you thinks of me anytime you looks at that 'and, boy, I 'ope you looks at it and reminds yerself what 'appens to folks who messes with Archie Miller—and I 'ope you counts yerself lucky that it was yer finger what was broke, and not yer neck."

He grinned at Billy and tipped him an exaggerated wink, then reached out and fingered the red neckerchief tied at Billy's throat.

"What's this?" he said. "Looks fancy. A girl give yer this, did she?"

Billy shook his head, and just about managed to murmur, "Flash Jim."

"Flash Jim?" Archie straightened up and bellowed with laughter. "*Flash Jim*? So it were a girl, then?" He shook his head and looked around, marking the other red neckerchiefs scattered through the crowd. "So that's what? Yer badge of honour? What d'yer call yerselves? The Red Roses?"

"We're Flash Jim's Lads," someone piped up.

In an instant, Archie's smile vanished, and he rounded on the speaker. "Flash Jim's Lads?" he snarled, then spat on the table. "So where's Flash Jim, then? Eh? Where's yer glorious leader? Just you all remember this: you may be Flash Jim's Lads, but Flash Jim's *my* lad now, so that means you're all mine. And don't you forget it."

A tense silence fell on the room. Those lads who sported red neckerchiefs were stirring restlessly, exchanging glances and shooting black looks at Archie. Those who didn't were edging away, and one or two near the door slipped out silently into the yard. A soaking in the rain was nothing in comparison to getting caught in a brawl with Archie Miller.

Archie sensed the tension in the air, and a smile spread across his face as he turned in a slow circle, searching out the troublemakers. Billy shrank back against the wall, grateful to be forgotten. If the lads did decide to pick a fight, he didn't doubt that Archie would come out on top, no matter how outnumbered he was; and when the dust had settled who was to say Archie wouldn't come for him next? He had reason enough, and if his blood was up, there was no telling what he might do.

But just as the first knives began to appear from sleeves and boots, there came the rap of knuckles on the kitchen door, and everyone turned to see Flash Jim leaning in the doorway.

The tension dissipated. The knives vanished. Archie relaxed, though a flash of disappointment passed across his face.

"Jim!" he cried, spreading his arms wide. "Thought I'd come to pay a visit. See how ye were gettin' on. You're lookin' …"

He paused, and made a show of examining Flash Jim, who had clearly just been woken from a drugged stupor: his eyes were red-rimmed, and he could barely hold his head up. His skin by now had taken on a yellowish tinge, and his hands trembled uncontrollably.

"… you're lookin' terrible," Archie concluded. He lowered his arms and shook his head, taking on the aspect of a concerned uncle. "Come now, Jimmy boy. You're not lookin' after yerself, are ye? All this … riotous livin'. Ain't doin' you any good. Best cut back, that's my advice."

"And since when was you my doctor?" Flash Jim managed to sneer, hauling himself upright against the doorpost. Long Paul hovered in the hallway behind him, ready to prop him up if he stumbled. "What d'yer want? Out with it!"

"Steady now," Archie cautioned him, wagging a finger. "You're fergettin' yer manners. That ain't no way ter talk to yer betters now, is it?"

"You ain't my better," Flash Jim replied. "Ain't nothing makes you better than me."

"Well, I'm in better health, for one," Archie replied. He pounded on his chest with a meaty fist. "Picture o' ruddy health, me! Reckon I'll live till I'm ninety at least. You … Well, I doubt you'll see thirty at this rate, my boy."

"I told you to say your piece." Flash Jim took a shuddering breath and brushed a lock of greasy hair away from his face. "Speak, or get out."

"All right. All right. No need to bust a vein. If ye want the truth, I'm here about the money." Archie shrugged apologetically. "There it is, plain as I can make it."

"What money?"

"The money I'm owed, o' course! You've been fallin' behind with repayments, Jimmy Boy. Now, I've been patient for a long while, but fair's fair, and it's time to pay up."

Archie extended a hand the size and shape of a shovel. Silence descended on the room once more. Looking around, Billy realised that one by one the regular tenants had all slipped away; the only ones left in the room were Flash Jim's Lads with their bright red neckerchiefs, along with Flash Jim and Archie.

Flash Jim's eyelids were drooping. He swayed on his feet,

and for a moment Billy thought he might collapse; but then he rallied, and his eyes opened wide as he drew himself up to his full height.

"You ain't getting another ha'penny out o' me," he declared. "This is *my* house, and these are *my* lads, and I—"

He got no further. With a sudden rush Archie sprang across the room and brought his hand down in a stunning blow on the side of Flash Jim's head. The lads rose up with a roar, knives flashing and crockery rattling as they seized whatever came to hand; but Archie had already seized Flash Jim's head in the crook of his arm, and with a roar like a lion's he stopped them in their tracks.

"All right!" he snarled, then took a deep breath and let it out. "Let's all just calm down shall we? One squeeze, and this boy's 'ead will pop off like a cork. So no funny business, eh?"

The lads subsided, though not without muttered oaths and curses.

"Tha's better," Archie said. He shifted his grip on Flash Jim's neck, though he did not loosen it. "Now. I can see we're in a bit of a pickle—some o' you may feel I'm bein' unfair, or that my reaction be disproportionate to the situation. Let me put ye at yer ease. I've a business agreement with Jimmy boy here—" he gave Flash Jim another shake, "—and part o' that agreement were a promise to pay the sum owed. Your glorious leader knew what he was gettin' into when 'e shook 'ands wi' me, and 'e knew the penalties fer goin' back on 'is word. That's all this is: purely business. It's nothin' personal against any o' you—so let's all just simmer down and try to work through this like gentlemen, shall we?"

He squeezed Flash Jim's head again, and leaned down to speak to him in a husky whisper loud enough for the whole room to hear. "What d'yer say, Jimmy boy? Can we be friends again?"

There was a pause, then the slightest of nods from Flash Jim. Archie Miller released him, letting him tumble to the floor. Long Paul darted in from the hallway and lifted Flash Jim up to sit with his back against the wall, where he closed his eyes and took deep, gulping breaths.

"All right now." Archie Miller clapped his hands together and sighed. "I can see it's a bad time. My fault really, fer callin' all unexpected like this. I shouldn't'a dropped in wi'out announcin' meself first. Figure I must'a startled ye, like. So here's what I propose: I'll give ye a week ter come up wi' the money owed. Tha's bein' generous—but I'm a generous man. Once the week is up I'll call on ye again. Consider this yer notice. All right? We all happy? Think ye can manage that?"

He didn't wait for a reply from Flash Jim, but turned and stalked to the door that opened on to the yard. He peered out, squinting at the sky.

"Rain's lettin' up," he said. "Tha's a good sign."

He pulled up the collar of his coat, then sauntered over to the fire, picked up his cap, and after inspecting it for a moment he pulled it down over his cropped hair. He took a final look around the room, winked roguishly, then sauntered through the back door, whistling tunelessly.

For a moment there was silence. Every eye turned towards Flash Jim, sitting with his eyes closed and his hands hanging limply by his sides. Beside him crouched Long Paul, studying his face with an expression of worry.

Billy held his breath. He could feel the moment hanging in the air, like a coin tossed for a bet, and there was no way of knowing which way it would come down. In an instant, everything he had gotten for himself over the past months could be snatched away, if Flash Jim broke, or the lads decided he was no longer strong enough to be their leader. And what then? Could he go back to a life on the streets? Could he make it on his own?

Flash Jim stirred and opened bleary eyes. He looked around at them all, then turned his head to Long Paul and beckoned him close.

"Send out word," he croaked. His voice was low, but it carried in the intense silence. "As many as will come. I've had enough of Archie, enough of bowing and scraping and paying through the nose. Come next week, we go to war."

23
To War

IN A MATTER OF HOURS the mood in the boarding house took a dramatic about-turn. Instead of the lethargy and listlessness that had marked the tail end of winter, the air was suddenly charged with furious energy. Lads marched to and fro, going out to carry messages and coming back with the replies. Flash Jim was calling in all the allies he could think of, mustering his troops, and drawing up battle plans.

In four days, he announced, they would march on Archie Miller and the Devil's Lads.

A meeting was called on the evening after Archie had come to call. In attendance were the heads of the four biggest gangs in the territories surrounding Flash Jim's new kingdom. Soapy Dave led the Five Ways Gang; the African Harry Black headed the Filthy Heathens; Alice Lamb represented the Coopers Lane Gang; and the Italian-born Gino Romano spoke for the staunchly Catholic Billingsgate Confessors, who took mass before they fought and unburdened their souls three times a week to a priest-in-residence.

At the meeting, the five leaders agreed to an alliance in

order to deal with the menace Archie Miller posed to the whole of London. He had been allowed to continue for too long, they said, and had gained too much power. All of them had some kind of contract with him whereby they paid him—some more, and some less—to be able to carry out their operations in peace, without fear of being taken over by one of his sponsored upstarts. Enough was enough, they decided. Archie Miller had to go, and Flash Jim was the man to lead them.

No one mentioned the fact that Flash Jim was himself a sponsored upstart, and that he had been responsible for the murder of one of the longest-serving gang heads in the area. These facts were conveniently swept aside, as each of the leaders present talked instead of the advantages that would come from filling the power vacuum left behind by Archie's demise.

The following days were a rush of activity, as messages went back and forth between the five gangs, weapons were stockpiled, and maps consulted. It was agreed that they would muster on the coming Sunday in Seven Dials, a cross-roads at the southern end of their combined territories, and from there march south, across the river at Waterloo, to Archie's home ground in Lambeth. Flash Jim estimated they had about two hundred bodies at their disposal, which seemed more than enough to overwhelm whatever forces the Devil's Lads might have waiting. And besides, they were keeping their plans a tight secret. The hope was to be able to take Archie by surprise, and to shed as little blood as possible.

Billy volunteered himself as a messenger during these days. He was small and quick, with a good memory, and he could be trusted to carry requests and information back and forth between the various headquarters without forgetting, getting lost or getting caught.

It was a good feeling to be useful for once, and to have people expecting him and listening to what he had to say. All Gerard had wanted to hear from him was, "Yes sir," or, "No sir," or, "Here's a shilling from the lady at number forty-three." True, he was only carrying other people's words now, but he was being trusted nevertheless.

So it was that he learned the secret ways between the territories, sometimes weaving down narrow streets, some-times scampering from roof to roof; and so it was that he saw the headquarters of the other four gangs: from the dis-used church occupied by the Billingsgate Confessors, to the warehouse loft where Harry Black's pickpockets roosted.

He saw, too, how they operated, some living off the items they stole and others making a living through more sophisticated crimes: financial swindling, or postal fraud. He was struck by just how well-organised the other gangs were in comparison to Flash Jim's Lads. They were industrious in their vices, almost businesslike, whereas the boarding house was a place of slovenliness and corner-cutting. Billy knew for a fact that many of the tenants were now short-changing Flash Jim, going behind his back to deal directly with the fences. Rubbish and refuse were piling up in the hallways and out in the yard, and a putrid stench permeated everything. Clearly, Old Sal had been responsible for a lot more than just keeping the books and dealing out punishments, and now she was gone the enterprise was struggling under Flash Jim's uneven leadership.

Nevertheless, what Flash Jim lacked in organisation he

made up for in sheer charisma, sustaining the war preparations almost single-handedly, and by Saturday afternoon the atmosphere in the boarding house was tense but expectant.

Flash Jim's Lads had congregated in the kitchen, where they sat sharpening knives if they had them, or filing edges on to belt buckles if they did not. Flash Jim was back at Old Sal's table, busying himself with a double-barrelled pistol. Even Young Sal had sensed the significance of events, and sat silently by the fire, dishing up soup to those who wanted it.

Billy had no knife and no pistol, and he sat in a corner and wondered what part he would have to play. Long Paul appeared and sat down beside him, nursing a mug of ale.

"How you keeping?" he asked. Ever since the night of the coup he had taken Billy under his wing, looking out for him and making sure he had whatever he needed. It was Long Paul who had suggested Billy put himself forward to be a messenger, commending him for his size and dexterity.

Billy nodded. "All right," he said shortly. He had never been in a real fight before—enduring beatings from Gerard did not count, nor did the frantic struggle with the men who had come looking for the silver spoon—and he did not know what to expect.

"You're nervous," Long Paul said, reading his face. "Ever seen a scrap like this before?"

Billy shook his head.

"The trick is to keep moving," Long Paul advised, "and watch your back. You can try to stick with me, if you like, but if you're watching me then you're not watching yourself or them. If someone comes at you, don't hesitate. You cut them, gouge them, kick, bite and cuss. Make yourself a weapon, and make them fear you. If you stop, or you show fear, they'll be all over you."

"You reckon …" Billy hesitated. "You reckon anyone's gonna be killed?"

"Most likely. Archie Miller, for one. But not you, Bill. It's not your time."

Long Paul flashed a smile and slapped him on the back reassuringly. Billy tried to return the smile, but it felt wrong on his face and it quickly faded.

"Got a tool?" Long Paul asked. When Billy shook his head Long Paul reached into his pocket and produced a folded razor normally used for shaving. "It's sharp enough," he said, handing it to Billy. "And most lads will think twice before coming up against one. Remember: keep moving, keep fightin'. Don't give 'em a second to think."

Billy unfolded the razor. The blade was spotted with rust, but the edge was still fine. He touched a thumb to it, and winced as a drop of blood welled up. Long Paul laughed.

"It's sharp," he said. "You'll do fine."

Billy did not sleep that night. He lay awake on his bed, fiddling with the razor and trying to picture himself in the thick of the fray, lashing out at enemies and avoiding their blows in turn. He couldn't see how it would be possible to escape without injury, and he wondered what his might be.

Again he massaged his broken finger, and the thought of Archie Miller gave him a surge of resolve. He was going to be a part of the fight that led to Archie's death, and any hurt he bore would be worth it.

It took him a long time to fall asleep, and when he finally did his dreams were of Clara and Tosher. They were snug and warm in a cosy kitchen, while he stood outside the window in the driving rain, surrounded by shadowed figures wearing red neckerchiefs. He banged on the window, trying to get their attention, but they just ignored him, and when he looked around he realised he was perched on a window ledge high above the ground, and below him was Archie Miller, looking up and smiling, waiting for him to fall.

The following morning the kitchen was crammed. Every one of Flash Jim's Lads was there, red neckerchiefs bright at their throats; and more besides, thieves and murderers who had aligned themselves with the lads in exchange for a scarf and a promise to share in the spoils when the battle was won. The battle, in their minds at least, was won already. The atmosphere was festive, the air alive with laughter and voices.

Billy sat and watched it all. He had woken early, roused from restless sleep, but as soon as he had sat up the dreams had faded, leaving nothing more than an impression of unease. His nerves had tightened as he dressed himself and thrust the razor into his waistband, but now he was here, surrounded by such fierce high spirits, his doubts began to melt away.

Some of the lads were daubing red paint on their faces, stripes and whorls that made them resemble the fierce American natives from Billy's Westerns. They saw Billy watching them, and one of them beckoned him over. They scored red lines down his cheeks, and the lads laughed when they saw him, and slapped him on the back, and Billy began to feel a warmth rising in him. He was truly one of them now; by the end of that day they would be brothers christened in blood, not merely by dint of a scrap of cloth.

At last Flash Jim emerged from his room, and when he walked through the door the kitchen fell silent. He was dressed in his finest, the whole of his face painted red, wearing a red waistcoat and red cravat beneath his long black frock coat. He had not worn a top hat that day, as he usually did when he dressed up; instead, a red silken scarf was tied around his head, which, combined with his high boots and dark eyes, made him look like a pirate or highwayman. A set of brass knuckles glinted on either hand, and a brace of pistols was thrust into his waistband. Long Paul followed behind him, carrying another two pistols, as well as a long rifle slung across his shoulder.

Flash Jim crossed to the fireplace, and every eye followed him. They all stood silent, waiting to hear what he had to say to them.

"Today," he declared, "is an auspicious day. Today is a day that will live in the 'earts and minds of the folk of London town for years to come. They'll be talkin' of this day to their sons and their grandsons, and when they do, the names of every one o' yer will be on their lips! Today you fight, not fer yerselves, fer money or fer fame—you fight fer justice, and fer freedom, fer the right to walk these streets with yer 'eads held high. You fight, because that fool Archie Miller thinks 'e owns your town. He thinks 'e owns *you*! He thinks 'e can walk in 'ere and make demands! Well, I'll tell yer what: today, you're the ones what gonna own him! You're gonna walk into his house, and you're gonna *tear it down*!"

A roar went up, fifty voices all joined in a savage war cry, and Billy's voice was joined with them. Flash Jim's words had electrified him, coursing through his whole body, vaporising any last tendrils of fear and filling him with wild exultation. He raised his voice, louder and louder, screaming defiance at their enemies and pride in his new brotherhood, and with a clenched fist held high Flash Jim passed through the crowd and out into the yard, leading them to war.

24
The Battle of Seven Dials

THE DAY WAS GREY and overcast, but for once the rain held off as Flash Jim's Lads marched out for Seven Dials. The streets were eerily deserted, even for a Sunday. Most people would be in church by now, or else shut away in their homes, but still it seemed strange how empty every window was, how lifeless the normally crowded roads.

Billy could not help but shiver as they marched down ever-widening roads into the heart of the city. Silence lay over everything, broken only by the distant chiming of church bells and the incessant tramp of fifty pairs of feet. It was as if the city knew what was coming, and was veiling its eyes.

Seven Dials was a crossroads in the heart of Soho, a place whose name was a byword for every kind of wretchedness and depravity. Over the years it had changed hands between a succession of gangs, but at present it was considered something of a no-man's-land, standing between the territories of the four gangs who had aligned themselves with Flash Jim. Usually it was crowded with every kind of life, but today as the gang arrived they found it completely deserted.

They tramped to the middle of the square, surrounded on all sides by dark streets leading off into the warrens of Soho, and stopped in the middle of the muddy road.

Silence fell.

Nothing moved.

Every shutter was closed, every door barred.

A dog barked in the distance; the sound echoed for a moment then died, swallowed up by the silence.

Long Paul sidled up to Flash Jim, slinging the rifle off his shoulder.

"They should be here by now," he muttered.

Flash Jim nodded and squinted down the shadowed streets. "Something's up," he growled. "And I don't like it. I want yer to—"

But what he wanted, no one would ever know. A loud crack echoed around the square and Flash Jim spun twice and dropped to the ground, lifeless. Long Paul screamed, "Ambush!" But before anyone could react, the air was split with a deafening volley of rifle fire. Three more boys fell, instantly dead.

The company scattered, boys and men fleeing heedlessly down the narrow streets. Billy ran with them, his head down and his heart pounding, still struggling to comprehend what had just happened. He was dimly aware of the knot of figures ahead of him suddenly skidding to a halt: a hay-cart had been pulled across the street, blocking their escape.

"Trap!" someone shouted, as a window above them was flung open and a small shape sailed overhead and landed in the hay. Flames blossomed, racing through the loose-packed bales and devouring the cart.

They ducked, shielding their eyes from the sudden heat, but before they could turn and run back the way they had come, every door on the street opened and a wave of bodies poured out, roaring and screeching as they descended on the helpless lads.

Chaos engulfed Billy. He had no idea where he was any more, or who was around him. Everywhere he looked he saw snarling faces, flashing knives, and fists and clubs descending on him. Instinct took over, driven by Long Paul's words: *Keep moving... watch your back... don't hesitate...* He ducked and squirmed, lashing out to left and right, not knowing or caring if he found his mark.

He struggled and squirmed, barging his way through the press until at last he stumbled out the other side and found himself in the open street. He did not hesitate, but darted away between the houses, ignoring the shout that went up behind him as he sprinted with all his might.

He did not risk a look behind; he could hear the crowd pursuing him, the thunder of their feet in the mud, the savage shouts and whoops, the clatter of steel. His lungs burned, his sides were splitting, and his legs were screaming at him to stop—but he could not stop. As soon as he stopped, as soon as he gave up, he would be dead.

He was back at the crossroads where the ambush had begun. Flash Jim's body lay face down in the dirt; as Billy darted past he grabbed one of the pistols that had fallen from the lifeless fingers, aimed it over his shoulder, and pulled the trigger. The blast of the shot nearly knocked him over, and the pistol bucked and spun from his hand. He swore, shaking scorched fingers; but the shot had done its job: there was a panicked shout from behind, and he heard the footsteps falter.

Billy did not falter. He pressed on, head down, arms pumping, racing down the first street he saw and praying it was not blocked like the other.

His prayer was in vain. Almost immediately he came upon another brawl, the two sides indistinguishable in the quantity of mud that had been thrown up on their bodies and faces. He skidded to a halt, and looked back for the first time, but the street was blocked with the mob that pursued him. The shot had slowed them, made them cautious—but still they came, a line of grim-faced men (and even one or two women) bearing down on him with murder in their hearts.

"Billy!"

He turned at the sound of his name. It was Long Paul, who was grappling with a man twice his size, wrestling for control of his rifle.

"Get outta here! Go! Scarper!"

Long Paul lost his footing and went down with the man on top of him, and disappeared from view.

Billy cast around desperately, his eyes scouring the surrounding houses, looking for any means of escape. There was none. Every door was barred, every shutter closed. He was trapped, and in a few more moments the mob would be on him, and he would be dead. It was just as it had been when Archie Miller had cornered him in the alleyway, just like the day he had tried to snatch the watch from the young dandy—and it was as this thought came to him that he knew exactly what to do.

He snapped the razor closed and thrust it into his belt, then turned and ran at the nearest doorway. A laugh sounded from the mob, as they saw him making what they thought was a futile attempt to get inside. The laugh died as Billy instead leapt and grabbed the lintel, then scrambled up and reached for the window frame above. The mob surged forwards, seeing their quarry escape, but Billy was already far out of reach of their clutching hands. He did not dare to pause, but climbed steadily, clinging on to windowsills and broken bricks, ignoring the cramping in his fingers and the ache in his chest. He knew as soon as he stopped he would fall, and that would be the end of him.

Finally the guttering was within arm's reach. Billy grabbed it, scuffing at the bricks with his shoes as he pulled himself up and on to the sharply sloping roof. Only then did he dare to stop for a second and look back.

Below him the street was filled with bodies. Most of the fighting seemed to have died down now; folk were milling around, nursing wounds or inspecting the fallen for anything to steal. Many of them were gazing up after him, their eyes startlingly white in their mud-and-blood-streaked faces. As Billy scanned their faces he could not help feeling a shiver of fear. If he had not escaped he would surely be dead by now, killed by people who had never seen him nor spoken to him before.

And why? What had happened, for these people to attack them? Were they part of a rival gang? Had they been sent by Archie? Had he found out about Flash Jim's scheming?

Then the crowds parted, and Archie Miller appeared through them, flanked by Soapy Dave, Harry Black, Alice Lamb, and Gino Romano, all equally dishevelled and stained from the fighting—and suddenly it became clear. They had never intended to march on Archie Miller. It had been a ruse from the start, some cruel game of Archie's, maybe in revenge on Flash Jim, or maybe as part of a grander plan. But whatever the cause, the plan had run its course. The deed was done. Flash Jim's Lads were no more.

"Is that a little Sweep I see?" Archie called up, shielding his eyes as he gazed at Billy. "Or mayhap it's a monkey escaped from London Zoo!"

A laugh rippled through the crowd, but Archie did not smile. His expression, as far as Billy could see from this distance, was one of intent contemplation.

"They're all gone, little Sweep!" Archie called. "All your friends. No more red neckerchiefs. No more Flash Jim. And by rights I should kill you too." He cocked his head to one side, and gradually the street fell quiet, the laughter dying away into restless silence. Archie stood gazing up at Billy on his perch.

"Aye," he said, and though his voice was quiet and contemplative, it carried in the still air. "I ought to do away with ye for once and all—but bless me if I don't want ter. There's something about you, Sweep. Yer a survivor. You don't die easily. And I like that. I could make use o' that." He sniffed, and nodded slowly. "Aye. I could make good use o' a lad like yourself. What d'yer say? Fancy a new master?"

In reply Billy seized a loose tile from the roof and threw it down as hard as he could. He aimed for Archie, but the tile went wide and struck Soapy Dave instead, who went down in a heap. Alice Lamb drew a pistol and aimed it at Billy, but Archie knocked her hand as she pulled the trigger, and even as Billy ducked the bullet whined off into the grey sky.

"Leave 'im!" Archie growled. "If 'e won't 'ave me offer then I'll kill 'im with me own hands. I won't 'ave 'im brought down like some duck in a shoot." He looked up at Billy again. "You best run along then," he said. "Run, run as fast as you can! And don't you stop while you can still smell the stench o' London Town!"

Billy saw Archie turn and mutter something to the lads nearby. A few of them looked up, then peeled off and disappeared into the streets surrounding the building. Billy turned and scrambled up the roof. He had no intention of meeting Archie again. All he wanted now was to get as far away as possible. It did not matter where, only that it was a place where Archie Miller was not, far from the Devil's Lads, the boarding house, and all the misery that had followed him from the moment he had left Clara and Tosher.

He reached the ridge of the roof and swung a leg over, then half-climbed and half-skidded down the other side. He could hear voices in the street below, shouts and calls of the chase, so with hardly another thought he kicked off against the gutter and launched himself clean over the gap, landing heavily on the roof on the other side. For a second his feet skidded on the wet tiles, then they found purchase and he was climbing up again. He did not think of what he had left behind; he did not think where he was going; he thought only of the climb, hand over hand up the steep slope, then over the ridge and down the other side again, leaping another street to another roof, up and over, down the far side, along a ledge, up a wall, over yet another roof, making his steady way over the rooftops of London until at last he reached a wide road and could go no further.

He found a handy drainpipe and shinned down it, landing with a thump in a muddy alleyway. Immediately he collapsed against the wall: his legs were trembling, and he could hardly hold himself up. He slid down the wall and sat with his back against it, his eyes closed, breathing deeply, trying to calm the whirling storm inside his head.

One thought kept coming back, over and over: *They're gone … they're gone …* Flash Jim, Long Paul, all the rest of the lads, gone forever, swallowed by the human tide that had engulfed them in Seven Dials. Only an hour earlier they had been laughing and joking, dreaming of their victory and dividing Archie Miller's spoils—and now they were dead, along with the brief life of comfort and privilege he had enjoyed, and he was alone once more.

He opened his eyes. He couldn't stay here. Archie Miller was determined to have him, alive or dead, and those lads of his couldn't be far away. Nowhere was safe now, at least not in London. He would have to leave the city, though he had no idea where he would go. The first thing was to get away.

He ducked out of the alleyway on to the road. It was a wide thoroughfare, busy even on a Sunday. No trams or buses ran, but the pavements were still crowded with people walking to and fro, most of them dressed in their Sunday best. Heads turned as he passed, and at first he wondered why; but then he glanced down at himself, and saw how his hands and clothes were stained with dirt and blood.

Suddenly he felt horribly exposed. He needed to get off the road, back into the shadows, find somewhere to wash, some new clothes to wear. As he looked around, his eye was caught by a pair of boys walking up the road towards him. They, too, were stained with dirt, and one of the boys' shirt was torn, and when they saw him their eyes lit up and their pace quickened.

Billy stopped. He was outside some kind of public

building—a music hall, or a theatre. The muffled strains of singing drifted out from within. He would have a better chance facing these boys in close quarters than out in the open where he could be flanked. He turned and ducked inside, and the last thing he saw as he glanced over his shoulder was the two boys hurrying to follow him.

25
'All Other Ground is Sinking Sand'

BILLY HAD A FLEETING IMPRESSION of gilded pillars and tatty red carpet as he hurried through the modest atrium, but he paid them no heed. He could only think of the two boys pursuing him, and of Archie Miller's threat.

A man on the far side of the atrium started to get up from a chair, but Billy ignored him and pushed through a pair of double doors. The music and singing swelled into a din as he stumbled into a cavernous auditorium—and there Billy stopped.

He could not help himself. The room was the largest he had ever seen, a cavern of light and sound. The floor of the auditorium sloped down towards a stage on the far side, where an arch leapt up into the heights, hung with crimson drapes and gold tassels. Between him and the stage were rows and rows of seats, packed with people in their Sunday best. At least, that was what he assumed: in reality the suits were shabby and the bonnets ragged, and many of the men had neither suit nor hat, but stood in their cleanest shirt with a handkerchief tied at their throat.

A gallery ran all the way around the sides of the auditorium, overshadowing the carpeted aisles. Billy peered out from underneath the part where he stood, and saw four or five tiers rising up to the gilded ceiling high above. Every inch of the building was packed with people, and the air was dense with the sound of their singing.

It was impossible to make out the words, but it was certainly not one of the songs Billy knew from the alehouse or Old Sal's kitchen: those were rowdy and lively, whereas this song was steady and serious, though the tune was oddly uplifting in its own stern way. The singers nearest to him were clutching pieces of paper in their hands, though only one or two were actually following the words printed there. The rest trailed behind, parroting what lyrics they could and filling in the rest with a cheerful, formless noise.

The stage at the front of the auditorium was bare, save for a rickety lectern at which an elderly man stood, clutching a piece of paper in his hands and singing along lustily. He had long white whiskers which quivered as he sang, and his whole body rose up with the emotion of the words.

Behind the man, a little way apart, stood two other gentlemen: one short and round, with rosy cheeks and a permanent cherubic smile plastered across his hairless face, and the other—

The other man looked oddly familiar, though Billy could not think why. He was as tall as his companion was short, and he had the air of a lord about him: a sort of effortless grace that made it seem as though he owned the auditorium and everyone in it. His long face was grave, and his dark hooded eyes travelled constantly around the room, scanning the audience restlessly yet not lighting on any one face in particular. It was as if he was looking for someone but had not found them yet.

A sound from behind cut into Billy's thoughts: a scuffle from the atrium, followed by an indignant shout; the boys must have entered the building. Without thinking, he darted to the right, scurrying along the curved wall of the auditorium towards another door near the stage.

Just as he was about to reach it, the singing ground to a halt, and the audience clattered into their seats. Billy froze, suddenly exposed, and turned to see the two boys standing at the back of the hall. They saw him at the same time, and grinned wickedly and pointed at him. It was hard to mistake their meaning: *We're coming for you.*

Billy ducked into the nearest row of seats, muttering an apology to the men and women whose toes he crushed and whose hats he knocked from their heads, and sank into an empty seat partway along. He hunkered down, pulling his head low into his shoulders, ignoring the scandalised expressions and tuts thrown in his direction. He was filthy, he knew, and he did not want to think of how much blood there might be on his shirt, but after a minute the tuts faded and the heads turned away, as the people around dismissed him as nothing more than a mannerless urchin and focused their attention on the stage.

Billy risked a quick glance behind. The two boys had been caught out by his sudden gambit, and had taken seats of their own a few rows back, from which they sat and glared at him. They would wait. All of them knew he was trapped: if he tried to run they would catch up with him in seconds, and no amount of witnesses would stop them from doing whatever it was they had planned. Or they would wait until the end of the performance to get him. They had time.

So Billy decided to wait, hoping that an idea would present itself to him before his time ran out.

The elderly man on the stage had begun to read from a massive book propped up on the lectern before him: "... and there wasted his substance with riotous living," the man read solemnly. "And when he had spent all, there arose a mighty famine in that land; and he began to be in want. And he went and joined himself to a citizen of that country; and he sent him into his fields to feed swine. And he would fain have filled his belly with the husks that the swine did eat: and no man gave unto him."

The elderly man fell silent. He glanced up at the crowds, his hands folded behind his back, and paused for a long moment before continuing:

"So begins the parable of the Prodigal Son," he declared. "A most marvellous account given by our Lord and Saviour: the life story of a young man, very similar, one might suspect, to many a young man here in this house today. Possessed of sudden riches, he departed, the Lord tells us, 'into a *far* country'—meaning, of course, that he wished to remove himself as far as he *possibly* could from the influence of his father ..."

The man droned on, but Billy barely heard any of it. He was acutely aware of the two boys sitting behind him, and his eyes kept darting to the door near the stage. If he made a dash for it when the meeting ended, would he reach the door before the boys caught up with him?

There was no chance of leaving now. The talk showed no sign of ending, and the whole auditorium was hushed, every eye turned towards the speaker and every ear hanging on his words. He was saying something about God, and Jesus, and sin, and gradually Billy realised he had stumbled into some kind of church meeting.

It was nothing like he had expected a church to be. Gerard had never taken them. Sundays were rest days, but all that meant was endless hours locked in the attic while Gerard went out drinking and gambling. Billy knew that other people dressed up and went to worship on these days, because he and Tosher had watched them from the gable of the House, or else passed them as the two of them sneaked through the streets looking for odds and ends to sell to Aggie. Now and then they had passed the imposing church buildings, with their steeples and windows and enormous iron crosses, and Billy had caught strains of singing or someone preaching—but they had never ventured inside, and now he understood why. If he had not been fleeing for his life, then an hour in such a place would have been the most boring hour he could imagine spending. The speaker's voice was a dry monotone, droning on and on with hardly a pause for breath. The room was warm, and the seat was comfortable. Billy had hardly stopped moving since the moment the first shot had been fired and Flash Jim had fallen; now his every muscle ached, and with his sleeplessness from the night before he was struggling to keep his eyes open.

He fought the tiredness—if he fell asleep now he might wake up with a knife at his throat—but it was like walking uphill. He kept blinking awake, realising he had drifted off. Scraps of dreams floated through his mind. He was back in the kitchen in the boarding house, with Old Sal sitting at her table, her face hidden under a grimy shawl; he was huddled under the arch with Tosher and Clara, who were frozen into icy statues; he was crouched at the window where the Unpardonables slept, watching helplessly as Archie Miller went from body to body, tying scraps of red cloth around their necks.

There was a sudden rush of noise as hundreds of bodies rose to their feet, and Billy jerked awake, realising that the meeting was over. Someone began to sing in a strong baritone, setting the pitch and speed for everyone else to follow:

"*My hope is built on nothing less, than Jesus' blood and righteousness; I dare not trust the sweetest frame, but wholly lean on Jesus' name ...*"

Gradually other voices joined in, some weaker and some stronger, the sound swelling into every corner of the high auditorium: "*On Christ, the solid rock, I stand,*" they sang: "*All other ground is sinking sand ... all other ground is sinking sand ...*"

After that the words became lost in the same formless noise as before, as some remembered how the song went and others hummed along to the tune. But for some reason the refrain stood out to Billy's ears, even through the cacophony: "*On Christ, the solid rock, I stand; all other ground is sinking sand.*"

To his surprise, these words burrowed their way through all the fear and pain and exhaustion, and pierced him in a place deep within. It was a place he hadn't even known he had, a dusty room behind a locked door in a deserted corner of his heart which had known neither air nor sunlight for many years.

A new and unfamiliar feeling began to stir, but Billy had no words to understand it. It was similar to the way he sometimes felt when he thought about the mother he could not remember, or when he caught a glimpse of a nurse carrying a sleeping baby in one of the houses they swept. Pain was a part of it, but it was not the pain of a beating from Gerard, or the pain of a broken finger; it was the pain of something precious that had been lost, something infinitely wonderful that he could not now recall.

It made him want to cry, and that made him deeply uncomfortable, and he thrust the feeling back down as deep as it would go, telling himself he had other things to worry about.

Then the song was over. The people did not take their seats, but stood with their heads bowed while the elderly man on the stage recited some kind of blessing about God the Father, God the Son, and God the Holy Ghost. This puzzled Billy, because he had always been under the impression that there was no more than the one God, but before he had time to think about it any more the people around him were gathering their things and filing out of the row of seats, and with a lurch of dread he realised the meeting was over.

He turned. The two boys had risen from their seats as well, and were standing to one side to allow others to pass. Their eyes, however, were fixed on Billy. This was it. He had to choose: run and hope, or stay and fight.

His hand strayed to the razor, still nestled in his waist-band. He found he was trembling. Fighting in the wild melee of the streets outside was one thing, where he could trust to luck to keep him from harm. In here it would just be him against the two of them, both intent on hurting him or worse.

The crowds were thinning now. The two boys pushed

themselves away from the wall and stalked towards him. They held weapons in their hands, but Billy could not see what they were. He looked around trying to decide which was best: to stay in the chairs to slow them down, or come out in the open where he would be able to run if need be.

The boys were almost on him. He tightened his grip on the razor. It would be here, then, and he would have to hope that picking their way through the chairs would make them cautious and clumsy.

"Come on, then," he said, raising the blade.

The boys looked at each other and laughed, and the sound was crueller than any war cry.

"Archie Miller sends 'is greetings," one of the boys sneered.

"He'd prefer you alive," the other added, "but we figure he'll settle for dead."

"You can try," Billy retorted. He held the blade towards them. It trembled and flashed in the gaslight.

The boys advanced, splitting off to take the row on either side of Billy, outflanking him. They had slowed now, and there was a deadly intensity in their eyes. One wielded a short-bladed knife, the other a thick cudgel. Billy tried to watch both at once, trying to think how he would take them, trying to make a plan of attack or defence. His hand was steady now. He was ready. He would have to fight, and he might have to kill. So be it. Better to kill than be killed.

The boys stopped and glanced at each other, then the one with the knife nodded to the other, and Billy saw them tense, ready to spring—

"Hey!"

A shout rang out from the back of the theatre. All three

boys turned to see a knot of men in blue uniforms crowding through the doors. They were armed with sticks, and as soon as the two boys saw them they turned and sprinted to the door near the stage, leaving Billy standing with his mouth agape.

The men—police officers, Billy finally realised—stormed after them, shouting and waving their sticks. Two of them peeled off to corner Billy, their sticks raised and their faces stern.

"All right, son," one of them said. "Put that down and let's have a chat, eh?"

Billy looked down at the razor in his hand, but he did not release it.

"Those two boys," he said. "They were trying to—"

"Look, son," the other officer warned. "We don't want to hurt you. Just put that blade down and let's talk about this."

Billy hesitated, then closed the razor and stuffed in into his waistband. He inched along the seats, eyeing the officers warily.

"This ain't got nothing to do with me," he said. "Like I said, they were—"

He got no further. One of the officers reached out and grabbed his arm, and before Billy knew what was happening he had been dragged from the seats and flung to the ground with his arm twisted painfully behind him, and the officer was kneeling on his back.

"Lie still now," the man snarled between gritted teeth, as Billy squirmed and kicked instinctively. "Cor, 'e's a wriggler and no mistake. Like an eel."

"Here. I'll sort 'im," the other replied. There was an explosion of pain in Billy's head as something solid smashed into his temple, and he fell still, dazed and silenced, his ears ringing.

"There," he dimly heard someone say. "That's the way to deal with 'em. They don't know no other language."

"He all right, though? That's a lot of blood."

"Nah. Most of it's some poor beggar's, I'll reckon. Who you been at with that blade o' yours, eh?"

Then another voice, stern and commanding, cutting through the both of them.

"What's all this? Unhand the child, for pity's sake! Can't you see he was the victim here?"

"Beggin' your pardon, sir, but this 'ere lad was about to engage in a full-on brawl with those two villains who run off just now. Some gangland squabble, I'd wager."

"Wager your money elsewhere, then," the commanding voice replied. "I saw this youth when he entered the building. He was clearly escaping from the 'villains' you describe."

"He was armed, your lordship …"

"As are you! Do you not expect the unfortunate souls who inhabit these neighbourhoods to be ready to defend themselves against attack? Unhand him, I say, and let me deal with him."

There was a long pause, then a sigh from the officer who had struck him, and the weight was lifted from Billy's back. A strong hand grasped his arm, but it supported rather than directed him, and the voice that spoke in his ear was as soft as it was authoritative.

"There, now," it said. "Let's get you sat down, shall we? Then you and I can have a little talk, and you can explain the cause of all this drama."

Shaftesbury

26
Two Roads

BILLY DID NOT RESIST as he was led through a door and down a short hallway, then through another door into a small room, where he was lowered into a thinly-padded chair. Through the blood streaming down his face he could see a large mirror occupying most of the far wall of the room, in front of which was a long worktop littered with pots and brushes.

"Here," someone said. A rag was handed to him. "Use this to staunch the wound. I'll have you seen to presently."

Billy took the rag and pressed it to the side of his head, wincing at the barb of pain. To think he had survived an ambush by Archie Miller, only to have his head opened by a policeman. And now he was sitting here with … who?

He blinked through the blood, and saw the vague shape of a tall person standing by the long mirror. The person wore a black suit and a white shirt, with a black tie at his throat. He looked like an undertaker, or a doctor. Billy blinked again, and wiped away the last of the blood, and finally the man's features swam into view.

It was the man from the stage. Not the elderly preacher, or the round gentleman with the permanent smile. This was the tall gentleman, the one who had appeared to own the room, the one who was strangely familiar to Billy. He felt like he had met him somewhere before, but for the life of him he still could not work out where.

"So," the man said, regarding Billy steadily with those lidded eyes. "Do you have a name, lad?"

"Billy," Billy said. He tasted blood, and spat to one side.

"No need for that," the man warned, though kindly. "I'll thank you to mind your manners around me, Billy."

If anyone else had spoken to him like that Billy might have taken offence—but there was something about the man, some steel in his eyes and in his voice, that persuaded him to hold his tongue. Billy was used to dealing with forceful personalities, people like Gerard and Archie Miller, and to a lesser extent Flash Jim and Long Paul; but they were bullies, and they held on to their power through fear and intimidation. This man was no bully, yet still he managed to exert his authority over the whole room, and Billy along with it.

"And what's been happening to you, Billy?" the man continued. "What brings you here with a pair of ruffians in tow? In trouble, are you?"

Billy shrugged. He didn't see what business it was of this man to pry into his affairs. And besides, he hardly thought he would understand. Not a gentleman like this. More likely he'd find a way to twist whatever he said into some kind of confession. Better to keep quiet and wait to make his escape.

"The officers tell me there's been something of a pitched battle down in Seven Dials," the man said. "You wouldn't happen to know anything about that, would you?"

Billy shook his head. The man laughed softly, then pointed at Billy's neck.

"What's this? Your affiliation?"

Unconsciously, Billy raised a hand, and his fingers caressed the red neckerchief there.

"'S nothing," he said roughly. "Not any more."

"Ah." The man nodded. "Another purge, then? There seem to be more and more of them these days. Is someone exerting their influence over the streets?"

Billy frowned. The man seemed to know more than he should about the goings-on of the London underworld. And just who was he, anyway? Billy knew there were criminals who dressed and spoke like gentlemen, and never got a drop of blood on their hands. They moved in the highest circles and mingled with great men, and no one ever suspected them of anything. What if this man was one of them, some-one higher than Archie Miller? Would he help, or would he just be another beast ready to tear him to shreds?

"Your silence tells me more than you think," the man said eventually. "It tells me you're scared. It tells me you're in trouble, and you don't know how to get out of it. It tells me you're trapped in a world of murderers and thieves, and you don't belong there."

"I ain't trapped," Billy muttered, unable to stop him-self. He could set the man straight on that count, at least. "I makes me own way."

"Yes, I can see that," the man said. "You made your way here, and you brought those boys with you. What did they mean to do with you, Billy? Were they aiming to kill you?"

"Let 'em try," Billy replied sharply, his hackles rising.

"Ain't no one gets the better o' me."

"And why is that? Because you kill them first?"

"Maybe."

"Have you killed many men, Billy? Perhaps with that razor of yours?"

Billy glowered at him. He knew what he wanted to say—to boast that he had killed scores of men—but for some reason the lie would not trip off his tongue in the way he wanted. And in the time it took to think this it was too late, and the man was smiling kindly in a way that made Billy despise him.

"No, I didn't think so," the man said. "You don't have the look of a killer to me."

"Met many, 'ave yer?" Billy threw the question at him out of spite, but the man just met it with another infuriating smile.

"More than you might think," he said. "I've met most kinds of men, Billy. I've met thieves, burglars, pickpockets, fraudsters, murderers, cheats and rogues of every stripe. And I don't see any of them in you. I see a boy who's lost, and looking desperately for a place to belong."

He fell silent and gazed steadily at Billy, who lowered his eyes and made a show of dabbing at the wound on his head. The man's look was intense, and it made Billy uncomfortable. He did not know what this man wanted from him. If he had wanted to arrest him, he would have done it already—so why was he asking so many questions? Did he want a confession? A confession to what? What did he think he had done?

"I would like to make you an offer, Billy," the man said, breaking the silence. "I would like to offer you a way out of this trap, if you will have it."

"I told you, I ain't trapped," Billy muttered. He had had enough of this interview now. He was uncomfortably aware of the passage of time—time in which Archie Miller's people would be spreading out, looking for him, forming a web of eyes throughout the city which would be increasingly difficult to escape.

The man hitched up his trousers and sat on a chair opposite Billy, folding one leg over the other and clasping his hands together. "But you *are* trapped," he said, in a matter-of-fact tone. "You are imprisoned—not by chains, or bars, or shackles—but by circumstance. By providence. By myriad occurrences, none of which are within your control, but all of which have conspired to drive you down this path you now walk."

The man stretched a hand in front of him. "Imagine it as a road, if you will, between high buildings. Others walk the road with you, sometimes ahead and sometimes behind. You meet, you talk, you part, and many of their faces you will never see again. Sometimes the road is pleasant to walk; at other times it is hard, and the stones cut your feet and the darkness blinds you. But it is the only road, and you must walk it.

"You know this road is leading you somewhere you do not wish to go—though none of your companions will ever talk of the destination. Every time you think of leaving the road you find the way barred, or else you take a turning which merely twists and turns until you find yourself back on the same road, only a little further ahead. You are weary of this road, and you wish you did not have to walk it; yet walk it you must, until you reach the end of it."

Despite his impatience, Billy found himself listening to the man's speech. There was a quality to his voice that was impossible to ignore, and a sure certainty in the way he spoke. He found himself listening against his will, and, as it had done during the song in the theatre, he felt something stir within him, something old and dusty and locked away.

"But now you and I have met," the man was saying. "And I am standing by a narrow gate, a gate which leads to a path. The path is narrow also, and steep, and at places it is beset with thorns—but at length it rises to a high mountain pass, and beyond those mountains is a fair green country where you may find rest. All you must do is leave the road and walk through the gate, and you will be free."

A suspicion began to stir inside Billy.

"You talking about religion?" he asked.

"As a matter of fact I am," the man replied, with another of his smiles. "At least, that is part of it. The other part is education, employment, a means of making yourself useful. Do you know much of the Lord God? Or of the Scriptures?"

Billy did not. He had never heard a word from the Bible, and the only time he had heard the name of God mentioned was as an oath from Gerard's lips when one of the little 'uns spilled soot or trod on his boots. In truth, he did not much want to know about religion—it seemed to involve a lot of going to places where people were expected to dress fancy, and dry words from dry men of the sort he had heard that day. And in the end, what good would it do him? He hadn't heard of religion putting bread on anyone's table, or ale in any man's mug. And if a religious life was supposed to be so much better, why did so many of those who had it look so miserable half the time?

He shook his head. "Never learned none of that," he said. "Never want to, neither. And I been in work before. I made myself useful, till I wasn't useful no more."

The man gave Billy a long, hard look. "Let me guess," he said. "You were a sweep?"

Billy shrugged. "What if I were?"

"And what happened? Surely you didn't outgrow the chimneys? A small boy like you—I'm sure your master had more than enough work for you. You must have earned him a good wage."

"I earned him plenty. Never got nothing for myself though, did I?"

The conversation was beginning to make Billy uncomfortable. He didn't want to think about Gerard, or Tosher, or any part of the life he had left behind. He didn't want to think about God, either. He needed to keep his mind on Archie Miller, and the business of getting away from him. There was no time for anything else.

"You gonna keep me here, then?" he said. "Only, I got places to be."

"Oh really?" The man laughed infuriatingly. "And where is that? Some crime to commit? Someone to fight?"

"It ain't nothing to you!" Billy snapped, his patience finally at an end. This man was no different to any other toff he had come across—he didn't understand, could never understand, the dangers and struggles of the street. His fists clenched, and his mouth hardened into a thin line. "I know yer type! You don't want nothing ter do with folk like me. Maybe you say you do, but you don't. You're only tryin' to make yerself feel good, or … or gettin' stories to tell at yer fancy dinner parties, how you helped them poor kids that one time. You don't want lads like me, lads that put up a fight and look after themselves. You wants the quiet ones, the ones that'll do as they're told."

He stood up, pushing back the chair with a clatter. His head swam, and for a moment he swayed. The man put out a hand to help him, but Billy snarled and flinched away.

"Steady," the man said softly. "Remember: temper, if ungoverned, governs the whole man."

"I don't need yer fancy words," Billy snapped. "And I don't need yer gate. There ain't no gate. There ain't no road. There's this life, and it's hard and cruel, and we got to make the best of it we can. All your religion and … and charity, and all that—well I don't need it. I ain't got time for it. It's all right for folk like you, folk who don't have to worry where their next meal's coming from. But not me."

The man stood up as well. He towered over Billy, tall and stern and powerful; but though Billy backed away from him, he did not feel the same air of menace as he had around Gerard. This man, he knew, would never strike him. He had probably never raised a hand in anger in his life.

"You're being a fool," the man said, and though his words were harsh his tone was soft and kind.

"And what if I am?" Billy retorted. "It's my life, ain't it?"

"I could compel you, you know," the man said. "There are police officers outside this door. I could have them arrest you and take you to a school for your own good."

"Yeah? An' drag me kickin' and screamin' to heaven's pearly gates? That'd make you a right old saint, wouldn't it? Bet your God would be well impressed with you then." Billy drew himself up, ready to fight the man off if he must. But the man made no move, just stood there and smiled.

They faced each other for a long moment: the tall gentleman with the stern, soft face and the heavy lidded eyes; and the small, scrawny boy before him, barely any meat on his bones, dried blood on his hands, eyes flashing, poised and quivering, ready to fight or flee.

Then the man shook his head with a wistful sigh. "I cannot force you," he said. "Much though I know it would do you good, it would go against my every instinct. But know this: if you ever should need help, I am willing to offer it."

He produced a small white card from inside his jacket and held it out to Billy, who hesitated for a second then took it. In neat black script across the front of the card was printed the word SHAFTESBURY, and on the back was an address.

"Come to that address at any time or date of your choosing, and present the card at the door," the man said. "You will be admitted, and you will find me ready and willing to lend you assistance."

Without waiting for a reply he turned and opened the door. Leaning out, he held a muttered conversation with someone outside, then nodded to Billy.

"You are free to go," he said. "God bless you, Billy. And I pray I will see you again before long."

He extended a thin, veined hand. Billy took it, and found the grip surprisingly strong. Then the man—Shaftesbury—gestured to the door, and Billy left the room, passing the two police officers who had arrested him, and made his way up a short corridor to an open door at the end.

He stepped out into the fresh, cold air. The door closed behind him, and Billy was alone once more.

27
The Chest

ONE THOUGHT FILLED Billy's mind as he scurried down a nearby alleyway, keeping off the main road and away from prying eyes: he had to leave the city. By now, Archie would have people everywhere looking for him. He had slipped through Archie's fingers three times now: after the fire at Aggie's shop, after the raid on the Unpardonables, and this was the third time. It no longer mattered how insignificant Billy was, or how little he affected Archie's schemes—it had become a matter of pride. Archie would have him dead by the end of the week, and the only way to avoid his fate was to get far, far away.

He knew vaguely that there were other cities, places like Manchester and Wales, but he had no idea how to get there, or what he would find when he did. That was without considering what he would do for food along the way. He could steal, of course, but he would rather not draw attention to himself. He had heard that thieves were being transported to the other side of the world now, to a place where men walked on their heads and the animals leapt about on springs. The idea didn't appeal.

And then there was the question of shelter, and where to sleep. It was still bitterly cold, even as winter was beginning to slip towards the icy fringes of spring. In the city there were plenty of holes into which he could worm himself, plenty of unattended carts, distracted shopkeepers, open purses and tempting pockets. He doubted the open road would be quite so accommodating.

Without prompting, the voice of the man called Shaftesbury came into his mind: "... *every time you think of leaving the road you find the way barred, or else you take a turning which merely twists and turns until you find yourself back on the same road ...*"

Billy thrust the thought away angrily. Right now he needed his head clear, not cluttered with thoughts of fate and destiny and all that nonsense. There was only one person who would be able to help him, and that was himself.

So it was clear, then. He would leave the city, but he needed money to support himself. Everything he had owned was back at the boarding house, including the locked trunk at the foot of his bed where he kept a small purse with a few pounds stashed away for emergencies. It wasn't much, but it would do for a week or two, just until he found his feet and learned the ways of the open road.

He looked up. He was far outside his usual territory, but he recognised one or two of the landmarks. This was Harry Black's patch—he was no safer here than anywhere else, and if he lingered in the open he would soon be seen and caught. He looked up again, his eyes travelling up the side of the building beside him. Well, it had worked when he escaped from Archie earlier, so why wouldn't it work now? No one would be watching the rooftops.

He untied the red neckerchief and let it drop into the dirt. It wouldn't do to have anything on him that could link him to Flash Jim, and the red stood out like a sore thumb. Better to be nameless and without allegiance, at least for now.

He flexed his aching hands, reached for a crack in the brickwork, and began to climb.

Many hours later, Billy sat on the ridge of a roof overlooking the boarding house yard, watching and waiting. He had been there since late afternoon, after spending a careful hour picking his way over the jumbled rooftops to this precarious perch, and now evening was closing in and the building was dark and silent. No lights burned in any of the windows. The kitchen doorway was a black hole, the smashed door hanging drunkenly on its hinges.

He had been waiting for at least three hours, huddled and shivering in the cold, but still he did not go down, not yet. He had seen Archie Miller get one over his enemies too many times to be caught out now. He would not have put it past him to post sentries in those open windows, guns trained on the muddy yard, waiting for any of Flash Jim's Lads who were foolish enough to come sneaking back.

Once or twice he had considered giving up the whole idea and making himself scarce; but each time the thought of being penniless and freezing on the open road had strengthened his resolve, and he had kept in place, waiting for nightfall.

He could see his own window, looking out over the yard. Two windows along from it, he could also see the opening to Flash Jim's room, and it was at this he had been staring for the last twenty minutes, turning a thought over in his mind. His trunk contained perhaps two pounds, all told— but Flash Jim also had a trunk, standing at the foot of his bed, and Billy knew for a fact that it contained much more than that.

Before Flash Jim took over, the trunk had belonged to Old Sal, and it had contained the bank balance of the boarding house, a small fortune in pennies, shillings and guineas. No one knew exactly how much was in there, apart from Flash Jim—but everyone agreed it was more than the wealth of everyone else in the house combined.

Billy knew he wouldn't be able to take all of it. But even a small bag of coins would be enough to keep him steady on the long road to wherever it was he was going. He knew where it was, and he was sure he could slip in, collect what he needed, and slip out again in a matter of minutes. It was worth taking the risk.

Another half hour slipped by, and still nothing moved. Billy's legs were cramping from remaining still for so long, and the night wind had begun to feel its way in freezing gusts over the rooftops. He decided he had waited long enough. It was time to make his move.

He slipped cautiously over the rooftops until he was above the boarding house, then gingerly lowered himself down over the guttering and slipped in through one of the upstairs windows.

The room was pitch black. Billy waited until his eyes had become accustomed before padding to the door, where he stopped and listened for a long time before easing it open.

The landing was darker than the room, but Billy knew the way. He knew which stairs were likely to creak as he crept down them. He knew which floorboards were loose on the landing below. He knew that Flash Jim's room was the third door along from the foot of the stairs.

And there he stopped again.

His heart was pounding by this time. He crouched by Flash Jim's door, taking deep breaths, trying to stay as quiet as possible. The house was still and empty all around him, but the darkness filled it, pressing down on him. He was alert to any sound: any creak, any scuff, the lightest footfall.

Slowly, he reached up and turned the door handle, then pushed the door so that it swung inwards. He closed his eyes, took one last breath, then peered around the door frame.

Nothing.

The room was empty. Only the bed stood in the far corner, the sheets draped messily across it and onto the floor. A bedside table stood nearby, on which were scattered the paraphernalia of Flash Jim's habits: bottles, matches, a selection of pipes.

And, at the foot of the bed, the chest.

Billy's heart quickened again when he saw it. A few more minutes and he would be free. He slipped through the door and scuttled across the room to the chest. To his delight it was unlocked: Flash Jim, like Old Sal before him, had placed his trust in a fearsome reputation rather than locks and keys.

His hands shook as he reached out and grasped the lid, then, with a swift movement, he lifted it up.

The jubilation evaporated. The chest was empty. There was nothing inside but dust and cobwebs. No gold. No money. Nothing.

Billy slumped back, numb with disappointment. All that effort, all that risk, for nothing. It was as if the ground had given way beneath him, and now nothing was certain. He was right back where he had started.

"Guttin', ain't it?"

He whipped round at the sound of the voice from behind him, and a wave of sickening fear rose up and overwhelmed every other feeling.

It was Archie Miller.

Archie stood in the doorway, swathed in shadow, filling every inch of the portal with his enormous bulk. His hands hung easily by his sides, and his manner was relaxed and open, but there emanated from him such a force of menace and evil that Billy was robbed of any strength that remained. His legs gave way, and he collapsed helplessly back on to the bed.

Archie took a step into the room, allowing what light there was to fall on his face. It was battered and scratched, new scars forming across old ones. One of his ears was crusted with dried blood, and Billy could see where a notch had been taken out of it.

Archie saw him looking and chuckled. "I ain't pretty," he said, fingering the wound. "But I'm more'n a match for you, boy." He glanced over at the open chest. "Not what you were hopin' for? Me neither. It were like that when I got 'ere. Seems ol' Flash Jim weren't holdin' out on me after all—he jus' spent the whole lot. Old Sal would never've done that. She understood how it worked. She knew she needed cash to keep her head above water. But Jim … well, I knew he were never cut out to lead. Takes a special kind o' person. You either have to know everything about everyone, like Old Sal, or you have to surround yerself with people who do, like me."

"Is that why you got rid of him?" Billy surprised himself with his boldness, but talking was the only thing he could do while he tried to think of a way out.

"Maybe." Archie shrugged. "Maybe I jus' didn't like 'im. Maybe 'e looked at me funny. Maybe I got bored. See, the thing is, I don't rightly know meself what I might do from one day to the next. Makes it harder fer enemies to get one over me. If I don't know what I'm gonna do, how's they gonna know?"

Archie took another step towards Billy, who held his ground despite the trembling in his legs and the cramping in his stomach.

"Like now," Archie said. "I'd bet all o' Flash Jim's spent cash that you don't 'ave the first clue what's about to 'appen."

Billy had a pretty clear idea, but he said nothing. His tongue was stuck to the roof of his mouth, and his throat had clamped shut.

"I know I should kill yer," Archie continued conversationally. "Me sense of honour demands it. But ..." He paused, and rubbed his chin thoughtfully. "But then I find meself wonderin'. There's something about yer, little Sweep, something that reminds me a lot of meself. I said it before, and I'll say it again: yer unkillable, or so it seems. No matter how hard I squash down on yer, you jus' spring right up again. I dunno why, but someone or something's got their eye on yer. And that makes me ... interested."

Billy swallowed down his fear. His mind was still racing, still thinking of escape. The window? He was only one floor up. Surely he would be able to jump down into the yard?

Then Archie reached inside his coat and pulled out an American-style six-shot revolver. It looked exactly like the ones from the illustrations in Billy's Westerns. He pulled back the hammer and levelled the gun at Billy's face, and as he looked down the black barrel Billy found himself strangely calm. There would be no escaping this time, no getting away from the wrath of Archie Miller. They had played a strange game of cat and mouse over the past few months, only to end up here. He might have known it would come to this. There was a certain sad inevitability about it.

"I jus' can't decide," Archie murmured. "So you're gonna have ter help me out here. Talk to me, little Sweep. Tell me what makes yer so special. Tell me what makes yer different to all the others I done away with in my time. Tell me why I shouldn't kill yer where ye stand."

Billy looked down the barrel of the gun. This was it. It had to be. After all the running, all the fighting, all the struggle, it had come down to this. Archie Miller had finally caught up with him. It was the end.

Except it wasn't. Because even as he prepared himself, the glimmer of an idea came to him. It wasn't much—barely even a full thought—but it was the only hope he had of escaping a bullet. And he wasn't ready to die, not yet. He was too young. He had barely begun. There had to be more. There had to be something better. He was not ready to give up on his life.

He took a deep breath, and did his best to steady his hammering heart.

"Because," he said, "I know a way to make you money. A *lot* of money."

The gun lowered. In the darkness, Archie smiled.

"Now you're speakin' my language," he said. "Why don't you come on 'ome with me, and we'll have a little chat, eh?"

28
A New Home

ARCHIE'S HEADQUARTERS were nestled in the heart of Lambeth, amongst streets and alleys that Billy had thought he would never see again. As he and Archie crossed Westminster Bridge, deserted in the pale moonlight, and turned off into the labyrinth of hovels that sprawled behind Waterloo Station, Billy was struck again and again by sights at once familiar and strange to him.

There were the washing lines strung low across the streets; the smouldering braziers standing on the corners; the seemingly innumerable pubs and gin-houses, all now shut up for the night; the shadowed bodies slumped here and there, whether drunk or dead only the morning would tell.

But for all that these things were familiar to him, they had also changed, as he had changed. His surroundings were smaller now, shrunken, robbed of the terror they had held for him only a few months previously. Where before he would have walked these streets with taut nerves and a sharp eye, on the lookout for trouble and ready to flee at a moment's notice, now he gave no thought to what might lurk. If anything, he had become the danger now—and nothing could be more terrible than the giant who walked by his side.

Archie owned several streets in the heart of the neighbourhood, which described a rough circuit around an abandoned warehouse and a few acres of scrubland. A wrought iron archway still spanned the entrance to the yard, rusted letters spelling out the name of the long-defunct former owner. As Billy passed beneath the arch he happened to glance up, and caught sight of two sentries sitting in empty windows high up on either side, rifles slung lazily over their forearms. They watched Archie and Billy closely as they passed, and Billy would not have been surprised if there were others watching, better hidden than these two.

"Welcome 'ome," Archie declared as they crossed the weed-strewn wasteland, the warehouse looming over them. "It ain't pretty, but it's a place to lay our 'eads."

He whistled sharply, and a moment later the great doors of the warehouse began to creak open, accompanied by the rumble of gears and the rattle of chains from within. Billy followed Archie through the widening gap, and as soon as they were inside the doors rumbled closed again, coming together with a final resounding boom.

The inside of the warehouse was a maze of wooden platforms and rickety staircases looming high overhead, some of which survived from its previous life, and many others that had been erected since. In time, Billy would come to learn its secret ways and hidden corners, where Archie Miller stored treasures long forgotten, and where he might come across something that had once been human, but had now withered away from a life far from the sun, consumed by opium or tobacco until it was a pale mockery of its former self. But on that first night all he could glean was a vague impression of empty spaces criss-crossed with beams, where torches burned in the distance and the air was filled with a never-ending rustle and whisper of muttered voices.

"This way," Archie said, leading him to a nearby staircase. "We'll find ye a corner to bed down, and in the mornin' I'll introduce yer to the lads."

Once again Billy's overriding impression was of battered timber, and guttering torchlight, and bodies either lying in drunken sleep or else propped up with a pipe or a glass. White eyes followed the two of them as they picked their way through the gloom, and still the whispers surrounded them, though Billy could not tell where they came from. At last, after ascending and descending several rickety flights of stairs, and crossing what appeared to be a bridge over a yawning chasm, they stopped in a place with a low ceiling where the bodies were lined in neat rows on either side.

Archie stepped over to one of the bodies and gave it a nudge with his toe.

"Sticks," he growled. "Get up."

The body groaned and rolled over. It was a boy a year or two older than Billy, with dark skin and bony arms and legs. He squinted up at them through the dim light.

"Mornin' already?"

Archie shook his head.

"You've a few hours," he said. He beckoned Billy forwards. "This 'ere is Billy Sweep. He's new. Make a space for 'im, and show 'im the ropes on the morrow."

"Right, Archie." The boy yawned and beckoned Billy.

"Kip down 'ere with me. We'll get you sheets and that in the mornin'."

Without another word he turned over and pulled the blanket over his head.

Archie chuckled. "You get your kip," he told Billy. "Sticks'll take care o' ye tomorrow. I'll call ye when I'm ready to talk about this idea o' yours."

Without waiting for a reply he turned and melted into the shadows, leaving Billy alone once more.

Billy barely managed to sleep. For one thing the place where he lay was cold, and the floorboards hard, and for another his mind was alive with thoughts and plans and fears.

He lay still beside the boy called Sticks, his arms folded across his chest, looking up at the shadowed beams of the low ceiling and wondering what was going to happen to him. His reply to Archie in the boarding house had been a desperate bid for his life; he had hardly expected it to work—and yet here he was. The problem was, the words he had spoken had been in haste; and in truth, he had no idea how to put them into practice. There was an idea there, but it was small and ill-formed. He would have to come up with something better before Archie summoned him.

It was, he reflected, a cruel kind of fate that kept on visiting him. He made plans, and took steps to lift himself up out of the misery and sucking darkness, and again and again he was only driven deeper down.

There had been Tosher's theft of the spoon, which had started it all; then there had been the decision to pawn the spoon; the decision to visit Clara; Gerard finding them, then those men; the gunshot in Aggie's shop that had caught Clara in the arm; Billy's return to the shop, and his meeting with Archie; and so many more, all of them leading him here, to this warehouse, lying amongst these thieves and murderers, under the thumb of Archie Miller. Any one of these things by itself would not have been enough to lead him to this point: it was the sum of them working together that had done it, every event turning on the next, the whole of his life moving inexorably to this point.

It reminded him of a clock he had once seen in a client's house. It had been a delicate contraption, all gold filigree, whose inner workings were exposed behind a glass case. Billy had been fascinated by the dazzling array of cogs and joints all meshing together, one working upon another, and another, and another, all to advance the fine-wrought hands around the filigree face.

That was how he saw the events of the past months: as an intricate machine patiently ticking, one event turning another, no incident working alone, and the result … What was the result? What was the point and purpose of this mechanism, the one that directed his life? The more he thought about it the more a feeling of looming dread crept over him. Because the honest answer was, he did not know. He had spent so long trying to survive, to stave off death, that he had not thought about *why*. Why did he continue to live? Why did he struggle? Why had he blurted out hasty words in an attempt to avoid a bullet from Archie Miller? Would it not have been better to meet his end, then and there? Why had he prolonged his misery?

He struggled with the question, but the longer it remained unanswered so the shadow it cast on him grew and spread, until he felt like he was suffocating under it. He was relieved when the darkness around him began to recede, as pale dawn crept through the warehouse. It did not banish the shadow, but it meant he could take his mind away from it.

Sticks stirred and yawned, stretching out his spindly arms and legs and elbowing Billy in the side. He turned his head and regarded Billy with bleary eyes.

"Oh yeah," he said. "The new boy. You sleep?"

Billy shook his head.

"No one does on their first night," Sticks said. "You'll settle in soon enough." He groaned and rubbed long-fingered hands over his face. "All right then. Let's find some breakfast."

Billy spent his first day with Sticks, in and around the warehouse. The boy was clearly not best pleased with having to play babysitter, but he was friendly enough, pointing out where to get food and drink, where Billy should relieve himself, and all the other things necessary for life with the Devil's Lads.

The warehouse itself was like a small town, a warren of seemingly unending rooms, passageways and staircases. Everywhere Billy went, following close behind Sticks, he saw men and women engaged in every kind of vice imaginable. Drunkenness was the least of it: gambling, fighting and dog-baiting were rife, as well as other sights that made him blush and turn away in embarrassment. Sticks was bothered by none of these things. He stepped over and around prone bodies, ducking the occasional fist if they strayed too close to a brawl, all the while relating the rules and regulations that governed their lives.

As far as Billy could gather, Archie Miller ran an operation much like Old Sal's, but on an industrial scale. Folk could lease parts of the warehouse for their own businesses, be they bars or gambling parlours or opium dens, and the Devil's Lads shared in the profits. At the same time, Archie took rent from the houses on the streets around the warehouse, as well as overseeing the activities of the gangs in his other territories and conducting 'business' of his own across the river.

The Devil's Lads themselves lived rent-free in the warehouse, and had free rein to eat and drink whatever they fancied, as long as Archie considered it reasonable. They paid with their service, robbing and burgling their way around the city and bringing the spoils back to be distributed.

"Archie'll find somewhere for you to fit in," Sticks assured him, as they sat on a platform overlooking one of the dog fighting pits, sipping from tankards of ale and chewing on cold mutton and cheese. "He's good at using us for our talents."

Billy did not reply. He already knew what Archie wanted with him. The only thing he did not know was when Archie would call on him, and exactly what he would say when it happened.

Below them, a roar went up from the crowd as a dog with a blunt muzzle emerged bloodstained and victorious from the bout. Its opponent lay still in the scattered sawdust until a disgruntled man stepped forward to drag the corpse away, clearing the pit for the next round.

29
The Proposal

ARCHIE'S SUMMONS CAME the next morning, while Billy and Sticks were eating a breakfast of bread and bacon on a step at the back of the warehouse. The sky was the clearest it had been for weeks, and the sun streamed down, warming the iron-hard earth and bathing Billy's upturned face.

Billy had just started on his second brown-black loaf when the door behind them opened, and they turned to find a weedy boy with black hair looking down at them. He wore the black cap that marked him out as one of Archie's messengers, and his eyes shifted restlessly between them.

"You Billy?" the boy asked.

Billy nodded. "Yeah. Who's asking?"

"Archie wants yer," the boy said, and turned and disappeared inside.

"You best go," Sticks said. "He won't wait for you."

Billy brushed the crumbs off his top and followed the boy through the door, only just catching up to him as he scuttled up a flight of stairs. They walked in silence, making their way through the maze of the warehouse to a part Billy had not yet visited, somewhere high at the back of the building.

Billy had been up for most of the night, trying to flesh out the plan he had blurted to Archie at the end of the barrel of a gun. It was workable, certainly, though Billy had never tried anything like it before, and it was not without risk. But there was no time to worry about that now. First he had to get through this interview, and then he could work out the finer details.

He followed the boy along a balcony overlooking a dingy bar, through what appeared to be some kind of hostel with tiny rooms containing a mattress and not much else, until they reached a quieter corner of the warehouse, somewhere near the roof, where the clamour of voices and the din of music did not reach. The boy stopped by a door and knocked softly.

"Come," Archie's voice growled from within. The messenger boy opened the door and stood aside to allow Billy to enter, and after a moment's hesitation Billy stepped through.

He had not known what to expect, but it was certainly not this: the room looked like a cross between a clerk's office and a respectable drawing room. Two large windows on one wall let in the morning sun, bathing the room in fierce light. The rest of the walls were lined with shelves, on which were stacked books and files with the spines neatly arranged. The floor was bare wood, but a large carpet covered most of it, in the middle of which were set three high-backed chairs in a loose circle around a low table.

Archie was sat behind a wide desk on the far side of the room, bent over a blotter and laboriously scratching numbers into a thick ledger. He waved a hand towards the chairs.

"Have a seat," he said. "Be with you in a minute."

Billy lowered himself into one of the armchairs, taking care not to turn his back on Archie. Archie finished writing the final numbers in the ledger, then sat up with a sigh before carefully capping his pen and placing it in a stand by his elbow. He stood, his head almost touching the ceiling, and came around the desk to take the chair opposite Billy. It creaked as he lowered himself into it.

"Now," Archie said, spreading his legs wide and throwing one arm over the back of the chair. "Let's talk business, shall we?"

Billy nodded, clasping his hands together in his lap to keep them from shaking. He was as sure as he was ever going to be about his plan, but around Archie Miller nothing was certain. There was no way of telling whether he would end the interview alive or dead.

"You made me a proposal, as I recall," Archie said. "How about you fill me in on a little more detail, and we'll see if you were worth me mercy?"

Billy swallowed down the lump in his throat. "All right," he said, trying to keep his voice steady. There was nothing for it now. "So like I said: I used to be a sweep, right?"

"Aye," Archie said. "I remembers, you used to work for that old thief Gerard, God rest his soul." He saw Billy's look of surprise and grinned wickedly. "Yer didn't hear about our poor Gerry? Never 'ad much luck, that man. Only went and got 'isself stabbed—a flesh wound, just the leg, nuthin' serious—but would 'e get it seen ter? Oh no. 'I'll be all right,' that's what he said—kept sayin' it, until those little rats of 'is found 'im stiff and cold one morning. I'm surprised they didn't eat 'im, 'e kept 'em so starved."

Billy stared at Archie. He was stunned. He didn't know

what to think. He didn't know what to feel. He had imagined so many times through his life what it would be like to see Gerard dead. He had expected to feel happy—or at the very least grimly satisfied. But now it had come he felt … nothing. Gerard was gone. That was it. It was a fact, the way the wetness of water was a fact, or the heat of fire. It just was, and he was not required to be pleased or dismayed by it.

Archie was watching him narrowly, a faint smile playing around his lips. "Cat got yer tongue, eh? I thought you'd 'ave a thing or two ter say. Disappointed it weren't by yer hand, perhaps? Well, that's that. Ain't nothing to be done about it. Gerry was a fool, and he died a fool. At least he were consistent. So. Enough o' that. Back to the point. You're a sweep, and you think you can use yer 'talents' to make me some money. That right?"

Billy nodded, took a moment to gather his thoughts, and laid out his plan in full. It was a simple one. Archie had the funds and resources to establish a sweeps' gang, which would stake out territory in the wealthier parts of the city, providing legitimate sweeping services to the houses there. The key, Billy explained as his confidence grew, was to be the most reputable and professional outfit in the city. That meant dressing the best, having the best and cleanest tools and equipment, and demonstrating impeccable manners and speech. In this way they would earn themselves a reputation, and in time gain more and more wealthy clients.

Once they had chosen a suitable target, the gang would return to the neighbourhood two or three weeks later, at night. Having already climbed up the chimney in the process of sweeping it, Billy would gain access to the roof and proceed to climb *down*, letting in a team of burglars who would then relieve the house of any valuables. Ideally, Billy would have already earmarked one or two big-ticket items for the team to pick up, things like jewellery or fine silver. When the job was done, it would be a simple matter for the gang to smash a window or two along the street to make it look like the work of opportunistic amateurs.

When Billy had finished speaking the room fell silent. Archie sat back, regarding him steadily. Billy hardly dared to breathe. With Archie, there was no way of knowing what would happen next. He would either walk out of here, or he would be dead—and he had no idea which.

"In and out, job done," Archie said at last. He nodded slowly. "I like the sound o' that."

"And if we play it right," Billy added, feeling a rush of relief, "you could double your takings with just one or two hits a month: nothing too obvious, always moving around, always careful."

"Double, you say?" Archie raised an eyebrow. "That's a brave estimate."

"I don't know." Billy shrugged. "But it'd be a lot."

"Aye. Aye, it would." Archie was still nodding, and now he stroked his chin, deep in thought. For another moment there was silence between them. Billy waited, his heart hammering. He was hopeful, but around Archie Miller hope didn't count for much.

Suddenly, Archie slapped his knee and stood up. "It's an accord," he declared. "I'll send one of the lads along to draw up a list of the particulars, and you can start spying out customers. Try Knightsbridge, Mayfair ... I reckon we'll be able to outdo any competition, an' if anyone becomes a problem I can always deal with 'em." He thrust out a meaty hand.

"Let's shake on it, eh?"

Billy hesitated. The memory of the last time Archie had shaken his hand was all too vivid. Archie saw the hesitation and roared with laughter.

"Still sore, are ye? Yeah, I remember that pinky o' your'n. Left me mark on ye. Well, don't fret. I know you won't cross me again, Billy Sweep. You and me goin'a have a fruitful partnership together. Here. Take my hand."

Gingerly, Billy reached out and placed his hand in Archie's paw, shuddering as he recalled the snap as his finger was bent backwards. Archie smiled and shook his hand once.

"There," he said softly. "Ain't nothing to fear no more, Billy Sweep. You're one of the Devil's Lads now, and the devil takes care of his own."

Later that afternoon Billy took himself out of the warehouse, passing beneath the rusted archway and making his way through the streets of Lambeth town. At first he had wondered whether he would be permitted to leave, but Sticks had laughed at his question.

"Ain't no one gonna speak against you if you're one of Archie's boys," he said. "You do what you want. This is your kingdom now."

So it was Billy found himself treading familiar streets, seeing familiar faces and familiar sights. It didn't take him long to find Aggie's shop, the buildings still blackened from the fire but occupied once more by sprawling families. The shop itself had a new owner, and the pawnbroker's balls above the door had been repainted in garish yellow. Of Aggie there was no sign.

Billy stood for a long time, looking around and

remembering the night it had all begun, so long ago now. So much had changed since then, within and without, and the new shop and the new faces only served to remind him that the past was gone, and he would never get it back.

Next he wound his way down to the street where the King's Head pub stood on the corner, then along to the door he knew so well, where a narrow flight of stairs led up into the darkness. He remembered every creak as he ascended. Even the smell brought back memories, startlingly vivid, of a thousand trips up and down these stairs, every day, morning and evening, following Gerard in and out.

To his surprise the door at the top of the stairs swung open at his touch. He ducked through into the attic beyond and surveyed the empty room, as more memories came flooding back. There was Gerard's mattress in the corner; there was the little 'uns corner, still littered with the soot-stained rags on which they had slept and cried the nights away. And there, in between, was the spot which he and Tosher had made their own.

He padded over and lowered himself to the floor, resting his back against the brick wall and gazing down the length of the loft. A soft wind sighed through the broken window high above his head, stirring the cobwebs in the beams.

So many changes; so many choices: each one another step along the road. So many twists and turns, all leading him back here. Had there been any choice in the matter? If he could go back, would he have done anything differently? Or was he destined to return, a little older and a little harder, his heart a little blacker and his hands a little more bloody?

On an impulse he rose and pulled himself up through the beams, climbing to the broken window through which he and Tosher had made their escape so many times. Out on the rooftop the wind was stronger, bringing with it dark clouds scudding from the northeast. It seemed to blow away the reverie into which he had sunk, clearing his head. He stood on the ridge and looked north, to where the dome of St. Paul's rose over the city, surrounded by a forest of chimneys disgorging a steady stream of pale smoke into the darkening sky.

There was no good wishing, no good in thinking 'what if?' He was what he was: and right now that meant he was one of the Devil's Lads, and that meant he had a job to do.

The chimneys were calling to him. It was time to go back.

PART III
OUT OF THE SMOKE

"Out of the depths have I cried unto thee, O Lord ..."
Psalm 130.1

30
A Vision of the Past

UP, UP, UP: arms aching, back breaking, soot falling all around him.

Squeezed in the pitch darkness of the narrow flue, alone save for the grinning spectre of Death, Billy toiled. Death clutched his scythe and hourglass, and said nothing. Billy ignored him. There was plenty of sand left. It wasn't his time.

Up, up, up: scraping, sweating, panting, coughing, smiling.

This was nothing like his old life, nothing like before. There was no rope around his ankle, no Gerard bellowing up at him to get a move on, no threat of a fire being lit below to force him on. He was his own master now, and he answered to no one.

Below him, in the sheet-swathed drawing room, his team swiftly collected the fallen soot and deposited it into clean sacks. Not for them the dirty sheets which Gerard had flung carelessly over the furniture, nor the hordes of snivelling little 'uns to bully and knock about. Billy had insisted that everything be clean and white, from the sheets to their overalls, and that their behaviour and speech should be impeccable. They had to be, he had explained to Archie, in order to give the best impression and secure the best clients. And Archie, smiling, had made sure Billy had everything he needed.

Up, up, up: scraping and scrubbing, arms dripping with sweat …

It was strange to be back at work. At first he hadn't known what to expect, or how he might feel. He had never hated sweeping, but he had never taken a great deal of pride in it either. It had just been something he did, something he had always done, something to be endured, and over the past few months he had almost forgotten what it was like.

But now he was back, up in the flues, he found that he was taking pride in his work, dirty and dangerous though it was. There was something comforting about being in the flue again, hidden from the outside world, cut off from the cares and worries of everyday life.

Not that he had many cares or worries, not any more. As one of the Devil's Lads he enjoyed privileges and free-doms he had never known before. The warehouse was his to roam around as he pleased; nowhere was closed to him, and nothing was forbidden. He stayed away from the opium dens—the smoke made him light-headed and nauseous—but he had quickly found his favourite gin bars, where he would sit and drink and occasionally play cards with the other regulars. They did not mind that he was no more than a boy. Age did not seem to matter in the warehouse; the most ancient sinner could be found side by side with the greenest newcomer, and both would be treated the same. The only currency was favour with Archie Miller, and for the time being Billy had that in spades.

Up, up, up …

He could smell fresh air above him now. With a final effort, pushing and scraping, he scrambled up the last section of flue and emerged from the chimney pot to hang by his armpits with his legs braced inside.

The day was old, the sun already low in the clear western sky. Billy closed his eyes and drew a deep breath. *This* was why he had loved this job, and why he loved it still: it was because of these moments, when he was caught for a few short minutes between the earth and the sky, with the whole of London laid out before him. Better, no one would complain about how long he was taking. He could stay here for as long as he fancied.

He looked up, taking in the wide cloudless sky. The first tendrils of night were creeping in from the east, chasing the setting sun, and as Billy looked he was struck like never before by the immensity of it all. He felt that he was gazing up into an upturned bowl, infinitely large, whose edges he would never be able to reach, no matter how far or how fast he flew.

And as he looked, a slow realisation began to creep up on him, and he became acutely aware of just how enormous it all was—the sky, the city, the earth itself—and just how insignificant he was in the midst of it all. It was as if he saw himself from high above, a mere dot in the centre of the sprawling city, and that city no more than a dirty smudge on the edge of England, and England an island shrinking against the coasts of Europe, and Europe tucked away in a corner of the vast globe of the earth, and the earth suspended in an endless void of stars.

The sheer scale of it all made him suddenly weak, and he slipped, and almost fell, only just managing to catch himself on the edge of the chimney pot. Another inch, and he would have tumbled and skidded down the flue to a certain crushing end.

He clung on for a moment, his heart pounding as he waited to catch his breath. The feeling of insignificance had evaporated, but the effects lingered, leaving him shaken and trembling. Only when his heart had slowed from a gallop to a walk did he lower himself carefully back into the darkness, to begin the long, slow descent.

The rest of the lads were just finishing packing away the soot when Billy arrived at the bottom of the shaft. Sticks was supervising them, and he gave Billy a nod when he emerged. Sticks, it turned out, was a talented housebreaker, and he knew a gravy train when he saw it. He had joined Billy's crew almost immediately, sharing Billy's insistence on absolute cleanliness and the highest of standards, and between them they had established the operation as a profitable slice of Archie's business.

"Made it back, then?" Sticks said. It was what he always said at the end of a job, pretending to be concerned for Billy's well-being. Usually Billy would reply with a laugh, a curse, or a punch on the arm—but today he was not in the mood for banter. He shrugged and began to pat himself down, scraping off the worst of the soot in silence.

Sticks made no remark—the lads were used to Billy's odd moods, whether it was falling into silent reverie, or else drinking himself to sleep of an evening. They put it down to him adjusting to his new way of life, and they knew nothing of the flashes of memory, or the odd dreams he still suffered, in which he was confronted by the ghosts of his past. Tosher, Clara, Gerard, Aggie, Old Sal, Flash Jim; they came to him in the deep dark hours between midnight and dawn, and no matter how much he fled from them they still found him, their mouths shut but their eyes accusing.

If anyone could guess what was going on behind Billy's eyes, it was Sticks. Sticks had quickly grown to be Billy's closest friend in the Devil's Lads, guiding him through the first housebreak of the operation, and handling the seemingly endless administration involved in bringing in large amounts of loot.

Archie was a stickler for procedure, and insisted on cataloguing and valuing everything that passed through the warehouse. At first the sheer amount of paperwork had overwhelmed Billy, but Sticks had sat down with him and gone through everything, and after an hour or so it had appeared more manageable. Through it all Sticks had kept up a more or less constant stream of jokes, and by the end of the task the two of them had been laughing together like old friends.

Since then they had stuck together, no longer out of necessity, but out of choice. Sticks had smoothed Billy's first few weeks in the gang, and Billy for his part had declined to take part in the occasional baiting Sticks endured from some of the others on account of his dark skin.

If Sticks suspected that Billy was in one of his moods again, he said nothing about it. They packed up the room, took payment, and returned to Lambeth in a silent convoy. Billy walked behind the others, pulling up the collar of the greatcoat he had acquired for a few pounds from the pawn shop in the warehouse. Normally they would have been laughing and joking, maybe even picking on one of the shoeshine lads on the corner to make sport for themselves; but today the rest of the lads could sense Billy's sour mood, and none of them wanted to get on his bad side. They all knew he was close with Archie, and the slightest word from him could mean the worst kind of trouble.

Only Sticks seemed unbothered. He sauntered along between Billy and the gang, hands thrust into his pockets, whistling a jaunty tune. Gradually he slipped further and further back, until he was alongside Billy.

"Penny for your thoughts?" he said at last.

"Nothing," Billy said. "Just had a bit of a slip, up on the roof, is all."

"Shook you, did it? Nah, I get that. Reminds me of the first time I got into a scrap alongside the Devil's Lads. Nearly wet meself. Big bloke came at me with a cleaver, an' I tell you, if I hadn't been quick …" Sticks drew a line across his throat with a long finger, and grimaced. "I'll say this for Archie: life is never boring when you're around him."

He laughed, and Billy's lips twitched of their own accord. That was certainly true. Life had never been more varied or more exciting—or dangerous. Archie was everything Billy had expected him to be: unpredictable and capricious, lavishing rewards on his favourites and punishment on his enemies. His favourite form of discipline was what was known as 'the Poleaxe': a single blow to the head which was usually enough to knock a grown man out cold, and which was occasionally deadly. Billy had seen it several times over the course of the past months, but he still shuddered to hear the crack of Archie's knuckles meeting some poor victim's skull.

But Billy had nothing to fear from Archie Miller—not for the present. The sweeping and thieving racket was bringing in rich rewards, and Archie only ever had smiles for him.

Yes. Life on the whole was as good as it had ever been. So why did he still not feel at peace? Why was he still so restless?

"Any marks today?" he asked Sticks, in an attempt to distract himself from the morose thoughts. They had turned on to a busy street, where the pavements were thronged with labourers on their way home from work. The boys weaved their way through stalls selling roasted peanuts and freshly-baked muffins.

Sticks shook his head. "I thought the third house, but they had a dog. I won't go to a house that's got a dog. Besides, we got, what? Four places to turn over? Five?"

"Five, with that one in Belgravia tonight."

"Right. That'll keep us going for a bit. Don't want to get cocky. Don't want to leave a trail."

Billy nodded, and stepped into the road to avoid a tight knot of men in tailcoats and top hats, who were standing and smoking foul black cigars. Before he could step back up onto the pavement again, however, he saw something that made him stop dead in his tracks.

It was Tosher.

There was no mistaking the bright shock of orange hair, the bulbous nose, the double-jointed neck. Tosher was dressed in a shirt and tie, and he was hurrying across the road at the side of a man with an enormous beard. As Billy watched them, frozen in shock, the man made a remark and Tosher let out a honking laugh—then an omnibus rumbled between them, and Billy was jolted back to life.

He took a step into the road, half thinking to follow them, but had to leap back immediately as a cart bore down on him. He stumbled and crashed to the pavement as the driver swore on his way past, and by the time he managed to get back up again Tosher and the man had well and truly disappeared.

"Bill, you all right?"

He turned to find Sticks frowning at him. For a second Billy stared at him, still struggling to comprehend what he had just seen; then he nodded tightly.

"I'm fine," he said. "Come on. Let's go home."

31
On the Job

SOON THEY WERE PASSING beneath the familiar iron archway with its rusted lettering, and crossing the weed-strewn
wasteland to the warehouse. The doors were wide open, the
evening's carousing already in full swing: music and light
poured out, mingling with the screams and laughter of men
and women. It would be many hours until the warehouse
slept.

The guards on the door nodded to Billy and Sticks as
they passed, and the boys returned the nods. Others might
be challenged, but they were Archie's favourites, and they
came and went as they pleased with no questions asked.

"Drink?" Sticks said, jerking a thumb in the direction of
their favourite haunt. Billy shook his head.

"Not tonight," he said. "I want to get some kip. Even my
bones are tired."

Sticks put a hand on his shoulder and looked him in the
eye. "You sure you're alright?" he said. "You were a misery
before, but now you look like you've seen a ghost. You're not
sickening for something, are you?"

"I'm fine," Billy assured him. "Just tired, I swear. You go. Have fun. I'll see you in a few hours. And don't drink too much!" he added, as Sticks grinned and disappeared into the throng. Billy knew he had nothing to worry about there. Sticks was a consummate professional when it came to his chosen trade: he wouldn't let his wits be dulled by drink, not when there was a job on that night.

That was the difference between being in Archie's gang and working for someone like Flash Jim: Archie treated crime as a business, and he insisted on the same standards as any bank or importer in the city. When you went to work for Archie Miller you went sober, and you didn't get caught. Following a strict code was how Archie had managed to build his kingdom up so far in such a short space of time, and you broke the code at your peril. No one who got their collar felt by the police ratted on Archie, firstly because they were too afraid of him, and secondly because they had the unfortunate habit of turning up dead in their cells.

Archie had reiterated this code to Billy when they began his plan for breaking houses. "No killin'," he had said, his meaty hand enclosing Billy's shoulder and his sharp eyes boring into Billy's face. "No killin' and no brawlin'. You get caught, yer runs, 'ear me? An' if yer can't run, yer keeps yer mouth shut tight. I'll not 'ave Bob Peel's lads stickin' their noses in our business. An' if you draws attention to yerself, well …"

He hadn't finished the thought, but there had been no need. Archie's code was to be kept, at all costs. It was more dear to him than the Ten Commandments.

Billy made his slow way up through the warehouse to the long low room which the Devil's Lads used for their billet.

A couple of the other lads were sitting and throwing dice in the corner, but Billy did not join them. He threw himself down on his mattress, closed his eyes, and tried to rest.

It was impossible. All he could think about was the sight of Tosher's bright orange hair, and the sound of that honking laugh. At first the shock had rendered him numb, and even though it was now wearing off he was still not sure how to feel, or what to think. Part of him was happy to find that Tosher was alive and well after all this time. But there was also a part that rankled at the thought of him being so healthy and happy; he had no right to be, after everything he had done and all the trouble he had caused.

True, Billy was in a better position now than he had ever been. He had more money to his name than he had ever thought possible—more money than he knew what to do with. But Tosher, it seemed, had stumbled across something no amount of money would ever be able to buy: some deep, innocent happiness, untroubled by anything in the world, safe and secure with no enemies and nothing to worry him.

Billy opened his eyes and rolled over. A small chest stood by the side of his bed, the lid secured with a padlock. He fished around in the pocket of his trousers and took out a key, and when he had unlocked it he opened the lid and rummaged around inside. Most of the contents were odds and ends—a tobacco pouch, a spare pair of soft shoes, a couple of handkerchiefs, a deck of cards, the razor Long Paul had given him—but when Billy's hand finally withdrew, it held a small rectangle of card, the edges battered, the printed letters faded but still legible: SHAFTESBURY.

He lay back, turning the card over in his hands. He did not know why he had kept it, nor why he could not bring himself to throw it away. It was just a piece of card, after all, and one he had no intention of using. And yet he was drawn to it at times like this, when he was unsure or afraid, and when the past loomed large in his memory. Perhaps it was a kind of insurance, something to keep nearby just in case things didn't work out; or maybe it was a reminder of a time when he had been alone and scared, friendless and powerless, and it helped him remember how far he come on his own, without help from anyone, even a lord.

Yes. That was it. The card was a talisman, a warning, telling him to go on and not look back. So what if Tosher was happy? So what if he had found a life for himself? Billy had made his own life, and it was a good one. He half hoped he would see Tosher again, just so he could confront him and show him what he had achieved, and to see the look on Tosher's face.

He tucked the card into his pocket and lay back. Time to stop thinking about the past. He had a job to do, and he would need all his wits about him to do it.

He woke as the clocks were striking eleven. The room was empty; the other lads were probably downstairs enjoying pleasant company and losing vast amounts of money at the card tables. Billy rose and dressed in his work clothes: soft shoes, black trousers and a tight-fitting black shirt. He paused, then fished around in the pocket of his day clothes for the card, which he transferred to the pocket of his work trousers. When he was ready, he made his way downstairs.

Sticks was waiting for him by the front door, along with the other members of the burglary gang: the Welshman Samuel Evans, Red Harry, and a hulking beast of a man known only as the Blagger. To Billy's surprise Archie was with them, a pint of ale in his hand and a long drooping pipe between his teeth. When he saw Billy he raised his glass in salute.

"Best o' health to ye," he declared. "And here's wishin' you a fine evenin'. You've made me a very happy man of late, Billy Sweep."

Billy nodded and flashed a tight smile, then turned to Sticks.

"Ready?" he said.

Sticks nodded. "Same as usual, Bill. In and out, no noise, no fuss. We'll break a back window tonight. Give 'em something new to think about."

"Right." Billy took a deep breath. "Let's go make some money."

Archie stood in the doorway and watched as they marched out over the wasteland, and when they reached the archway and Billy looked back he could see Archie's hulking form standing there still.

The city was still awake, the strains of pub music and shouts and cheers drifting through the chill spring air. Billy and his team crossed Lambeth Bridge and made their way up into the city, passing playhouses and music halls still alive with light and song. Gas-lamps hissed and glowed dirty orange through the murk. There were plenty of people out at that time, some worse for wear than others, but everyone made way for Billy and his companions when they saw the look in their eyes. They had an evil business that night, and the city knew it.

Belgravia was quieter: the streets were mostly residential, with palatial houses of white stucco standing tall and proud around private gardens. During the day these gardens bustled with activity, as the residents took a turn in the fresh air, or spread out picnic blankets on a Sunday afternoon. Now they were dark and silent, swathed in shadow.

The gang spread out, each taking a corner, shrinking into the shadows beneath lamp posts and under hedges, watching and waiting for the signal from the lookout.

Billy took up his post at the end of the street. It was the most exposed location, but he needed to be able to see the others. As soon as he got the all-clear he would dart down to the mews, the dark cobbled alleyway that ran along the back of the houses, where tradesmen delivered coal, fish, meat, vegetables, newspapers, candles, boot polish, and all the other thousand things that made one of these huge houses run smoothly. From there he would be able to climb up the rear of the house to the roof, and so to the chimney he had swept nearly a week and a half before, and down into the sleeping building.

He waited. Lights still burned in windows up and down the street. The sound of piano playing drifted out to him. A hansom cab pulled up, the wheels rattling and the horse snorting, and disgorged a laughing couple who stumbled arm in arm across the street and up the steps to one of the enormous front doors. The man was swathed in a thick woollen coat with a tall hat standing on his head; the woman was draped in furs and velvet, and her laugh rang out like a golden bell across the gardens.

Still Billy waited.

The piano fell silent. One by one, the lights began to wink out.

Still he waited.

A cat stalked carefully across the road, and froze as it caught sight of him. They regarded one another for a moment, then the cat darted away and flowed like water over a nearby wall.

Still he waited.

Stars glimmered overhead, their frosty light shining dispassionately from the empty void of night.

A low whistle sounded from down the street. At the signal, Billy immediately turned and ran silently to the entrance to the mews, then down along the backs of the houses, counting as he went. One ... two ... three ... four ... five ... Without stopping, he ran straight at the wall of the sixth house, his feet finding purchase on a low railing, his hands reaching for a windowsill, then up, up, up, barely thinking, trusting to instinct more than anything else, scrambling and leaping until with surprising suddenness he was at the roof and swinging himself onto the tiles.

He paused, catching his breath. That was the easy part. Now for the challenge.

A row of identical chimney pots stood on the ridge above him, squat and black against the stars. A wisp of smoke drifted up from one; the others were still and lifeless. Cautiously, Billy crept up the sloping roof to the ridge, where he stopped and narrowed his eyes, recalling the image he had fixed in his mind when he had swept this chimney the week before. If that way was south, towards the river, then *that* had to be east, which meant he had come out of *this* chimney pot. He sidled over to it and placed a questing hand against the rough clay; it was warm, but not hot. Good. His one fear was climbing down a still-hot flue: not impossible, but extremely uncomfortable.

He pulled himself up, and lowered first one leg, and then the other, into the round opening. It was always strange, going down the flue without having first come up, but this time as he lowered himself still further to hang by his armpits he felt an unfamiliar tightening in his stomach. A sudden flurry of what-ifs streamed through his mind: what if he got stuck; what if he woke someone; what if one of the servants was still up; what if he lost his way?

He shook the thoughts away. No time for that now. He had to focus.

With a final look at the slumbering city and the stars shining fitfully overhead, he lowered himself into the darkness.

32
The Blonde-Haired Boy

THE CLIMB WAS LONG, warm, and treacherous. Billy had spent hours that week studying the drawings he had made, memorising the twists and turns and branches. There were two other flues that ran into this one: two places where he had to make the right choice, or end up scrambling into the wrong room, maybe even a bedroom—or, if he was really unlucky, a bricked-up fireplace.

When the first fork came Billy paused, checking and rechecking the map in his mind, then lowered himself down the left-hand opening. He ignored the nagging finger of doubt that tickled him. This was the right shaft, he was sure of it.

At the second fork he stopped for longer, momentarily disoriented. He was trying not to confuse himself with the memory of all the other chimneys he had climbed that week. A small voice inside was urging him to hurry, reminding him that time was passing. How long had it been since that low whistle on the street outside? Ten minutes? Twenty? Thirty? An hour? He pushed the voice away. Time lost all meaning in the darkness, and he couldn't think about it now. All he could do was to keep climbing, and trust to his skills and instincts to carry him through.

He took the right-hand fork.

Down, down, down, bracing himself against the sides of the shaft, feeling the bricks much warmer now, though not so hot as some he had climbed.

Down, down, down, trying to make as little noise as possible, conscious all the while of the sleeping house mere inches from his stealthy progress.

Down, down—

His feet found purchase on something level: the smoke shelf, where he normally began his ascent. Relief flooded through him. He slithered the rest of the way down, twisting his body over the shelf and down into the hearth, where he crouched and waited, listening.

The house was dark. Silence lay over everything, broken only by the ticking of a clock on the mantelpiece above his head. Shadowed forms of furniture were scattered around the room—the same room which ten days earlier had been draped in white sheets and flooded with sunlight.

With agonising care, Billy removed his shoes and tucked them inside his shirt, laying his bare feet on the floor beyond the grate. He brushed as much of the loose soot from his shirt as he could, then stood up and peered around into the gloom. Again he listened, his ears alert to the slightest creak of a footstep on the stairs, the slightest squeak of a door handle turning.

Nothing.

At last he stirred, padding across the carpeted floor to the hallway. Here the carpet gave way to polished floorboards, over which a rug had been laid. Billy trod carefully, remembering which side of the hallway creaked, and when he reached the broad front door he gingerly drew the bolts back, turned the handle with the utmost care, and pulled gently.

The door did not move.

Billy turned the handle the other way and pulled again.

The door remained closed.

He tried pushing, then pulling again, all the while acutely aware of every tiny sound he was making. But it was no good. The door would not budge.

It was only then that Billy noticed the iron keyhole below the door handle, and with a plummeting sensation in his stomach he realised that the door was locked as well as bolted, and the key was likely with the housekeeper in one of the attic bedrooms.

He let go of the handle and stood back, fighting the first queasy tendrils of unease rising inside him. Fine. The door was locked. He should have seen that. He would just have to find another way.

He returned to the front room, and after a second's thought he crossed to the window. It was broad, and divided into two halves, one upper and one lower. Billy examined the catch between the two and found it opened easily, allowing him to raise the lower portion of the window.

The curtains stirred as the cold night air curled into the room. Billy held the window up and leaned out, giving a low whistle of his own. He waited, watching the street, and was rewarded by the sight of four shadows detaching themselves from walls and trees and prowling across the road to the house.

The gang ascended the steps to the front door and stopped, finding it firmly closed. Billy clicked his tongue to get their attention, and as one they turned to look at him. Sticks raised his hands in a mute question: *What's going on?*

Billy beckoned him urgently, pointing to the door and waving his hand to try to indicate that wasn't the way in. *You'll have to climb*, he mouthed, gesturing to the short section of wall between the front door and the window. Sticks looked at the wall, then looked down. There was a sheer drop to the basement level entrance, with a narrow flight of steps leading down to it. It wasn't far to fall, but far enough to break a leg if you landed wrong, and certainly far enough to make a noise to wake everyone.

Sticks shot a dark look at Billy, who shrugged. It wasn't like it was his fault. How could he be expected to know there would be locks as well as bolts?

Just come, he mouthed, beckoning urgently.

Sticks rolled his eyes, glanced at the others, then shook his head and swung a leg over the iron railing that ran up the steps.

It was a stretch, but he just about managed to hook his fingers of one hand onto the window frame. Hanging on to the railing with the other hand, he took a few deep breaths then pushed himself off and transferred all his weight to the windowsill, bracing himself with his feet on the wall.

For a moment it looked like he might slip and fall; but with a whispered curse he saved himself and scrambled up through the window and into the room, where he stood panting.

Billy kept his eyes down, avoiding Sticks' angry look. The three other men followed in quick succession, all of them glaring at Billy as if the whole thing was his fault. When they were inside they crowded round him, and in the barest whisper Billy directed them to the rooms on the ground floor where they would find the most valuable items.

The three men spread out, each bearing a velvet sack to hold the proceeds from the night's work. Only Sticks stayed where he was.

"What was that?" he whispered, his voice barely audible.

"Nothing," Billy whispered back. "It's fine. We're in."

Sticks looked at him narrowly. "It better be fine," he hissed, then slipped away into the darkness.

Billy lowered the window again. He didn't fancy having to make a quick exit that way. He would have to find the back door, and hope that it was merely bolted.

While the other four slipped silently around the ground floor, Billy made his way to the back of the house, down a short flight of worn stone steps to the kitchen. It was a large room, crowded with dense shadows; the only light came from the black iron range set along one wall. Warmth radiated from the range, seeping into Billy's bones, and he stopped and basked in it for a moment while his eyes adjusted to the gloom.

A stout kitchen table occupied much of the room, the kind of table that doubtless stood in many such kitchens all over the city. But as Billy looked at it, a sudden memory rose in his mind, the memory of another table in another kitchen. Clara's prone form lay on it, her bloody arm hanging uselessly by her side, and the shapes of Mrs. Lucas and the bearded Daniel loomed over her.

The image was so vivid, and so unexpected, that Billy flinched away from it involuntarily, and before he could stop himself he had knocked over a broom propped up nearby, sending it clattering to the floor. He swore under his breath and reached to pick it up—then froze as something stirred on the far side of the room, something that had lain swathed in a pile of dirty sacks, but now lifted its head and turned to look at him with bleary, sleep-muddled eyes.

It was a boy, not much older than him, with a head of tousled blonde hair. They stared at each other for a moment, the boy blinking in confusion, wondering what Billy was doing there, and whether it was just a part of his dream. But Billy could see the realisation dawning in his eyes, and when the boy grasped what was going on the natural thing would be for him to shout, or gasp, or make some kind of noise.

Billy's hand was gripping the broom handle. He had no choice. There was only one thing to be done.

When Sticks and the others entered the room ten minutes later, they found Billy sitting motionless at the kitchen table. Samuel Evans nudged Sticks.

"What's up with 'im, then?"

"No idea," Sticks murmured. "Been like this all afternoon. Bill. Hey, Bill."

He shook Billy, who started in shock then looked at them as if he had forgotten who they were.

"You all right?" Sticks said. He peered at Billy, then nodded to the Blagger. "Something's up with him. Gimme your sack. You take Billy, and let's get outta here."

The huge man lumbered over to Billy and lifted him out of the chair. Billy followed mutely, allowing himself to be led out of the back door and into the yard.

Sticks was the last to leave the room. Before he pulled the

door closed he stopped and swept the kitchen with an exacting gaze, looking for anything out of place, any clue as to their presence there that night. There was a single shoe lying in front of the range, but it wasn't one of theirs. Probably left by the kitchen boy when he went upstairs to bed.

When Sticks was satisfied there was nothing, he slipped out and closed the door after him, leaving the kitchen in darkness.

33

'Attack in Belgravia'

THEY RETURNED, AS USUAL, to a heroes' welcome. Archie was waiting for them, and shook them all by the hand personally, congratulating them on another job well done.

But Billy didn't hear Archie's praises, or his noises of approval as the sacks were opened to disgorge the night's haul: silver, mostly, with one or two gold trinkets and a fine pearl necklace that had been left in a box on the side. He didn't feel the slap on the back that Archie gave him, or the crushing handshake. He didn't see the smile plastered across Archie's flat-nosed face, or the looks of grudging respect cast in his direction by the onlookers.

All he could see was the face of the boy in the kitchen, his eyes widening as realisation dawned, his mouth opening to cry out ...

A hand clasped his arm, and he turned with a start to find himself standing alone with Sticks. Everyone else had long since gone to drink the last few hours of the night away.

Sticks was frowning, but not out of concern. "What're you playing at, Bill?" he hissed. "First you come over all funny this afternoon, and then you forget about a door lock? And when we found you in the kitchen—what was all that about? What had you bin doin'? Huh?"

"I …" Billy trailed off as the blonde-haired boy's face swam into view again, eyes wide, mouth open. He shuddered. "Nothing," he replied gruffly, shaking off Sticks' hand. "Nothing. I need a drink."

But before he could walk away Sticks had grabbed his arm again, and this time the grip was firm.

"No you don't," Sticks growled. "You don't get to leave. Not after tonight. You're distracted, and you're makin' mistakes, and when people make mistakes on Archie Miller's business, they tend to die. So you're gonna tell me: what's goin' on with you?"

"I said nothing!" Billy shook his arm roughly, and when Sticks refused to budge he swung his fist and caught Sticks a blow on his cheek. Sticks let go at once, more surprised than hurt, but then his jaw tightened and he lashed out with a punch of his own, catching Billy across the eye and sending him staggering backwards.

The two boys faced each other, panting hard, their fists balled: Billy trembling with pent-up aggression, ready to take whatever Sticks gave him, and Sticks equally taut, his jaw working with barely contained fury.

For a moment it seemed they would definitely come to blows; but then Sticks relaxed. He stepped back, shaking out his hands and spitting on the ground.

"You sort yourself out," he said, pointing a long finger at Billy's face. And after a final steady glare he turned and walked away.

Billy woke the next morning to a pounding headache and a dry mouth. He groaned and rolled over, wincing as a lance of pain shot through his temples.

"You're up, then."

Billy opened one eye to find Sticks sitting crossed-legged on the bed beside him, scribbling on a piece of paper with a fountain pen. Sticks dipped the pen into a bottle of ink balanced on one knee and continued writing.

"Jus' doing the accounts," he said. "Can't leave Archie waiting, can we?"

Billy threw an arm over his eyes. "What time is it?"

"Time you were getting up," Sticks replied. "There's work to be done."

"Not today," Billy said. "I've got a headache the size of Big Ben, and it's poundin' my head like a bell and all."

"Too bad." Sticks scribbled a final line and laid down his pen, blowing gently on the paper to dry the ink. "Archie's orders. He wants us back on the streets."

"It's too late. No one's going to want a sweep at this hour."

"We'll find someone. Bill?"

Billy lifted his arm and squinted at Sticks, who was gazing at him seriously.

"Archie knows something's up," Sticks said, and now there was something in his voice Billy had never heard before: fear. "He saw how you were last night—he'd be a fool to miss it—and I reckon he's testing you. Wants to see if something's gone wrong with his golden goose. Don't give him any excuse, Bill. Get up, get dressed, and let's hit the streets. We need more marks, and the only way we're gonna do that is by sweeping chimneys. All right?"

Billy squinted at Sticks for another moment, then he

nodded.

"All right."

He rose, wincing each time he moved his head, and managed to find a basin to dunk his head in. The cold water made him gasp, and when he had towelled himself off he felt marginally more alive. A mirror hung above the basin, cracked and pitted but clear enough for him to see his reflection staring back at him. To his surprise there was a cut over his left eye, which had already swelled up.

"What's that from?" he asked Sticks, turning and pointing it out.

"You really don't remember?" Sticks snorted. "You got in a fight, and you lost. You must have drunk more than your fair share not to recall it. Don't you remember anything from yesterday?"

"I remember the job," Billy said, turning back to inspect the cut in the mirror. "I remember the front door was locked, and you had to use the window. And then—"

He stopped. Suddenly he felt as if he had been doused in cold water again. He remembered. How had he forgotten? Blonde hair, wide eyes, an open mouth ...

"Bill?"

Sticks was standing behind him, his reflection staring accusingly.

"What happened on the job?" Sticks said softly. "What did you do?"

"Nothing," Billy replied. He brushed past Sticks, kneeling by his bed and taking deep breaths. Behind him, the floorboards creaked.

"Don't hide it from me," Sticks said. "Whatever happened, whatever you did, I need to know. I need to know if I need to be worried. I been too long in this gang to be comfortable around a liar. Liars get a man killed."

"I …" Billy closed his eyes. His head was pounding, and all he could see was that boy's face. What had he done? He couldn't quite recall. All he could see was the boy's shocked face, and his own hand gripping the broom handle. He felt sick, and dizzy. His stomach churned. He gritted his teeth and breathed deeply.

"It's nothing," he repeated. "I swear."

"You best hope so," Sticks replied. "For both our sakes."

They made their way up to Knightsbridge, avoiding the area they had visited the night before. It was past lunchtime, and by all accounts they should have expected slim pickings, as most housekeepers preferred to get sweeps in early. But as usual they found that their name preceded them, and housekeepers opened their doors eagerly to 'the smart young lads' they had heard so much about. They were relieved to be confronted with a clean and professional outfit rather than the half-drunk, filthy master sweeps they were used to seeing, with their rabble of silent apprentices trailing miserably behind.

One lady hesitated for a long time, turning the business card over in her rough red hands.

"You know it's illegal to use climbing boys now, don't you?" she said eventually. She was clearly unwilling to be found on the wrong side of the law, but Sticks had a smooth tongue, and he had met enough housekeepers now to know how to deal with them. After a brief negotiation, and not a little flattery, she gave in, only insisting that the police hear nothing of it.

"Boys are the best way, after all," Sticks assured her. "And it's us who'll be doing the climbing—and if we're all right with it then it can't be wrong, can it?"

The housekeeper agreed, reluctantly, but the frown remained on her face.

They swept two chimneys that day, and made appointments for several more. Billy kept quiet, and he and Sticks exchanged hardly a word. There was a palpable tension between them, and it only deepened as the day wore on.

It was with relief that they finished the second job and began making their way back through the streets towards the river. Their route took them through Belgravia, and as they walked they could not help but notice that there were more police around than usual. They soon found out why.

They were passing a newspaper stand when one of the other lads nudged Sticks and hissed, "'ere. Ain't that the place you turned over last night?"

Billy looked, and to his horror he found that the front page of the newspaper was plastered with an engraving of the house they had robbed the night before, beneath the headline: ATTACK IN BELGRAVIA.

"Get us a copy," Sticks commanded, and when the lad brought the paper to him he snatched it up and began reading the front page furiously. After a moment he lowered it, and his eyes found Billy.

There was silence. Around them the hustle and bustle of the street continued, but between Billy and Sticks was a great void, and Billy found that he could not hold Sticks' gaze. He looked down at his feet, feeling a black cloud of shame lowering upon him.

"Bill," he heard Sticks say. He looked up to see an

expression of furious disbelief plastered across the other boy's face. Sticks shook his head and held up the paper. "What did you do?"

Before Billy could begin to think about how to answer, they were interrupted by another lad running up to them. He wore the black cap of one of Archie's messengers, and his face was grim.

"You best come back," he said. "Boss wants a word."

34
Survival of the Fittest

THIS TIME, WHEN THEY PASSED beneath the rusted iron archway, one of the guards peeled off and followed them with a loaded rifle in his hands. He kept the rifle down, and walked a little way apart, as if to indicate that they weren't exactly in trouble, just under observation—but Billy saw Sticks' nervous glances, and the sweat glistening on his forehead.

The other boys in the gang had long since disappeared, not wanting to stick around while there was a summons from Archie Miller in the offing. So it was just Billy, Sticks and their guard who ascended the innumerable staircases to the hallway outside Archie's office at the top of the building.

The guard knocked, and when a muffled shout of "Enter!" came from within, he stood to one side and nodded his head towards the door.

Billy was shaking so much he could hardly stand. The enormity of what he had done was finally beginning to dawn on him. Not for what had happened to the boy—the article in the paper had stressed that his injuries, while severe, were not life-threatening—but because of Archie's code. *No violence ... don't get caught ...* These were the foremost commandments, and he had broken them both, or near enough. They had not been caught, but they had been detected, and now the police would be alert to any burglaries in the area.

Sticks pushed open the door, and Billy followed him inside mutely.

The room was just as Billy remembered it from the day he had put the scheme to Archie. Only this time Archie was not sat behind the desk, but stood at the wide windows looking out over the scrubland surrounding the warehouse. He was dressed only in his shirtsleeves, the cuffs rolled back to reveal forearms like weaver's looms, his trousers held up by brown suspenders.

"Evenin', Archie," Sticks said nervously. "We heard you wanted to see us, so—"

Archie raised a hand. Sticks fell silent.

For a long while no one spoke. Archie continued to stare out of the window, while Sticks shuffled his feet and clasped his hands together. Billy stood and stared at the carpet. He knew what Archie was going to say, and he knew that whatever happened they wouldn't get out of that room without some form of punishment. The only question was whether he would walk out of the room at all.

At last Archie turned and fixed the pair of them with a steady gaze. He wore an expression of pained disappointment, like a father faced with a pair of unruly sons.

"You read much?" he asked.

Sticks frowned. Whatever he had expected, it wasn't this.

"I'm a reader, me," Archie said. "I resolved a long time ago to read as much as I can, and to learn as much as I can. There's been many wise men in the world, with many wise things ter say about how ter make your way. An' I figure, why not avail meself o' their wisdom? What's the point in thinkin' I know it all, when plainly I can't?"

He crossed to his desk, where he picked up a bulky volume and held it up for them to see. "'On the Origin of the Species,'" he declared, reading the title aloud. "A very interestin' little number, by a feller called Darwin. Lots o' very interestin' ideas in there, stuff ter make yer hair stand on end, if yer really think about it. Know what he says? That life is a war, and every man and beast is in the fight, whether they want it or not. In this war there's winners and losers: the winners live, and the losers die, and by and by the winners get stronger and stronger, and so the species benefits. It takes time, mind you, and a whole lot o' patience—but in the end there's no argument, nothin' to plead, and no beggin' fer mercy. You do what you need to do, and you survive. Simple as that."

He flicked through the pages of the book, then replaced it on the desk and paced over to the circle of chairs in the middle of the room. He sat, lowering his enormous bulk into one of the chairs with a creak. Billy and Sticks stayed where they were.

"Some animals are very good at this war," Archie continued. "Take the shark, for example. A shark can smell a drop of blood in an ocean, he can find a wounded animal from miles away, and he can bite another fish clean in half without so much as blinking. All the other fishes fear the shark, for his speed and ferocity, and his mouthful o' knives. He has no natural enemies. He fears no one. The only way he'll die is when he gets old and grey, and his natural time comes. The shark has been winnin' for so long that he doesn't know how to lose."

Archie held up a finger. "But," he said, "a shark has one weakness: he must keep moving. His body works in such a way that he has to keep water flowin' through those gills o' his, otherwise he'll suffocate and drown. It's a curious fact, ain't it?"

Archie looked between the two of them. Sticks nodded, and remained silent.

"I like ter think of meself as a shark," Archie said. "I can smell trouble from a mile off, and I know when a man's at his weakest. That's when I strike, and I got knives too—plenty of 'em. I ain't got no natural enemies, and I don't fear any man. This city is my ocean, and everyone in it's afraid o' one thing: me. See, I'm good at this war too, and I been winnin' at it for a long time. But I gots ter keep movin': I gots ter stay ahead of the game, and that means I can't stand for anythin', or anyone, that'll slow me down."

He leaned forward, fixing Billy with his steady gaze.

"Look at me, boy," he growled, and Billy was forced to look up and into his eyes, though it was the very last thing he wanted to do.

"You made a mistake on the job las' night," Archie said softly. "Then you made another right after. The first mistake was raisin' a fist to that lad, whoever 'e were. But I might've overlooked it, I might've been forgivin', if it hadn't been fer the second—and that were keepin' it from me."

He narrowed his eyes, and there was a look of reproach in them. "How'd yer think it felt for me to have to read about my own operation in the papers? Chief constables mouthin' off, sayin' as how they're gonna catch this monster, an' MPs chimin' in, sayin' as how this city's not safe ter live in any more." He gave a barking laugh. "As if it were safe before! But now you got the toffs rattled, thinkin' they'll all be murdered in their beds afore the week's out, and all they can talk about is gettin' dogs and guns and night watchmen—and all o' this is gonna slow me down."

Archie lifted a thick finger, like an iron bar. "Now you listen to me, and you listen good," he said. "We got a good thing goin', you and me. We both get a good deal out of it. I gets my money, and you gets a home and a family. The longer this goes on for, the better for you and the better for me. Which is why I'm goin' ter give you one chance, and one chance only, and I'm gonna look the other way this one time. We're gonna lay low fer a while, and when we starts up again there's gonna be a new order to things, but you'll keep yer life, and a bit o' my favour. But if you ever—*ever*—pull something like you pulled last night, and bring down the heat on one o' me operations, I will *finish* you. Understand? I will finish your life, Billy Sweep, and no one will remember you was even born."

Billy nodded miserably, and Archie sat back with a satisfied nod.

"Good," he said. "I likes to be clear with my people. No misunderstandings, no confusion. And I likes you—I said that before, didn't I? Which is why we're talkin' about this like gentlemen, rather than solving our problems like thugs. You got a lot to learn, Billy Sweep, about life in my ocean. And you'll do well to remember who are the sharks and who are the minnows."

He stood and tugged on his shirt, straightening it out, then stepped forwards until he towered over the pair of them.

277

"Now, I'm a merciful man," he said. "But I do want you ter remember this lesson. So I'm gonna have to deal out some kinda punishment. You understand that, right?"

Billy nodded, trying to keep his legs from giving way entirely. He didn't want to imagine what a punishment from Archie might entail.

"Right." Archie nodded slowly. "But like I said, I'm fond o' ye, so ter show how much ye mean to me, I'm goin' ter go easy on you today. How's that sound?"

"Sounds good, Archie." Billy nodded again, relief flooding through him. "Thank you."

"You're welcome," Archie said, beaming.

Then he turned to Sticks and smashed a fist hard into the side of his face.

Sticks dropped to the floor, where he lay unmoving on the carpet. Archie gave his hand a shake and stood gazing down at him for a moment. Billy was frozen in shock, reeling from the suddenness of what had just happened.

"There ye go," Archie said, sniffing and nodding in satisfaction. "Consider yer trespasses accounted for. Go have a drink, get yerself back together, and be ready for work tomorrow. You hear?"

Billy did not reply. He could not take his eyes away from Sticks, who was lying still immobile on the carpet.

"Billy?" Archie's voice roused him, and he blinked and looked up to find Archie gazing placidly at him. "You hear me?" Archie repeated.

Billy nodded dumbly.

"Good. Now get on out. I'll have the girls clean this up."

Billy turned and stumbled to the door, leaving Archie standing over Sticks' unconscious form.

35
A Wrong Turn

UP, UP, UP, scraping, chipping, scouring, brushing. No longer did he think about what he was doing. He worked like a machine, dull-eyed, heavy-hearted, a shell of a boy, emptied of everything he had once been.

Up, up, up, inch by inch, foot by foot, trying to think of nothing but the flue above him and the drop below, trying to ignore the spectres of the past that floated around him.

They crowded thick now: Gerard, Aggie, Clara, Old Sal, Flash Jim, Long Paul, the blonde-haired boy … and now Sticks. All lives that had been ruined by him, or lost around him, their faces solemn, their eyes accusing him. *It's all your fault,* they seemed to say, their voices ghosts of whispers, softer than the sighing of wind in bare trees. *We had lives, and then you came, and now we have none.*

And Tosher. His face loomed largest, though his eyes did not accuse. Instead, tears streamed down his face, while his words echoed mockingly: *I'm not like you. I can't go back out there. I'll die. But you'll be all right Bill. You'll be all right …* Billy gritted his teeth and hacked at the filthy walls. *You'll be all right.* That's what he had said. *You'll be all right.* Well, he wasn't all right, was he? Yes, he was alive. Yes, he was whole. But what had been the cost? Piece by piece, inch by inch, his soul had been chipped away, until now he could feel nothing inside but an empty black void.

Up, up, up … He could not remember which chimney he was in, or which house. He was no longer in charge of the crew—following the interview, Archie had replaced him with the Blagger, and relegated Billy to just another member of the gang, to do as he was told and keep his mouth shut— and now there was nothing for Billy to do but climb: up the flues by day, chipping and scraping; down the flues in the dead of night, weaving his way through pitch-black mazes, trying to remember where he was and what day it was, and which house they were robbing. Opening doors, opening windows, letting in the Devil's Lads to thieve and plunder while he kept watch and prayed that no one would wake.

They were out most nights now, falling into a routine, spreading themselves out, varying the false trails they left behind. Sometimes they would smash a window on the way out; sometimes they would leave the back door unlocked, and make it look like carelessness; once, for a joke, the Blagger set a fire in the drawing room, and the gang ran whooping and shrieking with laughter down the street as cries of terror and alarm rose from behind them.

And everywhere the Devil's Lads went, Billy went with them: silent and solemn, keeping to himself, surrounded by his ghosts, hardly knowing where he was or how long he had been doing this.

He paused and pressed his aching legs hard against the opposite wall, supporting himself while he caught a breath.

There was no brush in his hand, he realised. That meant it was night, and he was breaking in. Down, not up. Down, down, down.

The days and nights had long since blended together in one long tapestry of exhaustion, going out late, working into the small hours, coming back to the warehouse to collapse on his sheets, only to be roused by the Blagger three or four hours later, demanding he get up and get ready for work. Billy did not argue. The memory of Sticks' unmoving form kept him in line. That fist had been meant for him, he knew. The only thing that had diverted it onto Sticks had been Billy's usefulness to Archie, and that usefulness was the only thing keeping him alive now.

That, he had realised, was what Archie had seen in him: nothing he respected, nothing he admired. Archie had seen only profit to be made from his dexterity, something to be used and exploited. Yes, Archie had wooed him and flattered him, ensuring his loyalty and service; but in the end it would always have come down to this. Archie Miller did not surround himself with people: he collected tools, and when a tool ceased to be useful he threw it away.

So Billy made himself useful, and kept quiet, and never looked Archie in the eye. And so he had lived.

Down, down, down ... Surely he should have come to a turning by now? He paused again, gasping for air in the enclosed space, feeling it unusually close around him, struggling to picture the map in his mind. But there were so many now, so many houses they had robbed, so many pounds of silver they had whisked away, so many boxes of jewellery, so many candelabras, so many cutlery sets, so many dishes and plates. Everything blurred together, the lines smudged with glass after glass of fiery gin. No. No turnings yet. But what about below? Was this a single flue? Were there any turnings at all? And which house was this, anyway? The one in Kensington? Knightsbridge? Mayfair? So many houses, so many crimes, so many stains on his soul.

Down, down, down, nowhere to go but down. Descending, so it felt, into the depths of the earth, lost forever in a never-ending shaft, cursed to climb for his remaining days, never coming to the bottom, never able to rest, never stopping until the earth swallowed him up.

And perhaps that was right. Perhaps that was what he deserved. Not for him a wife, a family, a graceful decline and a peaceful end. No. Only the flues, up and down, up and down until they ate him alive.

Down, down—

He stopped.

There was no more flue. No more down. Only a surface thick with soot and filth, on which his feet scrabbled for a second before he slumped, exhausted, and did not rise.

He had missed a turning. The realisation came with a dull thud in his chest. There was no other explanation. But which one? How many had there been? There were usually at least two or three in any chimney, and if he had taken the wrong fork at the very first turning he would have to climb all the way back up, or else try another fork at random and risk ending up in someone's bedroom, or behind a boarded-up fireplace.

He struggled to his feet, but as soon as he stretched his hands up they met something solid above him, and as he felt around he understood what had happened. He had done the unthinkable, and dislodged a plug of soot and ash which was now jammed into the narrow opening above him.

He closed his eyes. He should have known this would happen, sooner or later. And when the time came he had expected to panic, to be afraid. But he felt no fear. He felt nothing. It was quiet here. The space was enclosed, but not claustrophobic. He could struggle, and try to dig his way out—but he was tired; so very, very tired. All he wanted to do was lie down and rest. Perhaps if he closed his eyes he would drift off and never wake up—and would that really be so very bad? Even as the thought brushed across his mind it was followed by a wave of uneasiness, a stirring inside him, the urge for survival. No. This couldn't be the end. This couldn't be it. Surely there was more sand in the glass, more days for him to see.

The uneasiness rose into his chest, blossoming slowly into a flicker of fear. What if he did fall into endless sleep? What lay beyond? He had heard rumours and whispers, words like 'heaven' and 'hell' spoken as oaths and imprecations; but he felt sure that if there was such a place as heaven, with angels and clouds and harps and such, he would not be welcome there: not a filthy climbing boy with a litany of sins to his name; not Billy the sweep, who had hardly done a good deed in his life.

He could see it now, looking back along the road he had walked all these years: never once had he reached out in kindness to anyone, not even to Tosher or Clara. No matter how pleasant he had been, no matter how hard he had tried to live peaceably, in the end he had always been looking to himself, to his own survival, to the next meal, the next drink, avoiding the next punch or the knife in the dark. What good did he have to his credit? What would he have to say to any angel that met him? What reason could he give to be admitted through the gate?

No. If he was to die, it was the pit for him, that half-understood place of fire and brimstone, a valley of unimaginable horrors. And he did not want that—but neither did he want to live, enduring this grinding cycle of sleeping, waking, climbing, descending, drinking, eating, and sleeping again, only to wake the next day and repeat it over and over. It was a living hell, an endless circle, a path he could not leave; and now he sensed that he was nearing the end of the path, and he had nothing to show for his walk.

And as the realisation of the utter futility of his short and miserable life dawned on him, Billy slumped down in the dark, hidden away from every mortal eye, unknown to the world. There was no point in continuing the struggle, not if all he had to look forward to was more of the same. Better to stay here, and wait for the inevitable, and hope that whatever came was better than what he had left behind.

He bowed his head, and his shoulders shook and tears brimmed in his eyes, and his muffled sobs echoed up the empty flue to be lost in the emptiness above.

He had come to the end, and there was nothing to do but wait.

36
The Calling Card

"MY LORDS," LORD SHAFTESBURY declared, "we can no longer sit idly by and pretend to ourselves that the world is as it should be. Every day, countless children trudge to the workhouses, to the mines, to the chimneys, their bellies empty and their spirits broken—or else they rise with mischief in their hearts, determined to earn their daily bread at the expense of honest men and women. Every day countless children face the prospect of injury or death beneath the tools of their trade or the conditions in which they work; every day such children must endure grievous abuses at the hands of their masters and mistresses, men and women who view them as no more than commodities to be used up."

Shaftesbury paused and swept the chamber with his searching gaze. On the benches opposite, his political opponents shook their heads and muttered to one another, some of them smiling indulgently while others glared at him with open hostility. Shaftesbury ignored them. He was used to it.

"Would that these children enjoyed the care and consideration given to the dray horse, or to the sheep roaming the hillside," he continued, his voice rolling around the wood-panelled hall and rising to the darkened rafters. "Would that their masters valued them half so much as they value the machines at which they toil, or the coal which they help bring to the surface, or the coin their efforts put into those already heavy pockets!"

A chorus of protest rose to meet his words. He continued, raising his voice over the din: "My lords, how can we continue to call ourselves a Christian country when Christian charity is relegated to a few meagre societies, struggling to survive from day to day on handouts from the general public? Charity should be enshrined in law—the laws whose purpose it is to protect and empower those very people who at this moment are so grievously abused by the same! And those laws, when enacted, should be enforced with the full authority of the Crown, and not be allowed to wallow in neglect, openly transgressed at every turn!"

He raised a hand, in which he clutched a thick sheaf of paper. "I have here but a sample of the many reports which have been compiled on the living conditions and privations endured by adults and children alike, the length and breadth of this country, merely in order to swell the profits of their masters! My lords, I urge you to peruse these reports, after which I am sure you will agree with me that legislation such as the Chimney Sweeps Act must be enforced, and indeed that the law must be changed still further in order to shield these innocent children from further abuses!"

He finished speaking amidst a roar of voices, some in agreement and some against, the two sides of the chamber bellowing at each other until the Lord Chancellor called the session to some kind of order.

Shaftesbury sat through it all, wrapped in stony silence. He had fired his volley; there was no use following it with sticks and stones.

The house moved to other business, and other lords spoke on this piece of legislation or that Act of Parliament; and when the session was over, the House rose with a clatter and dispersed from the chamber in ones or twos, discussing the issues of the day and arranging dates for further meetings.

Shaftesbury gathered his papers and made to join them, but when he heard his name called across the chamber he stopped. He looked around, and his gaze lighted on a large, jovial man with enormous bushy whiskers who was waving to him from the floor of the chamber. He beckoned for Shaftesbury to join him.

"Well spoken today," the man said, as Shaftesbury drew near. "Very moving. Very touching."

Shaftesbury inclined his head graciously. "You are too kind, Prime Minister."

The Prime Minister, Lord Palmerston, was as large as Shaftesbury was thin, and as booming as Shaftesbury was reserved. He had a reputation for making light of matters— but he was also known for doing the right thing if he could, and Shaftesbury respected him for this.

"I trust you will be sufficiently moved to review the reports yourself?" Shaftesbury said pointedly.

"Oh, of course. Without a doubt. It's a shocking business. Really, it is." Palmerston shook his head and clasped his hands behind his back. "You're doing quite remarkable work with this whole business. We're all most indebted to you."

He paused. Shaftesbury sensed there was more to be said.

"But …?" he prompted.

Palmerston laughed. "You can always see through me, Shaftesbury. Yes, there is a 'but'. Not a big one, mind. All I was going to say was … well … go easy, eh? Take your time. These fellows are like a flock of pigeons—come at them too hard and they're likely to panic and take flight. I know you're doing your best for these young 'uns, but just remember to rein it in now and again. If nothing else you'll do yourself an injury, and I can't afford to lose you!"

"Of course, Prime Minister." Shaftesbury replied coldly. "I shan't trouble you any further."

"Oh, come, come!" Palmerston clasped him by the hand before he could leave. "I've offended you. I see that. I don't mean to malign your integrity, of course. No one can fault your selfless dedication to these poor creatures, and by all means continue this crusade of yours. I'm not asking you to keep quiet—speak up, speak out, keep bringing these Bills to the House—but just … give them some time, eh? Time to come round. And don't despair if they drag their heels. They're just trying to make sure that the laws we pass are robust enough to be effective."

"I understand, Prime Minister," Shaftesbury replied. "And I am well aware of the often glacial pace of proceedings in these chambers. But you will forgive me if my patience frays now and again, when I read almost daily reports of children having limbs amputated, eyes put out, and lives taken, while we sit in this room and debate the difference between this word and that in a Bill which could alleviate their suffering. Meanwhile, the masters who inflict this suffering continue to do so with impunity, sneering at what laws we have and comfortable in the knowledge that they will not be prosecuted under them."

Shaftesbury tightened his grip on Palmerston's hand, and lowered his voice so that the other man had to lean in to hear him: "I am a patient man, sir, and I will continue to be patient. And I value your support in all my endeavours. But I pray you remember that for every day we delay, lives are lost, and those the most innocent amongst us."

Palmerston nodded seriously, and tightened his own grip in reply. "It will be done," he said. "God has given you the strength and the determination, and He will see it through."

They regarded each other for a moment, the one broad and the other gaunt, then with a flicker of a smile of gratitude Shaftesbury turned and strode away.

It was late by the time Shaftesbury returned home, and he was exhausted from a day of committees and interviews with various societies and foundations. Often he felt he passed all his time apologising to well-meaning people on behalf of the church or the government, and having to explain to them why the money or the resources were not available to support them. Such days left him spent, wondering whether his best efforts could still be in vain, in the face of the towering apathy and ignorance which he encountered from his peers.

He had looked forward to a quiet dinner and an hour or two with his wife, but when he opened the door to the drawing room he found it occupied by a man in the blue uniform of the Metropolitan Police force, standing to attention by the fireplace, and he knew with a heavy heart that the day was far from over.

"Officer," he said, motioning for the man to sit. "Please.

I'm sure your day has been as long as mine. I see no need to weary ourselves with ceremony."

"Thank you, your lordship," the officer replied, though he waited until Shaftesbury had lowered himself into a high-backed armchair before perching on one himself.

"So," Shaftesbury said. "To what do I owe the pleasure …" he glanced at the stripes on the man's shoulder, "… sergeant?"

The man shifted uncomfortably on his seat, his fingers drumming on the helmet perched on his knee. "Well, you see, sir— I mean, your lordship …"

Shaftesbury raised a hand. "'Sir' will do."

"Thank you, sir. Well, I'm afraid it's rather unorthodox. If I may explain?"

"By all means."

"Well, sir, the force has been investigating, for some time now, a series of burglaries around the city. Always in affluent areas, always very neat and professional. You might have read of the Belgravia incident? Well, we think it's the same gang responsible. Usually the perpetrators try to throw us off the scent by making it look like a random attempt— break a few windows down the street, leave the back door open as if it were the maid's fault, that sort of thing.

"Anyway, it's had a few at the Yard a bit baffled. These houses are fairly secure, as you'd imagine; and besides that, no one's ever seen these ruffians break in, though once or twice they've been caught breaking *out*."

"I find it eternally fascinating," Shaftesbury interjected, "the extent to which the criminal mind will go to avoid earning money by honest means. However, you'll forgive me if I fail to see the connection between these entrepreneurs and myself."

"Ah," the sergeant said. "Well, all this is by way of saying that we hadn't a clue how they were going about all this—until this morning, when a young lad was found trapped behind a bricked-up fireplace in a house in Kensington. It was sheer chance they found him, on account of his weeping, sir. Well, the family fetched a mason out and they took down the wall, and lo and behold the lad fell out, all over with soot and half-dead. They reckon he had climbed down the chimney during the night and taken a wrong turning, which led us to suspect that's how these bandits had been gaining access to these houses. And what's more, sir ..." And here the sergeant reached into his breast pocket and pulled out a small grubby rectangle of card. "What's more, he was carrying this."

Slowly, Shaftesbury reached out and took the card. He recognised it instantly, recognised his own address even through the filthy smudges that obscured most of the writing. And on the front of the card, printed in neat black capitals, one word was clearly visible: SHAFTESBURY.

"Fascinating," he murmured, turning the card over in his hands. Was it possible? Surely anything was possible. Was it probable? No—but in the workings of Providence there was no such thing as probable or improbable. There was only what was, and what was not. And what he could not deny was that this was the same card he had handed to a young boy in the back room of a theatre on a Sunday morning over three months ago.

"So you recognise the card, sir?" the sergeant was saying.

Shaftesbury looked up at him. "Oh, indeed," he said. "It is one of mine."

"And is there any possibility you might know the young

man in question? Would you happen to know why he would have your card on him?"

"I believe I do know him, yes. Not intimately, but we met. And he had this card because I gave it to him, and I told him to come to me should he ever be in need of assistance." Shaftesbury glanced back down at the card, and at his own fingers smeared with traces of soot. "Where is he now?"

"Being held at a local station, sir."

"And what is his condition?"

The sergeant frowned. "Sorry, sir?"

"His condition. His health. From what you say I understand he had been trapped for some time. Has he been seen by a doctor?"

"Well, not exactly, sir …"

"Very well." Shaftesbury stood up, and the sergeant shot to his feet. "I shall send a man with you, and he will make arrangements for a doctor to attend to the boy. In the morning I shall speak to the authorities on his behalf so that we may determine what is to be done with him."

"I'm sorry, sir. Did you say a doctor … ?"

"Yes, sergeant. A doctor. Or did you intend to allow him to die in custody?"

The sergeant's mouth opened but nothing came out. His eyes looked around in mild panic.

"I am aware the boy is a criminal," Shaftesbury assured him, moderating his tone for the sake of the man's nerves. "But whatever he has done, he is also a child and a human being, made in the image of God—and for this reason we owe him a duty of care. There is justice for him to face, of course, but I very much doubt it will be achieved by his perishing in a cell before he has had a chance to stand trial."

The sergeant struggled with the thought for a moment, before giving up and giving a small bow. "Yes sir," he said. "I'll make sure the doctor is allowed to see him."

"My thanks, sergeant." Shaftesbury nodded. "If that is all … ?"

The sergeant bowed again then headed for the door, grateful for the excuse to leave.

When he was gone, Shaftesbury stood for a long time in silence, gazing down at the card in his hands. Then, with some effort, and using the arm of the chair for support, he lowered himself to his knees on the deep carpet, bowed his head, and, clutching the card so tightly that it buckled in his fingers, he prayed.

37
Life into the Dead

BILLY OPENED HIS EYES.

He was dead—that much was plain. He had died in the flue, trapped in the cloying darkness, suffocated by the soot and dust. His limp body was probably still there, slumped behind a bricked-up fireplace where it would never be found. And he was ... where?

He raised his head and looked around. This didn't look like his idea of either heaven or hell. There were no clouds, no angels, no golden harps and gates of pearl; but neither were there any flames or demons, or souls suffering in torment. Instead, he lay in a narrow bed in a small room with a low beamed ceiling and one window, through which a bright spring sun shone. Maybe the preachers had been wrong, after all. Maybe he was in some heathen afterlife, and everything he had ever heard had been a lie.

He tried to sit up, but a sharp pain stabbed him in the chest, and he gasped and fell back, coughing so hard he doubled over in the sheets. The cough did not die away; it intensified, as did the stabbing pains, until he thought his lungs had caught fire.

As he struggled to breathe, thrashing on the bed, he was dimly aware of a door being flung open and rough hands seizing him and forcing him on to his side.

"That's it," a voice said gruffly, seeming to come from miles away. "Get it out. That's the way."

With a final hacking burst that nearly split Billy in two, the cough died away, leaving him trembling and exhausted. He opened his eyes blearily. Black and red flecks speckled the pillow and sheets.

"There'll be more," the voice said. "Get used to it."

Billy tried to turn over to see who had spoken, but already the speaker had stood up and crossed the room to the door.

"Wait …" Billy croaked, flapping a hand uselessly.

"Just rest," the speaker said. "You've been through plenty."

The door closed, and Billy felt himself sliding once more into a void of unconsciousness.

When he woke again it was dark. A lamp burned somewhere nearby, filling the room with a flickering orange-red light.

This time he did not try to sit. He didn't want another coughing fit, and instinct told him the best thing to do was to keep as still as possible. Instead he lay and looked at the ceiling, listening to the rasp of his own breathing in the silence.

He was not dead—sense and reason told him that. Clearly something had happened, some kind of rescue, and he had been brought here by his saviours, whoever they were. But he had no idea where 'here' was.

He was not sure how to feel about his reprieve. In the

bricked-up flue he had resigned himself to death, even if he had not wanted it, but now the awful inevitability of that fact had passed, he found that he was empty. He felt nothing: no relief, no disappointment, no elation, no sorrow. He just *was*—a boy lying in a bed, lungs breathing, heart beating, while around him the seconds of his life ticked over.

"Bill?"

The voice startled him. He turned his head, searching for the speaker. It was not the same voice that had spoken to him earlier: it was younger, softer, familiar …

His eyes lighted on a person sitting in a chair in the far corner of the room. It was a boy, long and thin, with gangly legs and a too-large nose. His hair was plastered down on his head, but by the light of the lamp Billy could see that it was a dull orange colour.

Billy's heart quickened as the boy leaned forwards, bringing his face into the light.

It was Tosher.

"You're up, then," Tosher said, grinning. "Thought you'd sleep forever, Bill. We was all worried about yer. Most thought you wouldn't make it, but I told 'em. 'Not our Bill,' I said. 'He's a fighter. You'll see.' And here yer are!" He fell silent, the grin still plastered across his knobbly face.

Billy stared at him. This had to be some kind of dream. He had left Tosher in the kitchen of the house where they had taken Clara, left him sobbing piteously by the fireside, left him for the hell of the streets and the merciless rule of Archie Miller. How could he be here?

Tosher gave a snort of laughter. "Bet it's a bit of a shock, seein' me here an' all," he said. "Bet mine's the last face you thought you'd see, right?"

Billy opened his mouth to speak, but no words came out. There were no words, none that were adequate, at least.

"It were a bit of a shock fer me, too," Tosher continued, blissfully unaware of Billy's struggle. "Seein' you bein' brought in an' all like that, all black and limp. Like a sack o' coal, you were, I don't mind sayin'. Hardly breathin', neither. Didn't think I'd see you again, and there you were, large as life!" He shook his head. "I was right pleased to see you. Couldn't think what you been through, neither—out on the streets all through the winter like that? Cor, you must'a seen a thing or two!"

Finally Billy found his voice. "What ..." he began, but immediately choked and coughed, and the cough took hold, and he doubled over again and hacked and spluttered until he thought his lungs would burst. Eventually the attack died away, and he rolled over with tears in his eyes, panting and gasping, to find Tosher staring at him with wide fish-like eyes.

"You all right?" Tosher said.

Billy glared at him. What kind of a question was that? He swallowed, though his mouth felt like he had just eaten a plateful of sand, and tried again:

"What ... do you mean?" he managed to croak.

Tosher gave a snort of nervous laughter. "What do you mean, what do I mean?"

Billy swallowed again. The effort of talking irritated him. Tosher's laugh irritated him.

"What ... did I ... see?" Every word was a stone in his throat.

"Oh! No, I meant ... just ... you must'a seen a few things, y'know 'out there', on the streets. Right? Got in a few scraps?

Had a few adventures?" Tosher shook his head dreamily. "Sometimes I wish I'd gone with yer, Billy. Just imagine it, eh? The fun times we'd'a had?"

Billy stared incredulously at Tosher's faraway expression, at the face of the boy who had abandoned him to the cold and the snow; and as he stared, something rose up inside him. It was something deep and dark, something with teeth and claws, something that had been slumbering the whole time he had lived on the streets. It had reared its head now and again—under the arch, when he had kicked that boy to make a path for Clara; in the battle at Seven Dials, when he had slashed left and right with his razor; and in the dark of the kitchen in the house in Belgravia, as his fingers tightened around the broom handle and the blonde-haired boy looked at him in dawning horror—and it came again now, only there was nothing to tether it, no leash to hold it back. It came roaring and spitting, howling and gnashing, a frenzy of rage and hatred, and as it enveloped Billy he rose from the bed and launched himself at Tosher, his hands clawed, his eyes wild, his throat raw with a ragged scream.

He fell on Tosher's startled face, scratching and gouging, kicking and swearing, pouring out upon his head all the pain and fear he had kept bottled up inside. He hated Tosher. He hated him for choosing to stay, for loving Clara, for being happy and healthy and clean and fed, for having a bed to sleep in and a roof over his head, for not understanding what it had been like, for thinking it had all been some kind of game.

And most of all, Billy hated Tosher for stealing the silver spoon in the first place, and for setting all the events of the past months in motion. So he beat his fists down on Tosher's head, not caring how much it hurt, not caring about the tearing pain in his chest and the pounding in his head; and he only stopped when the door burst open and strong arms seized him, flinging him back onto the bed.

He was dimly aware of someone shouting at him, of a brief scuffle followed by the door slamming so hard it shook the room. But the cough had seized him, racking his body again and again until he thought he would suffocate, and he lay on his side and wished that he could die.

Daniel burst into the kitchen, dragging Tosher with him.

"Enough!" he bellowed, startling Mrs. Lucas, who was standing by the fire and tending to a kettle. Daniel thrust Tosher in front of him, pointing a quivering finger at the scratches covering his face. "That boy is a menace! Look what he did to Tosher here! If I hadn't come in when I did, I dread to think what would have happened!"

"Daniel—" Mrs. Lucas began, but he raised a hand and cut her off.

"Nothing doing, Mrs. Lucas!" he growled. "You won't persuade me this time! I've had enough of taking in every waif and stray that comes begging at our door! Our rooms are full, and our purse is empty! We are doing all we can, and more, and this boy has no place in it! He's naught but a wild animal, and he belongs on the streets with others like him, not in here with respectable folk!"

"But Daniel—"

"I mean it!" Daniel's great beard quivered with the strength of his feeling. "I want him gone, Mrs. Lucas! Christ taught us to be wise as serpents as well as harmless as doves, and it is not wisdom to have such a boy in our house! All that'll happen is that he'll bring down the other boys, you mark my words! The next time I see his lordship the earl I'll have a thing or two to say to him, just you wait and see!"

"*Daniel!*" Mrs. Lucas snapped, her eyes wide and her face red. Something in her tone stopped him short, and he slowly turned his head and followed her pointed gaze to where Lord Shaftesbury sat on a chair in the far corner of the kitchen.

"Good evening," Shaftesbury said, inclining his head politely. "I see my visit is not before time."

Shaftesbury

38
The Ragged School

WHEN THE DOOR OPENED AGAIN, Billy did not bother turning to see who it was. He lay on his side, wheezing for breath, clenching and unclenching his fists in helpless fury. The rage that had engulfed him had not subsided; it boiled and seethed, welling up each time he pictured Tosher's stupidly grinning face.

The visitor did not speak, but Billy heard quiet footsteps pacing across the room, the chair being set upright, then a body being lowered into it.

The room fell silent.

Billy closed his eyes, wishing the person would just go away. He did not want to talk. He did not want anything: he did not want to be here, but neither did he want to be back on the streets; he did not want to die, but neither did he want to live. He longed simply for darkness to take him, a long slow sleep with no dreams and no waking, into which he could sink eternally, never to rise.

Seconds ticked by, stretching into minutes. The visitor said nothing, and apart from the odd little breath or shift in the chair, Billy would have forgotten they were there. Eventually, after what felt like an hour, the fire within began to die down, and as it left him Billy realised just how weak and weary he was. His outburst had drained him, and now even to shift his weight was agony.

"Hello, Billy."

His heart stopped.

"You've certainly been through the wars, haven't you?"

Billy felt as if every bone in his body had been broken, but he didn't care. He had to see this with his own eyes before he would believe it. He turned himself over slowly, grimacing with the pain. When he had finally turned onto his side, and he saw who was sitting in the chair, all he could do was stare in utter astonishment.

Anthony Ashley Cooper, the Seventh Earl of Shaftesbury, inclined his head graciously and allowed a tiny smile to tug at the corner of his mouth.

"I'm glad to see your strength has returned, at least," he said.

Billy was stunned. Seeing Tosher had been a shock, but this was so astonishing that he had neither the words nor the thoughts to express it. Of all the people he had met in his life, this man was the last he would ever have expected to see, and no matter how he struggled he could not think why he should be here now.

"I see you appear to have lost your voice." Lord Shaftesbury crossed his hands over one leg and leaned back in the chair. "Though I wouldn't blame you. I imagine the dust and fumes did their work well. You must be in pain."

"I'm not ..." The words caught in Billy's throat, and he coughed, but it was not so fierce this time, and when it was over he cleared his throat and tried again. "I'm fine."

"Clearly," Lord Shaftesbury said. "You're made of sterner stuff than most, Billy. And I don't doubt your resolve. But I must beg you to refrain from exerting yourself, at least for the present."

Still he stared, searching for the right words to say, the right questions to ask: How had this man found him? Why was he here? Why should he have concerned himself with someone like Billy: a sweep, a thief … and worse. His chest tightened, as it always did when the memory of his darkest moment returned to him, and he had to bite his lip to hold back the tears of self-hatred. With an enormous effort he hauled himself up in bed, leaning against the backboard as his lungs struggled for air. "How …?" he began, but again his breath failed him, and the words dissolved into a hacking wheeze.

"Please." Shaftesbury raised a hand. "Be still. I can see you have questions, and I also gather from the state of your friend downstairs that there are matters which still need to be resolved. Let me do what I can to illuminate you as to your immediate circumstances, and then maybe we can talk a little of other things."

He reached over and took a glass of water from the table by the window, which he handed to Billy. After Billy had drained it, they sat for a moment in silence. Billy watched him, waiting for answers, waiting to see what was to become of him.

"I must confess," Shaftesbury said, "that I was as surprised as anyone might be when I arrived home to find a police officer in my study. Still more surprised was I when he presented me with this."

He reached into his coat and pulled out a grubby scrap of card. Billy recognised it instantly. It was the same card he had been given by this man in the back room of the theatre, the same card he had carried with him ever since, never knowing exactly why.

Shaftesbury looked at the card for a moment, turning it over in his hands, before continuing: "This police officer told me a remarkable tale," he said. "I shan't bore you by recounting it, for I am sure you are familiar with the details. Suffice it to say the story included a series of daring burglaries by one of the city's most notorious gangs, and concluded with the discovery of a boy, half-suffocated, behind a bricked-up fireplace in one of the finest houses in Kensington. The card was found amongst the boy's effects, and it was in turn conveyed to me. It is curious, is it not, how Providence manages ever to surprise us, even when we think we have seen all there is to see in this world?"

He fell silent again. Billy said nothing. For one thing, his lungs still felt as though burning matches had been stuck into them, and for another, he had a feeling he knew where this was going. There was talk of police, and clearly this man knew what he had been doing in the flue where they found him. Surely they knew about the blonde-haired boy as well, and Archie, and everything he had done. Surely this was all leading to a dock, and a judge's frown, and a dark cell in a grim prison.

And yet he was here, in this room, in a warm bed, and he was talking to a lord rather than a policeman. There was more to be told, and so Billy waited to hear it, torn between hope and fear.

"I visited the station," Shaftesbury said, "along with a

physician, who informed me that you were as near to death as one can be without crossing through its waters: on the very bank of Jordan, as it were. However, we were presented with something of a dilemma. Of course I recognised you from our encounter in the theatre, and I was determined to do what I could to help you; but at the same time you were suspected of burglary, and of being a notorious gang member. I could not simply ignore the law and whisk you away, and so another method of salvation had to be found—and it was.

"Did you know that the law makes a special allowance for children found to have fallen in with evil company? I know, because I insisted on such an allowance myself. Rather than a custodial sentence, they may instead be transferred to a ragged school, in the hopes that they will learn to be of use to society rather than a scourge. It was under such a dispensation that I sought to extricate you from the judicial system, and as you see," Shaftesbury looked around at the room and smiled, "I was successful."

"So this is a …" Billy struggled to recall the term. "What, a poor school?"

"We call them 'ragged schools,'" Shaftesbury replied. "Most are simply day schools, opening their doors each morning to whichever waifs and strays may turn up, and seeking to educate them a little in reading and writing, and whatever arithmetic they can manage. Some, such as this one, also offer boarding to a limited number of students in the most desperate of circumstances—such as yourself, for instance."

Understanding dawned. "And I can't leave?" Billy said. It was more a statement of fact than a question.

Shaftesbury shook his head. "For the time being, no. It is, however, preferable to the accommodation you would be otherwise enjoying. I hope that you will come to see the benefits of such lodgings, especially inasmuch as they will afford you the opportunity to learn a useful trade, and perhaps move on from the mistakes of your past."

Silence fell in the room. Billy looked down at his sheets and frowned. So he was under arrest, and in a cell, of sorts—but he was alive, and the cell was the most airy and comfortable he could ever have imagined. There was not much he understood about all of this, but one thing was clear: this was nothing compared to what he deserved. By rights he should have died in that flue, trapped beneath the soot and dirt. He had been spared—why, and by whom, it was not clear to him—but now he was here he had no idea what to make of it.

His confusion must have been evident, because Shaftesbury cleared his throat and said, "Now you understand how you came to be here, and what your prospects are, perhaps it would help to know a little about who I am, and why I am taking such an interest. I am what is called a peer of the realm—do you know what that means?"

Billy shook his head.

"It means I spend much of my time in a large room with very important men, deciding what the laws of this land shall be." Again, Shaftesbury permitted himself the shadow of a smile. "Such meetings would, I expect, be exceedingly tedious to most people, and I confess I find myself uncommonly distracted through many of them. But occasionally I have the opportunity to stand up and speak to these men, and when I do I make it my business to speak on behalf of the poor and needy.

"I have spoken in my time on the matter of the lunatics, those poor souls whose minds are broken, and who are too often cast into places little better—if not worse—than a common jail, where they are left to rot in obscurity and the diseases from which they suffer are left wholly untreated. I have spoken about the lives of the children who are forced to work in the deepest mines, hidden from the sun for endless hours, alone in the dark beneath miles of crushing rock and earth, forgotten and unloved. I have spoken about the children who toil in factories, sweating and weeping over all manner of machinery, beaten and starved, their lives little better than the animals that work the fields, until an accident cuts them short and they are cast away. And I have spoken about the lot of the climbing boys."

Billy's head snapped up in surprise. Shaftesbury nodded.

"Yes," he said. "You never thought that there were men who interested themselves in the lives of boys like you, did you? Well, rest assured that for the most part you would be correct. There are precious few in positions of power who feel that any such creatures—the lunatics, the miners, the factory workers—are worth the spending of five minutes' speech in the Houses of Parliament. But for myself, I find such indifference abhorrent. It goes against my nature as a Christian, as a man in a position of authority, and as a human being. The neglect of aid to the sufferer, when one is in the position to give it, is tantamount to inflicting the suffering itself.

"I know about you, Billy, inasmuch as I know about countless boys like you. I know about the darkness, the choking soot, the heat, the beatings, the cruelty, the starvation. I have seen it with my own eyes, and I have wept over those who endure it. I have made it my life's work to reform the laws of this country to a point where no child will have to experience the deprivations which have been forced upon you. Alas, there is far to go, and often I feel it is a Sisyphean endeavour—that is, utterly hopeless," he added, seeing Billy's frown.

"So why do it?" Billy rasped. "No one does anything for free. I learned that on the streets. Why you trying to help folks like that? Why you helping me? I ain't got nothing to give you. Ain't none of us got nothing to give you."

"Why?" Shaftesbury nodded. "A pertinent question. Why indeed? I have my money, I have my family, I have a comfortable life. I have visited the palace, and spoken with the Queen and the Prince Consort. I travel Europe, and meet the crowned heads. I have enormous influence over the lives of the citizens of this isle. Why would I waste all my wealth and power and influence on folk who have never asked for it, and who, if the other powers at work had their way, may never see the benefits?

"To answer your question," he said, crossing his legs. "Let me tell you a story."

39

A Light in the Dark

"Imagine a boy," Shaftesbury said, "born into a wealthy family, his father a landed gentleman, heir to a vast estate, with a lineage going back to the time of Queen Elizabeth. This boy will never have to labour for his daily bread, will never be homeless, and will have every opportunity in life.

"And yet the boy is unhappy. Why? Because his parents do not love him. His father is a bully, who alternately beats him and neglects him, and his mother is more concerned with the pleasures of society than with the welfare of her children. Both parents regularly leave their brood in the care of the servants, who treat them little better. The father has frittered away most of his fortune, and so there is precious little food on the children's plates. They are often cold, always hungry, and desperately unhappy.

"Soon the boy is sent away to school. At last, he thinks, he will have a reprieve from the hardships of life in the familial home. He is wrong. The treatment he receives at the hands of his schoolmaster is as bad as, or worse than, that of his father. The boy suffers equal cruelty at the hands of his classmates, who are encouraged by the adults to fight, cheat and steal. So our boy is caught in a dilemma. He does not wish to stay at school, but neither does he want to return home. There is nowhere he can turn."

Shaftesbury steepled his fingers and gazed shrewdly at Billy over the tips of them.

"You may be wondering why you should care for this boy," he said. "It is better, surely, to be beaten in a fine house by a man with an ancient name, than in a freezing garret by a drunken stranger? And after all, will the boy not one day become a man, and the head of this noble family? He will have sons of his own, upon whom he can shower the love and devotion absent from his youth. Or else he will be free to beat them also, visiting upon the children the sins of the father. In either case, you may think, why should this boy complain? He is free, after all, and his life will be a long one. Whatever struggles he may experience, this boy will never know anything close to the hardships you have endured.

"But misery is a strange thing. It cares not for one's surroundings, nor for one's station in life. It comes not from without, but from within, growing and spreading from the heart throughout the whole person. No amount of money can alleviate it, nor can the prestige of a family name erase it. Misery is misery, wherever it is found: whether in the grandest palace or in the filthiest mineshaft. And the misery of a child is surely the worst kind, for children are incapable of bringing it upon themselves. Such misery is imposed on them by those around them, by neglectful parents and abusive masters, by indifferent rulers and unloving clergy. And once they have been brought so low, there is nothing upon this earth that can lift them up again.

"So you see, this boy is not so very different to yourself. His setting may be grander, his education more robust; but stripped of these trappings he is just a boy, and a boy in deepest misery.

"But," and here Shaftesbury raised a finger, "there is one light in the darkness of his existence, one candle that burns beside him in the long gloomy tunnel down which he must walk. This light shines in the face of a woman, poor and simple, whose duty it is to care for the boy in the place of his parents.

"To the miserable boy, the sight of this woman is like the sun rising after a long night of terror. Her plain speech is sweeter to his ears than the finest symphonies of Mozart or Beethoven, the touch of her calloused hands softer than the finest Egyptian cotton. Why? Because she loves him, in her halting and clumsy way. And because she loves him, she tells him from whence her love flows: from the very heart of the God who died for her, hanging on a tree and suffering for her sins. It is from her that the boy learns the name of Jesus; it is from her that he learns a simple prayer of repentance; and it is under her care and guidance that he finds in Jesus Christ a Saviour from his youthful sins.

"The woman has given the boy the greatest gift one human being can bestow upon another: the gift of the Gospel. For through this gift he can be assured, no matter what ills may come upon him in life, there waits for him a glorious home in heaven, to which he hopes one day to go."

Shaftesbury paused, and his eyes drifted, gazing through Billy to someone far beyond. Billy held his breath. He was trembling, he realised, transfixed by the man's words. Through all his life he had only ever thought about survival, existing from one day to the next, fending off the ever-present spectre of Death. And yet here this man was talking about something else, something more than just fighting and surviving.

He felt as if he was standing on the crest of a rooftop, looking out over a dark and smoky city and waiting for the sun to rise. Below him was nothing but filth and futility, a never-ending cycle of struggle and pain; above him was a clear sky of bright stars; and before him, beyond the distant hills, the first faint promise of dawn. His heart raced, and he lay still and listened as Shaftesbury continued:

"In time this woman leaves him, and makes her journey to that far country to be with the Lord she loves. The boy is destitute, alone in the world—but only for a time, because there burns within him a flame which no sorrow can extinguish, a bright and burning hope of eternal salvation, and the certainty that he will one day see her again, standing by the side of the Lord of Glory.

"And in her kindness she leaves him a token to remember her by: a pocket watch, neither grand nor glorious, not set with precious stones or inlaid with gold; but a possession most dear to him ever after, for it reminds him daily of the best friend he ever knew."

Shaftesbury paused, then reached into his own pocket and drew out a watch on a long chain, which he held in the palm of his hand. It was small, the case a little scratched here and there with use, but nevertheless carefully polished and free from smudges.

"It isn't much to look at, is it?" Shaftesbury murmured. "And yet it is more dear to me than all the gold and jewels of the whole British Empire. For this watch holds for me the memory of the time I found the greatest friend any man can possess: not a nursemaid, or a fellow to watch his back on the dark and dangerous streets, but the Lord God Himself."

He replaced the watch in his pocket and sat back, folding one leg over another.

"So my time at school continued," he said. "I had lost my dearest earthly friend, but I had another, who was heavenly, and though I confess I was no saint, I dearly wanted an opportunity to prove myself in His service.

"My opportunity came sooner than I thought. I was a youth of fifteen years old, progressing well in my studies, if occasionally indolent. One evening I was walking the streets of the town in which my school was situated, thinking on the future and my place in it, when I was disturbed by the most atrocious drunken singing I had ever heard in my life. I did not have to wait long to discover the source of the racket, for in the next moment there emerged from a side street a rabble of fellows bearing a box upon their shoulders. They were weaving back and forth across the road, tripping over their own feet and singing songs of the filthiest sort.

"As I watched, one of the men stumbled and lost his grip on the box, which fell into the road and spilled its contents. To my horror, I realised that the box must be a rude coffin, for what emerged from it was the corpse of a man. His compatriots—for that is who they must have been, bearing his coffin to the graveyard for interment—swore at their friend and proceeded to return the body to its casket, before lifting it again and continuing on their way.

"I was horror-struck. No words can communicate the disgust and despair I felt at such a display. To see a man, created in the image of God, bearing an immortal soul and made to worship the Almighty forever in the courts of heaven, subjected to such indignity. I swore to myself, then and there, that I would do everything in my power to ensure that no human being should have to suffer such indignities again.

"In time I entered politics, and the Lord presented me with countless opportunities to prove my resolution. I took them, and He has guided me ever since."

Shaftesbury looked narrowly at Billy over the tips of his fingers. "So you see why I do this work, Billy," he said. "Not for glory, nor for fame. Neither of these rewards are offered to me by society. Rather, I am ridiculed by many and pitied by many more, and my opponents in Parliament do all they can to silence my voice. When I propose a law that will protect millions, and bring them out of ignorance and hopelessness into a place where they may have the opportunity to read the very Word of God for themselves, I am called 'agitator', and 'troublemaker', or else I am told I have a romantic disposition with no understanding of the realities of life.

"No, I will have no praise from men—and what praise I receive, I would gladly exchange for a few pounds more to open another school, or to fund the release of a dozen more children from slavery in the factories. Rather, I do this because I must, because we are all creatures in the hand of the Creator—and what Christian man could do any other?"

He looked down at his hands, where the card and the watch lay, one in each palm.

"You are but one boy, Billy the sweep," he said. "And you may consider yourself not very significant in the grand scheme of things. But the Lord has seen fit to lead you through myriad paths to this room, to this meeting between you and I, and I cannot believe it is for naught. I have no place for luck in my life—it is an evil word, conceived by men who wish to forget that there is a throne in heaven, and one who sits upon it and conducts the affairs of the world with wisdom and with judgement—but I believe in divine coincidence, and I believe in the purposes of God. You have been given an opportunity—for education, for a useful life, for gainful employment; but also for something far greater, if you will have it. There are those in this place willing to love you in the way I was loved, all those years ago, not with soft looks and embraces, but with the clear words of the Gospel. All you must do is accept that love, and hear their words, and act upon them. It really is that simple."

"Is it though?" Billy said. His heart still quivered with the stirrings of hope, but at the same time a shadow lay over him, and the whispers of his ghosts echoed faintly in the recesses of his memory. "You don't know what I been through. You don't know what I done. I been in a lot of trouble, and I fallen in with some bad folks. I been bad myself—real bad, more bad than I ever thought I would be …" His voice trembled, and to his shame he felt tears pricking at his eyes. He dashed them away angrily.

"It ain't that easy," he said, biting back a sob. "You come in here and you talk about love, and God, and heaven, and mercy—but your God don't want me. And these folk in this place, I bet they're Christian folk, and they don't want me neither. I done … There was this boy, see—"

Shaftesbury held up a hand, silencing him. For a moment neither one of them spoke, and they faced each other in silence: the lord sitting bolt upright in the chair by the window, and the boy in the bed, battered and bruised, shaking with the emotions coursing through him.

"I don't doubt," Shaftesbury said at last, "that you have seen and done many terrible things. You forget that I, uniquely, am well acquainted with the struggles of the poor. I have walked the streets. I have seen their lives. I have spoken to them, wept with them, comforted them, held the dying. Now consider this: if I, a mere man, am prepared to offer you a second chance at this life, what does it say about the Master whom I serve, whose heart is immeasurably greater than mine, and whose depths of love I cannot begin to fathom? There is mercy for you, Billy: here in this house, and also in the throne room of heaven. There is hope, also, for a new life, a better life, one which will benefit many others besides yourself."

Billy stared at him, still biting his lip, his mind still in turmoil. Unbidden, the words of the song he had heard in that theatre so long ago rose in his mind: On Christ, the solid rock, I stand; all other ground is sinking sand ... He had been sinking ever since the night they fled from Aggie's shop, and it seemed that no matter how hard he struggled he was sinking still.

Now, at last, he could sense something solid beneath him, an end to the sinking, a rock on which to stand. And yet he was afraid to put his trust in it, because what if this, too, ended in ruin? What if, after putting his trust in these people, and accepting their help, he just ended up hurting them like he had hurt so many others already?

"You're unsure," Shaftesbury said, breaking into his thoughts. "Even now, at the end of your hope, when the hand of help is being offered to you, you shy away from it.

Why? What holds you back?"

"I'm bad news," Billy said gruffly. "I been bad news for a long time. Seems no matter what I do, I end up hurting people, or people get hurt. So what if I stay 'ere? So what if these people take me in? What about when Archie Miller comes lookin' for me? What'll happen to them then? Cause he will come lookin', I guarantee it. Archie Miller don't like loose ends."

"Something tells me that will not be the case with you," Shaftesbury replied. "The police are keen to speak with you further regarding this Mr. Miller, and the workings of his operation. They are particularly interested in the existence of certain records related to your burgling activities. I gather it is rare for them to have such an opportunity, and I think your words may prove invaluable to finally bringing him to justice. I will pray for their success, and your safety."

He rose, stooping his head under the low ceiling.

"I have said all I can," he said. "If you are still not persuaded, then there is nothing more for me to do here. I gather there are others who wish to speak to you about this; I hope they will have more success."

"You mean Tosher?" Billy shook his head. "Nah. Tosher won't want to talk to me. Not after what I done to him."

"You may be surprised," Shaftesbury replied with a smile. "And it is not just Master Tosher who is waiting to see you."

Before Billy could ask what he meant, he had slipped through the door and closed it behind him.

The room fell silent. Billy lay back on the bed, staring at the ceiling. His head was filled with everything and nothing: he could not settle on any one thought. His heart, too, was in turmoil. Deep within him a door was opening, shedding light on a dusty room in a forgotten corner of his soul; but Billy did not know if he wanted that door opened at all. There were things hidden in there, crimes and deeds he would rather keep locked away forever, and yet he suspected that the only way to be free of them at all was to let that light fall on them, and find a way to unburden himself. He shuddered to think what he would see within himself, when the full extent of what he had become was uncovered.

A bell rang, somewhere below him, and the sound was followed by a rushing and thudding and clattering of footsteps, all muffled by walls and floorboards. Then, through the glass of the window, he heard a shout and a laugh, followed by more voices: children's voices, singing songs and chanting rhymes.

He rose from his bed with an effort, set his feet on the floor, and after steeling himself he stood up and tottered to the window.

He found himself looking down on a yard wedged between tall buildings. His room was maybe two or three floors up, and from his vantage point he could easily see without being seen. The yard was crowded with children of all ages, all dressed in a similar fashion: grey shorts and white shirts for the boys, and grey pinafores with white blouses for the girls. They were all engaged in play, some throwing a ball, some skipping over a rope, others rolling hoops. They were all clean, healthy, and—strangest of all—they were happy.

It was only as Billy watched them play that he realised he had never been truly happy in his life. He had laughed with Tosher, delighted in mischief, taken pride in his work for Old Sal and then Flash Jim, and he had lorded himself over the Devil's Lads. But happiness—true, honest, pure joy such as he had seen on Tosher's face that day on the street—had always eluded him. Now it was within his grasp, and all he had to do was reach out and accept it—but somehow it felt that this was the hardest thing he had ever done in his life.

The door opened behind him, and Billy turned. Tosher was standing in the doorway, an anxious smile hanging lopsidedly on his face, and the scratches and bruises of Billy's assault on him as vivid as the red hair that stuck out in a halo around his head. But it was not on Tosher that Billy's eyes fell, and it was not the sight of Tosher that made his chest tighten and his heart race.

Instead, it was to the girl who stood beside Tosher that Billy's eyes were drawn, as with a magnet. Her skin was dark, and she wore a plain grey dress and a white blouse, the right arm of which was empty, folded over and pinned at the shoulder. She smiled when she saw Billy, and her smile was like the sun rising after a long night of terror.

"Hello, Billy," said Clara. "It's been a while, hasn't it?"

Epilogue
"Our Earl's Gone!"

THE GIRL SAT on her uncle's shoulders, craning her neck to see over the crowds that thronged the thoroughfare of Piccadilly Circus. It was a warm summer's day, and the whole affair had the feel of a carnival. Her uncle had already warned her once not to leave his side—it was too easy to get lost in a crowd, he said—and by now the place was so thick with bodies there was no other choice for him but to carry her.

She brushed back her tightly curled bronze-brown hair, which as usual was blowing in her face. The other children teased her about it sometimes, called her 'mop-head' and other names like it; but her father had taught her a long time ago that people would point and stare, and that it just meant they were ignorant and she was to feel sorry for them.

Ahead of her, over the heads of the heaving throng, she could see the sight they had all come for: an enormous tent-like structure of draped canvas, tied with a garish red ribbon that looked comically out of place. Her uncle had insisted they come to see it being unveiled. It was, he had said, something she would remember for the rest of her life.

A band struck up, playing a jolly tune that battled with the cries of street vendors and souvenir sellers, and was all but defeated by the deafening chatter of the crowd. It was nearly time.

"Can you see all right?" her uncle asked, from somewhere around her dangling knees.

She nodded. "Yes. I think they're about to start."

"Tell me what you see."

She looked up, eager to do the job as well as she could. "There's a line of people coming up on to a stage on the right," she said. "They're all dressed in fine clothes. Must be lords or something. One of them just said something to the band." The music stopped suddenly, though the chatter around them continued. "Now the same man is coming up to the front. He's saying something … I can't hear what it is."

She strained, turning her head to catch the man's words over the hubbub around them; but though she saw his distant mouth moving, and one hand gesticulating, the speech itself was lost in the wind.

"He's finished talking now," she said after a while. "Now he's got a pair of scissors. He's turning … he's cutting the ribbon around the tent …"

A cheer went up all around them, washing like a wave from the front of the crowd. Most people weren't sure what they were cheering for, but they cheered all the same.

"The tent's coming down," the girl said. "It's falling … there's something inside it …" Her eyes widened. "It's a statue!" she cried. "A statue of a man with wings, standing on one leg … the other leg's stretched out behind him … he's holding a bow … it's beautiful!"

She could feel her uncle nodding in satisfaction, and his hands gripping her legs tightly.

"Well done," he said. "I can imagine it exactly."

When the event was over and the crowds had dispersed, the girl went with her uncle to have a closer look at the statue. As they walked hand in hand—slowly, to account for her uncle's limp from the curve of his spine—she felt the usual eyes on her, saw the usual raised eyebrows and the usual startled expressions. She ignored them, and remembered to feel sorry for their ignorance.

As they neared the statue, they passed a group of men in rough clothes and battered caps who were standing and looking up at it. Their faces were dirty, their hands stained from a life of hard toil, and under any other circumstances she would have been scared of them. But today there was no hardness in their eyes, none of the cruelty she might have expected from such men. Instead, there was a profound sadness.

"Well," she heard one sigh to his fellows. "Tha's it, then. Our earl's gone."

"What did he mean?" the girl asked her uncle, as they stopped at the foot of the statue and gazed up at it. The sun beamed down, lending the bronze a deep brown-gold lustre. The eyes of the figure looked off into the distance, through the buildings and the traffic that surrounded them, gazing at something she could not see.

"Hmm?" Her uncle had not been listening, lost in his own thoughts. "What was that?"

"The man back there," the girl said. "He said, 'Our earl's gone.' What did he mean?"

Her uncle smiled sadly and rubbed at the little finger of his right hand, the way he always did when he was deep in thought.

"To answer your question," he said. "I need to tell you a story. It's a story about a boy, a troublemaker, who made a lot of bad decisions and got in with a lot of bad people in his time. He was a thief, a liar, a cheat, and nearly a murderer, once. But that wasn't the end for him. Because, even though he was walking down a road that would lead him to a very bad place, there was a man—an earl, no less—who showed him the way out of it, through a narrow gate and up a steep path, to an ancient hill and a rugged cross, where that boy found peace and new life. And this statue right here was erected in memory of that earl, because he didn't just help that one boy, he helped hundreds of thousands of boys and girls, and men and women, when no one else wanted to."

"Is it a true story?" the girl asked, her eyes wide.

"Of course," her uncle replied. "All the best stories are true."

"And did you know the boy yourself?"

Her uncle chuckled. "I did indeed," he said. "And your mum and dad did, too. Here, I'll tell you about him on the way home."

He reached out to take her hand, which was soft and copper-brown, and she grasped his littlest finger, which was twisted and bent inwards, and together they walked away until the traffic hid them from view.

THE END

Author's Note

This book is a work of fiction. Billy, Clara, Tosher, Archie Miller and the rest of the cast—with the exception of Lord Shaftesbury himself—come from my imagination. However, the kinds of people on whom they are based were very much real, and the circumstances of their lives reflect the conditions in Victorian London.

The book itself is not set in any particular year. Instead, I chose to set the story in the vague time period of the 1860s, and I have borrowed characters and events from throughout this decade, and a little of the preceding one, in order to present a sketch of the kind of man that Shaftesbury was, and the work he undertook. It is not intended as a strict biography; for those who are interested, I can recommend 'The Poor Man's Earl' by John Pollock as an excellent resource.

As there is a meeting of fact and fiction in these pages, I thought it might be helpful to highlight some key facts, and to provide some historical context.

On Contemporary Events

In the 1860s Queen Victoria was on the throne of England, ruling over an Empire that stretched across most of the world, taking in large parts of Africa, Asia (including much of India), Australia, and territories across the Atlantic in North America.

America at this time was engaged in the Civil War. Abraham Lincoln was President, until his assassination in

1865, and the emancipation of slaves was still underway. The western territories of America were still very much wild, and it is from this time that tales of cowboys and Indians come, popularised in lurid novels and 'Penny Dreadful' magazines of the kind that Billy so loved.

In London, Sherlock Holmes would soon be solving cases in the short stories and novels by Sir Arthur Conan Doyle. The Metropolitan Police force had been formed only a few decades before, and organised policing was very much in its infancy. Because of this, crime rates were incredibly high, and at times the streets of London (and many other cities around the United Kingdom) more closely resembled the Wild West than many would have cared to admit.

Gangs of London

Unemployment and poverty were rife in Victorian cities. In this environment gang culture flourished, each gang presiding over a territory which they defended fiercely. Pitched street battles were not uncommon, usually as retaliation for a perceived insult or as the result of a challenge. The Battle of Seven Dials is an invention of my own, as are the Devil's Lads, Flash Jim's Lads, and the rest of the gangs mentioned in the book. Their colourful names, however, are drawn largely from historical sources, because the truth is stranger—and often more inventive—than fiction.

Old Sal's boarding house is based upon contemporary accounts: many such boarding houses were in operation around the city, catering to the lowest and most helpless in society. It is not inconceivable that their owners were engaged in the kinds of organised crime I have depicted.

As shocking as some of the events depicted in these pages may be, where I have taken liberties with the historical record, it has been to omit rather than embellish. The reality, almost invariably, is far worse than anything I have written, and the crimes in which these gangs (most of them youths or children) were engaged were, for the most part, unspeakable.

It is important to remember that this is the context in which Lord Shaftesbury (and many others) worked, rescuing countless children from a life spent in misery and fear, or from a constant escalation of violence simply in the name of survival. The value of his work cannot be overstated.

Climbing Boys

The 'climbing boys', as young chimney sweeps were called, were only decisively outlawed in the year 1875, following decades of campaigning by Lord Shaftesbury and others like him. In this time, numerous Acts of Parliament were passed and revised, all without any great effect. Real change only came about when the mounting death toll turned the tide of popular opinion, and the dwindling trade and increasing trust in 'new' technologies (in reality decades old) finally put the spectre of the climbing boy to rest.

The details included on this matter in the book are wholly accurate, although once again they have been extensively censored, the stark realities being far too harrowing for a young people's novel. Suffice it to say that Billy's conclusion of climbing boys being "cheap, replaceable, and soon forgotten" is a fair and accurate summary.

Above: "Tall buildings rose all around him, their windows thick with grime. Across the yard was the kitchen door, from which the smell of stew and the sound of a drunken fiddle drifted over to him."

(Photo courtesy of Royal Academy of Arts, London; photographer: Prudence Cuming Associates Ltd)

Right: "Gerard was the closest thing to a father Billy had ever known—if a father was a drunk with squinting eyes, yellow teeth, and a wiry black beard as thick as the brushes that were his livelihood."

(Photo: LSE Library)

Lord Shaftesbury
A Biography

Lord Shaftesbury was born Anthony Ashley Cooper in 1801. His father was Cropley Ashley Cooper, the Sixth Earl of Shaftesbury, and Anthony's childhood was one of "great severity, moral and physical". Anthony's parents spent their time and money on themselves, and their children were often hungry and cold, left in the care of the servants while the parents went out socialising.

Anthony's only real friend in his childhood was his nursemaid, a lady called Maria Millis. She was a Christian, and she taught him the Gospel from a young age. She also taught him a simple prayer of repentance, which, though he promised numerous times to repeat it to his biographer, died with him. It was during this time that Anthony came to know the Lord as his own Saviour, and he continued to love and serve Him for the rest of his life.

When Maria died she bequeathed to Anthony a pocket watch. He treasured this simple gift, and would often take it out and show it to those he met, and tell them the story of "the best friend that ever I had".

At the age of seven Anthony was sent to school at Manor House in Chiswick, where he was beaten and bullied by teachers and peers alike. After five years of this grim existence

(Photo: Wellcome Collection)

he was moved to Harrow, which was a far better experience. It was while at Harrow, between the ages of fourteen and fifteen, that he saw the sight which was to motivate his work with the poor and needy in later life.

While walking home late one night, Anthony heard drunken singing coming from a side street. As he watched, he saw a procession of men emerge, all of them drunk, bearing a coffin on their shoulders. To his horror, the men stumbled and dropped the coffin, spilling the corpse onto the ground. In that moment Anthony resolved to do all he could to ensure that no human being would have to endure such degrading treatment.

Anthony entered politics, becoming a Member of Parliament aged twenty-five, and inheriting the Earldom and a seat in the House of Lords at the age of fifty on his father's death. Throughout his life he fought tirelessly on behalf of those who had no voice, passing legislation in support of people with mental illnesses, children working in factories and mines, and chimney sweeps.

He was a pioneer of the Ragged School movement, which

set up free schools for children who could not afford an education, and an enthusiastic supporter of the Sunday School movement which has brought the Gospel to many millions of children who would not otherwise have heard it. His advocacy for the poor—which was unusually strong for a man of his position—earned him the informal title of "the Poor Man's Earl".

When he died in 1885, thousands lined the streets to watch his hearse go by. One bystander was heard to cry, "Our earl's gone!" The Shaftesbury memorial was erected in his memory, and it stands in Piccadilly Circus in London to this day. But perhaps the best and most lasting memorial is the undeniable effect he has had on the education and welfare of children throughout the United Kingdom, and the many hundreds of souls who came to repentance and faith in the Lord Jesus Christ as a result of his spiritual endeavours.

Right: The Shaftesbury Memorial Fountain, Piccadilly Circus

"It's a statue!" she cried. "A statue of a man with wings, standing on one leg … the other leg's stretched out behind him … he's holding a bow … it's beautiful!"

Left: A typical ragged school. Children would be taught reading and writing, as well as a useful trade. Bible lessons were also common.

Right: Shaftesbury Avenue in central London, a lasting testament to the influence of Lord Shaftesbury's work on the history of England.

Year	1801	1801-08	1808-13
Age	Born	0-7	7-12
Shaftesbury's Life	Born in London, named Anthony Ashley Cooper.	Brought up in London. Anthony is neglected by his parents; his only friend is his nurse, Maria Millis, who teaches him the Gospel.	Sent to Manor House School. Described it in later life as "bad, wicked, filthy."
Historical Event	The United Kingdom of Great Britain and Ireland is formed.	Napoleon is crowned Emperor of the French. First steam locomotive. Britain declares the slave trade illegal.	Beethoven performs his Fifth Symphony, Jane Austen publishes 'Pride and Prejudice'.

1813 -16	1826	1833	1840
12-15	25	32	39

		Introduces the 'Ten Hours Bill', designed to limit the amount of work that children can be forced to do. His opponents in Parliament try to change the bill to make it weaker. Shaftesbury must continue to fight to bring it into law.	
Goes to Harrow School. Sees the pauper's funeral with the drunken coffin-bearers and decides to campaign on behalf of the poor.	Enters Parliament as MP for Woodstock.		Supports a bill in Parliament banning the use of climbing boys (chimney sweeps). The law is not enforced, and children continue to work in this dangerous job.
Napoleon is exiled to Elba, escapes, and is defeated at Waterloo. Mount Tambora erupts - the largest volcanic eruption in recorded history.	Samuel Morey patents the internal combustion engine (car engine).	Slavery Abolition Act bans slavery throughout the British Empire.	New Zealand is founded.

Year	1844	1851	1853
Age	43	50	52

Shaftesbury's Life	Becomes president of the Ragged School Union.	Anthony's father dies. Anthony becomes the Seventh Earl of Shaftesbury. Introduces another bill into Parliament to outlaw the use of climbing boys. The bill does not become law.	Introduces another bill into Parliament to outlaw the use of climbing boys. The bill does not become law. Shaftesbury continues to fight!
Historical Event	First publicly-funded telegraph line in the world. The first message is, "What hath God wrought?" (Numbers 23:23).	The Great Exhibition in London. Herman Melville publishes 'Moby Dick'.	'Twelve Years a Slave', by Solomon Northup, is published by David Wilson. Crimean War begins.

1858	1864	1875	1885
57	63	74	84

Introduces yet another bill into Parliament to outlaw the use of climbing boys. The bill does not become law.	Passes the Chimney Sweepers Regulation Act, which has more power than previous laws. But this law is still not enforced properly.	Helps to pass the Chimney Sweepers Act, which is enforcible by the police. The use of climbing boys finally comes to an end.	Dies in Folkestone.
Construction of Big Ben is completed. (1859 - Charles Darwin publishes 'On the Origin of Species').	First railway track in Indonesia is laid. (1865 - Abraham Lincoln assassinated).	HMS Challenger surveys the deepest point in the Earth's oceans, the Challenger Deep. 26 million people in India die due to famine.	Karl Benz produces the first car with an internal combustion engine. Louis Pasteur creates the first successful rabies vaccine.

1893: Shaftesbury Memorial erected in Piccadilly Circus, London.

About the Author

Matthew Wainwright lives and works in Greenwich, south London, and is a husband and father of three lively girls. He has spent many years working with children and young people as a member of the Metropolitan Tabernacle Baptist Church (Spurgeon's), and in his career as a Communication Support Worker for young deaf people.

Want to know more?

Visit the author's website for activities, games, and resources for:

- teachers
- home schoolers
- Sunday Schools

Scan to see!

MatthewWainwright.co.uk